ST. MARTIN'S

MINOTAUR
MYSTERIES

GET A CLUE!

Be the first to hear the latest mystery book news...

With the St. Martin's Minotaur monthly newsletter, you'll learn about the hottest new Minotaur books, receive advance excerpts from newly published works, read exclusive original material from featured mystery writers, and be able to enter to win free books!

Sign up on the Minotaur Web site at:
www.minotaurbooks.com

ELECTRIFYING PRAISE
FOR JENNY SILER'S NOVELS

Flashback

"The complex puzzle of a life forgotten powers this beautifully written spy novel . . . An air of lyrical melancholy hangs over the novel . . . The plotting is deft, the characters believable and, in the end, Eve finds who she was, even if she remains unsure of what that means or what she will become."

—*Publishers Weekly*

"Unexpected depths of both intrigue and emotion, all of which keeps *Flashback* a cut above its genre."

—*Houston Chronicle*

"Eve is a winning character—and Siler's prose remains as bracing as in her earlier books."

—*Seattle Times/Post Intelligencer*

"Siler has outdone herself in *Flashback*."

—*The Denver Post*

More . . .

"Fans will think Ludlum with this exciting thriller starring a wonderful protagonist who ensures that the plot freshens up the trite amnesiac victim in peril. The story line is exciting . . . A terrific taut thriller."

—*Midwest Book Review*

"Tight prose and a quicksilver plot complete the package. Siler knows how to write an absorbing page-turner. *Flashback* is every bit as much fun as her last [*Shot*]."

—*Library Journal*

"A welcome addition to the Grit-Lit boys' club. Siler can slice and dice and talk tough with the best of them . . . The action is swift, the setting is exotic, and Siler's riffs on memory are memorable."

—*The Baltimore Sun*

"Relentless pace and some clever plot twists keep you guessing in this *Bourne Identity* update."

—*Mystery Lovers Bookshop News*

Shot

"*Shot* is everything a thriller should be: spare enough to keep the tension constant, but brimming with fully realized characters who are heroic, in part, because of their flaws; smart enough, with its biochemical warfare–centered plot, to keep the reader guessing, but never didactic . . . Damn good fun."

—*Entertainment Weekly*

"*Shot*, the third of Jenny Siler's riveting suspense novels, showcases her strong female characters and superbly paced plotting . . . The pieces come together fast and furious in this sharply written and timely novel evocative of the best of the 'noir' genre."

—*The Baltimore Sun*

"Quirky characters, a quicksilver plot, and chase scenes aplenty . . . In Siler's dirty but redeemable universe, everyone ends up on higher ground."

—*Publishers Weekly*

"A sizzling nail-biter, ratcheting up the suspense with each page, keeping the reader guessing during the entire tension-filled trip."

—Mary-Ann Tirone Smith, author of *Love Her Madly*

"Sit back and enjoy the intrigue. *Shot* is riveting story-telling."

—Lynn Hightower, author of *High Water*

"Siler hits her marks with quick, fast takes packed with telling clues and sharp details."

—*Kirkus Reviews*

"Siler's latest crime novel features not one but two of the strong female characters that have become her trademark . . . The path they take from drawn weapons to uneasy alliance against secretive and powerful foes makes this a substantial and suspenseful thriller."

—*Booklist*

Iced

"Poetry with attitude."

—*The New York Times Book Review*

"Jenny Siler writes like a hard-boiled angel, prose as dazzling as cut stones, characters as polished and complex as diamond facets, and a plot as compelling as unbridled greed."

—James Crumley, author of *Bordersnakes*

"The first thing you notice about Jenny Siler's atmospheric novel *Iced* is the elegance of the prose laid against the rough-and-tumble exterior of her protagonist. The result is a novel that works on two levels, that of a terrific thriller layered with imagery and passages of soulful, beautiful writing. Siler's first book, *Easy Money*, was a huge critical success and put the author on the literary map. *Iced* will keep her there. Here is a major talent."

—*The Denver Post*

"Gardner's unshakable moral foundation gives her depth and likability as she untangles a knot of murder and mayhem with roots in a plane crash decades ago. It's a bleak, intricate story. And Meg Gardner's a keeper."

—*The Baltimore Sun*

"One of the new talents in tough-gal crime fiction . . . She handles the hard-boiled writing style with a natural grace, never sounding forced or stagy . . . It effectively reveals Gardner as a complex soul, faithless and dour, as rugged as the Montana wilderness."

—*Publishers Weekly*

Easy Money

A *New York Times* Notable Book

"Once in a blue moon, a new writer speaks up in a voice that gets your attention like a rifle shot. Jenny Siler . . . has that kind of voice. . . clean, direct and a little dangerous . . . An intensely vivid piece of writing."
—Marilyn Stasio, *The New York Times Book Review*

"In her first novel, 27-year-old author Jenny Siler has shown tough-guy thriller writers how a woman does it. And she packs some punch . . . A terrific thriller."
—*The Wall Street Journal*

"A triumphant debut . . . Siler's persuasive take on the underground world of deviant behavior, and her ability to channel that world through an introspective female protagonist, mesmerizes as it thrills."
—*Publishers Weekly*

"Breezy, cool violent action debut featuring a two-fisted, pistol-packing tough gal courier chased by bad guys across a shattered, washed-up-and-left-for-dead American heartland . . . A bumpy, bloody road trip into a dark past and darker present from a writer who may have what it takes to be a genre star."
—*Kirkus Reviews*

Also by Jenny Siler

Easy Money

Iced

Shot

Available from
St. Martin's/Minotaur Paperbacks

FLASHBACK

Jenny Siler

St. Martin's Paperbacks

NOTE: If you purchased this book without a cover you should be aware that this book is stolen property. It was reported as "unsold and destroyed" to the publisher, and neither the author nor the publisher has received any payment for this "stripped book."

Published by arrangement with Henry Holt and Company.

FLASHBACK

Copyright © 2004 by Jenny Siler.

All rights reserved. No part of this book may be used or reproduced in any manner whatsoever without written permission except in the case of brief quotations embodied in critical articles or reviews. For information address Henry Holt and Company.

Library of Congress Catalog Card Number: 2003055254

ISBN: 0-312-93316-9
EAN: 9780312-93316-6

Printed in the United States of America

Henry Holt hardcover edition published 2004
St. Martin's Paperbacks edition / August 2005

St. Martin's Paperbacks are published by St. Martin's Press, 175 Fifth Avenue, New York, NY 10010.

10 9 8 7 6 5 4 3 2 1

ONE

Sister Heloise got up from her place at the back of the nave and made the sign of the cross. It was compline, her favorite of the hours, and normally she stayed till the sweet and bitter end, till most of the other sisters had left and the chapel was dark and hushed. But tonight, with Eve gone, there was the work of two to be finished before bed.

"Your anger has overrun me," she heard Sister Magdalene read as she turned and headed for the door, "your terrors have broken me." It was the end of the Eighty-seventh Psalm, the prayer of the gravely ill.

"They have flowed round me like water,
they have besieged me all day long.
You have taken my friends and those close to me:
all I have left is shadows."

It was a dark prayer, Heloise thought as she stepped out into the cold air, dark and beautiful at the same time. What was it St. Benedict had said? Something about living constantly with death. The door swung closed behind her, muffling the voices of the other sisters. "I cry out to you, Lord, by day and by night. Alleluia."

It was the first week of Advent, the fifth day of December, and winter had closed in tight. There was a white rime of frost on the grass and on the bare tree branches. A thin shard of moon hung in the crystalline sky. In the time-carved niches of the stone church wall dozens of red votive candles flickered and glowed.

Pressing the flaps of her wool coat up around her bare neck, Heloise started across the icy lawn toward the priory kitchen. There were thirty-five of them, plus some two dozen visitors from a women's church group in Dijon who'd be arriving in the morning. That made sixty mouths to feed, some twenty-odd loaves of bread she'd need for the day, not to mention the usual breakfast. She'd be up half the night.

From the farm just below the convent came the sound of a dog barking and another answering, both of them urgent and purposeful. Monsieur Tane's two watchdogs, most likely running off the fox. It was not like Heloise to begrudge any creature a meal, but the sisters had lost three good laying hens in the last week and she found herself hoping the dogs would succeed. She had a soft spot for the guileless birds.

Protectively, she glanced toward the dark shape of the henhouse. Everything was still and quiet. Or was it? Halfway across the yard she stopped walking and stood in the lacy halo of her own cold breath. She had heard something. She was certain of it. A stutter in the pea gravel on the far side of the priory. Was it the fox, chased up the hill and looking for an evening snack? Or just one of the sisters, forgoing compline, out for a late stroll or a cigarette? Heloise sometimes found herself tempted to do the same.

The noise came again, and this time Heloise was certain it was human and not animal, someone walking on the gravel drive. Satisfied, she reached into her coat pocket, pulled out her heavy ring of keys, and continued forward. She'd have to remember to bring some bones down to the Tanes in the morning, a small reward for the dogs. She let her thoughts drift back to her baking. If she was quick in setting everything out to rise, she'd be able to get a few good hours of sleep.

The sound came again, closer this time, and the nun turned her head to see a dark figure coming around the corner of the priory. Heloise squinted, trying to read the person's features in what little light the building's windows offered. No, it wasn't one of the sisters. It was a man, definitely a man. He ducked into the shadows and disappeared.

"Monsieur Tane?" she called, receiving no answer.

Heloise felt suddenly afraid, a little girl alone in the dark. *Keep us safe, while we are awake.* She whispered the first lines of the canticle to herself and picked up her pace. The keys jangled in her hand.

And then, quick as a fox, he was upon her. Heloise started to scream, but a gloved palm covered her mouth.

"Quiet," the man whispered. His face was streaked with black greasepaint, his eyes hidden behind strange glasses. Robotic, Heloise thought, inhuman, to see in the dark. He looked like the characters in the American action films Sister Claire liked to watch. He grabbed the nun's coat, pulling her close to him.

Keep us safe, Lord, she prayed silently. Gripping the keys, she brought her right fist up hard to his face. The metal caught against the glasses, pushing them up, and his head snapped back. When he looked back down at her, she could see his eyes, the pale skin of his lids shining in the darkness. One of the keys had ripped his cheek, and he was bleeding. But she had accomplished little more than to make him angry.

"The American," he growled, pinning her arms to her sides. "Where is she?" He was foreign, his French slightly accented, though she couldn't tell how.

Heloise shook her head, trying to understand what he wanted.

He brought his face down toward hers. "Where is she?" he demanded, so forcefully that she thought he would hit her, but he didn't. Instead, he turned his head and looked toward the church, and Heloise looked with him. On the frosty lawn, heading slowly toward the chapel, were some dozen dim figures. In the hands of each man was a long black rod. Guns, Heloise thought. She tried once more to scream, but the man's hand tightened over her mouth.

Inside the chapel the sisters were saying an antiphon to Our Lady. Heloise could just make out Magdalene's call and the louder chorus of responses. The man started forward, dragging Heloise with him. In a single clear instant everything she might have felt was replaced by the knowledge that unless she did something to help herself, she was about to die.

Opening her mouth as wide as she could, she clamped down on the man's gloved hand and sank her teeth into the leather. He flinched, his arm relaxing instinctively, and Heloise jammed her knee up into the soft flesh of his groin. The man moved backward slightly, the look on his face more astonishment than anything else. Kicking him hard in the shins with her work boot, Heloise wrested herself from his grip and started for the tangle of woods that bordered the convent.

Run! she told herself. She could feel the man behind

her, but she didn't look back. *Keep us safe, Lord,* she prayed again, her eyes on the dark trees, her arms and legs hammering her forward, her boots slipping on the hoary grass. There was a small explosion on the ground next to her, then another, and the muted sound of gunfire. Then suddenly she was in the dark underbrush, careening downward over roots and rocks.

TWO

TWO

What is the first thing you remember? The taste of the ocean, the cold shock of snow, or the face of your mother, young as she was and is no more? The first memory I have is of the hour I came into this world. Before that, there are just the ghosts of what I've forgotten.

I arrived on All Saints' Day, a little over a year ago, to a busload of aging virgins on a muddy roadside in Burgundy. How I got there is a mystery to all of us. What I remember is the smell of cattle, the rain-blurred outlines of twelve dark heads against the gray sky, and an unrelenting pain in the left side of my head. What they remember is a scraped-up body in a ditch, a face clouded by blood and bruises, and a young woman who fought them off in gutter English.

Later, the doctors would use the word *miracle* when referring to the single bullet that had pierced the bones of my skull. The tiny piece of lead that by all rights should have killed me had instead navigated the folds of my brain as deftly as a surgeon's blade, sparing my life, sparing my eyesight, sparing everything but the most mysterious of connections, the tender filament of memory.

What little I know about myself is only what the living body can tell, and that is not much. Not surprisingly, it's the mouth that says the most, and mine reveals that I was once loved, or at least well cared for. I have three fillings, no wisdom teeth, and a neat patina of decay preventative sealant on my molars. Someone paid for braces in my adolescence. On my upper left incisor is a cosmetic bond, and beneath it, a yellow scar in the enamel from a fall I took as a child. I have envisioned this mishap so many times now—a summer day, blue sky, green grass, the cool metal of the monkey bars, and a faceless father on a bench in the distance—that it has come to seem like a truth. And who's to say it isn't?

A very American set of teeth, a dentist in Lyon remarked, and given all the other evidence, my North American English, and the U.S. labels in my clothes, it would seem that he was right.

Except for the catastrophe that birthed me, I've come through life so far relatively unscathed. On the outside of my right ankle is a simple birthmark, three black dots that, if connected, might form a lopsided triangle. The skin on my upper arm is smooth, unblemished by the circular scar of a smallpox vaccination, confirming the fact that I was born no earlier than 1971. I do have one old scar, the healed remnants of a laceration that is at once my body's greatest mystery and its biggest clue. It's a small mark, unseeable unless one is looking, from a cut that was made on my perineum to allow a baby to pass through.

A child! Think of all the things you've forgotten and wish you hadn't: the exact weight and shape of your first kiss; the last time you saw your father, your grandfather, loved ones who aren't coming back. And yet, how could you forget your own child? How could you not remember such a thing? When they told me in the hospital, I insisted there had been a mistake.

The doctor who examined me was a woman, small and slightly round, with a spattering of fading freckles. Finally, she brought a mirror and held it so that I could see the scar, the faint, pale line of the episiotomy.

Whether my appearance in that field was accident or design has so far been impossible to determine. In the beginning it seemed inevitable that someone would come looking for me, and the violence of my arrival suggested that someone might not have the best intentions. Better not to advertise, the police had said, and so, other than a discreet correspondence with the U.S. Embassy in Paris, the nuns' discovery was kept quiet.

Don't worry, the U.S. consul told me confidently. People don't just disappear without someone wondering where they've gone to. Especially not people with children, people who have been so obviously cared for. Yes, I thought, hoping he was wrong, not knowing this past year would prove him so, and that in the end I'd wish him to have been right.

All I could feel then toward the dark life behind me was a flush of fear, a dread not just of those who might hurt me but of my own capacity for rage. Though I needn't have worried. In the thirteen months since that All Saints' Day no one has come forward to claim me. Not a soul has inquired about a brown-haired, blue-eyed, young American with a scarred front tooth.

The life I have now, and everything in it, including my name, has been given to me by the sisters. It took them some time, but in the end they settled on Eve. The first, they told me, the name given by God. It seems fitting to me, this moniker of one so irreparably divided from the life she once knew. Though often my own separation seems far more powerful than sin.

It was snowing in Lyon, a weak effort, flakes sputtering down from a low blanket of clouds, but snowing nonetheless, with the promise of more to come. Out the window of Dr. Delpay's office I could see the city's rooftops in their various shades of gray, flannel and slate, ash and charcoal.

"You're still planning on going?" Delpay asked from across the room.

I nodded, turning away from the window to face him. "I spoke to the consul last week. He's making arrangements."

"Do you know where they'll be sending you?"

I shook my head. I hadn't given the idea much thought. Somewhere quiet, I thought now, with mountains and pine trees, and the earnest and honorable people you see in movies about the American West. "It'll take some time. There was talk of finding me a sponsor. It's all a little tricky, the bureaucratic side of things."

"You seem relieved by that."

Yes, I thought, though I didn't say it. It had been my decision, my idea to go to America, and yet I was guiltily happy to put it off.

Delpay settled into his chair. He was a kind man, fatherly in a no-nonsense way, not coddling, just always quietly there, and I didn't want to disappoint him.

"You know, you don't have to leave," he offered.

I thought of the few Americans I'd known, the consul and his red-haired secretary, a group of Benedictine sisters from Michigan who'd spent two weeks at the abbey.

They were all foreigners to me, loud and overly friendly, and yet somehow suspicious at the same time. I couldn't imagine a country full of these people, could not imagine this place as my home. But it was, and somewhere in it, among those strange people, was a child. Mine.

"Yes," I said, "I know."

Delpay nodded, as if understanding some deep and complex problem. "What are you afraid of?"

I turned back to the window, touched my forehead to the glass, and peered straight down into the street toward the glazed hoods of the cars below, the pale pedestrians huddled against the wet December chill. I could taste Delpay's vasopressin in the back of my throat, the bitter pungency of the drug.

The doctor waited patiently for my answer. I heard him shift in his chair. The old radiators came on, clunking and hissing. Down below, a woman emerged from the front door of the hospital and climbed into a waiting cab.

"I had the dream again last night," I said, "the old one."

"The warehouse?" Delpay asked.

I nodded. It had been months since I'd last had the nightmare, and Delpay and I had chalked it up to the piracetam he'd prescribed when we had first begun to meet. I'd had the dream almost nightly then, a terrible, suffocating vision in which I was trapped in a deserted warehouse, running from someone or something.

"And the ending," Delpay prodded. "Still the same?"

"Yes." Instinctively, I touched my hand to my throat and felt the unblemished skin there. In the dream it was not so. In the last panicked seconds of my nightmare a blade flashed in the warehouse's dim light, then arced toward me, slicing across my neck. Again and again I woke to the great gaping throat of death, my fingers scrabbling to stanch the flow of blood.

In the end, we'd stopped the piracetam, and the dream

had stopped as well. Now it was back, and I shuddered at the memory.

"And the man?" Delpay asked. "Are you still seeing him?"

"Yes," I told him. The man was a newer vision, no less persistent than the warehouse had been, and almost as disturbing.

"Tell me about him."

"I have," I said, turning once more from the window.

Delpay smiled. "Tell me again."

"It's the same as it always is," I explained. "We're up high, on a roof, I think. There are mountains around us."

"And the writing?"

"Yes. On the hillside. There's something written on the hillside."

"Can you read it?"

I shook my head. "It's not a language I know."

"But the letters? You can read the letters."

"No," I said, the frustration showing in my voice.

"It's okay. Tell me about the man. Is he young? Old?"

"He's young, close to my age, I think."

"He's an American?"

"I don't know."

"What else?"

I turned back to the window.

"What else, Eve?"

"He's dying."

"Why?"

"He's been shot. There's blood everywhere." I swallowed hard, trying to clear my throat of the vasopressin tang, trying to rid my head of this memory I didn't want.

"What else, Eve?"

"I'm holding a gun in my hand, a pistol. I'm the one who has done this."

"You don't know that."

I turned to face Delpay once again. As much as I wanted to believe him, there was a part of me that was certain I was right. "It's the only thing I do know," I said.

I was late leaving the city. A theater near the hospital was showing a new American movie, and I went after my appointment, as I often did, hoping to catch a glimpse of something familiar on the big screen. My first few months at the convent I'd spent much of my time watching Sister Claire's collection of American movies, trying to kindle a spark of recognition. Occasionally, I saw places I knew, or at least thought I knew: parts of New York City, the desolate landscapes of the old westerns, or *Sleepless in Seattle*'s rain-washed waterfront. But the rest of America, from the apocalyptic sprawl of Los Angeles to the arctic landscape of *Fargo*'s Upper Midwest, seemed completely alien to me.

The matinee let out at four, and by the time I picked up the Miles Davis CD Heloise had asked for and stopped at Sister Theresa's favorite chocolatier, it was rush hour, the streets clogged with evening commuters. I had to battle my way out of the city in the convent's rusty old Renault.

I was still hungover from my meeting with Dr. Delpay. My throat was dry, and there was a black hole of pain in the back of my skull. It had been several months since we'd introduced the "miracle drug" into our sessions, and so far there had been no miracles, none of the sudden breakthroughs we'd hoped for. Just this same bloody memory, one I wished I could send back to the oblivion from which it had emerged. And now the piracetam dream was back as well.

It was dark when I got off the highway and headed for Cluny and the little hill towns beyond. The Renault's heater rattled and shook beneath the dash. I brightened my headlights and careened north on the narrow road, past sprawling vineyards, the grape wood bare and gnarled, each plant clipped and tied neatly for winter, limbs spread out, like bodies crucified.

The road dipped through a small village, a handful of stone houses huddled together around a café. I slowed slightly and watched the settlement slip by. The few windows that were lit shone like stage sets: a woman at her stove, a man smoking, a dozen green bottles on a shelf. It was six-thirty by my watch. If I pushed it, I could be at the convent well before seven. I shifted and punched the gas pedal, coaxing what speed I could out of the old engine, and turned onto the even narrower road that led up to the abbey.

As I neared the Tanes' farmhouse, I eased my foot off the gas and peered past the Renault's headlights, watching for the two retrievers. They were good dogs, but suicidally stupid, and had the bad habit of darting out of nowhere. There was no sign of the creatures tonight. The Tanes' house was ablaze with lights, each window shining with an uncanny force. Two large spots on the old carriage house illuminated the yard and the driveway. A party, perhaps? Though there was nothing festive about the glare. Monsieur Tane's white Peugeot was the only car in the drive. I blinked, heading back into the darkness toward the convent.

As I came around the last curve, I could see the stone priory and the chapel beyond. Something was wrong there as well. The abbey's grounds were bathed in light, the winter trees casting stark shadows on the frozen ground. Half a dozen cars and several police vans were parked on the gravel apron outside the priory. A handful of figures lingered in the cold, all men as far as I could see, some smoking, some talking on cell phones. I recognized most of them as local police.

There was an air of tired catastrophe to the scene, the
drama long since over and the players waiting for their
next move. I parked the Renault behind one of the vans
and got out, my heart beating in panic. It was Sister
Magda, I told myself, finally succumbed to all those cigarettes and the goose fat she liked to spread on her toast,
but even as I thought it I knew what had happened was far
worse.

One of the men, an inspector named Lelu, started toward me. He had on a parka and, beneath it, a rumpled
coat and tie.

"What's happened?" I asked.

"There has been a terrible tragedy," he explained. "I'm
so sorry." Shaking his head, he pulled a pack of
Gauloises from his coat. "I can find no easy way to say
this." He tapped the cigarettes against his left palm, wor-
rying the pack like a string of prayer beads. "There has
been a massacre."

It was a funny choice of words, the meaning so insane
I had trouble processing it. "I don't understand," I said.

"A massacre," he repeated, "here at the abbey. The sisters . . ." He paused.

"The sisters?" I asked stupidly. My legs felt like rubber
bands.

Nodding, he put his hand on my arm. "Please," he said
gently. "You cannot stay here tonight. Madame Tane is
expecting you. Sister Heloise is there as well. I will have
someone take you down the road, and if you are capable,
we will need to ask you some questions."

"Yes. Of course." I felt nauseous, dizzy, and off balance. I took a step toward the Renault and put my hand on
the hood, trying to keep myself upright. "And the others?" I asked. "Where are they?"

Lelu glanced behind him and motioned for one of the
other men to join us. "Mademoiselle," he said, turning

back to me, "I don't think you understand. You and the sister are the only survivors."

One of the inspector's assistants drove me down to the Tanes'. He was young and nervous, more a farm boy than a cop. He seemed slightly stupefied, crippled by whatever he'd seen at the convent. We sat in the Tanes' kitchen, and I answered what questions I could.

No, I could think of no one who might have had a reason to do something like this. I could not even think of a reason. Yes, I went to Lyon twice a month to see my doctor. Yes, I always spent the night before my appointment. There were certain medications that needed to be taken. Delpay could vouch for me. No, I was not a Benedictine myself. I'd been with the sisters a year, running things in the kitchen. And before that? I'd lived in the States.

Where? The young man wanted to know. He had spent some time in Florida, he explained, brightening, I supposed, at the thought of beaches and sunshine.

Around, I told him, my usual cover. I smiled weakly. Never Florida, though.

He looked up at me, suddenly understanding, finally hearing whatever slight tic it was in my accent that still betrayed me. "Oh," he said, "you're the one, the American."

I nodded and smiled.

When we finished, he excused himself to go back up to the convent, saying there would likely be more questions, but for now I should try to rest.

Madame Tane brought me a glass of Armagnac. She was a sweet woman, in her own rough way, round and hard from years of farm living. Her children were grown and gone, scattered to desk jobs in Paris or Toulouse. She sometimes came to the priory kitchen when I was working, more, I thought, for conversation than for the sugar or yeast she would borrow.

She sat down across from me at the kitchen table, took my hand in her coarse paw, and watched me take a sip of the brandy.

"Where's Heloise?" I asked.

"Upstairs," Madame Tane said. "She's sleeping."

"Do you know what happened? How she managed to get away?"

"She escaped into the woods." The old woman lifted her hand and crossed herself. "She must have hidden there all night. It wasn't till late this morning that she came to us. That's when we called the police."

I shivered, thinking of the damp swath of forest behind the abbey, how cold the last few nights had been. "She's all right, though?"

Madame Tane nodded. "Bruised and badly shaken, but not hurt, thank God."

I took another sip of the Armagnac. It was warm and thick, and I could feel it in my belly. "May I go up?" I asked.

"Of course." Madame Tane stood, and I followed her out into the old farmhouse's front room and up the stairs to the second floor. At the end of a narrow hallway she stopped and put her hand to her lips.

"Here," she whispered, indicating a closed door. "I've made a bed up for you as well and left some towels. There's a bathroom next door. Monsieur Tane and I will have dinner soon. We hope you'll join us if you're not too tired."

I nodded. "Thank you."

"I'm sorry," the woman said; then she turned and started back toward the stairs.

I put my hand on the knob and quietly opened the door. The bedside lamp was on, casting a warm circle of light on the room's two twin beds. In the bed on the right, her legs curled protectively into her stomach, was Heloise. She woke at the sound of my footsteps and opened her eyes, staring at me through the fog of sleep.

"Eve?" she said.

"Yes." I crossed to the bed and bent down beside her. "Sorry to wake you."

She sat up, propping her shoulders on the headboard, resting her hands on top of the quilt. There was a long red welt on her right cheek, and the backs of her hands were raw and scratched. She'd been the dearest to me of all the sisters, and though I felt guilty thinking it, I was relieved that she was the one who had been spared.

I put my hand gently on hers. "You all right?"

She nodded, and I could tell she was fighting back tears. "There was a man," she said. "I left compline early. I was going to the kitchen."

Her hair was loose around her face. I reached up and brushed a stray strand from her cheek. Normally, we took that walk together each night, from the chapel to the kitchen to finish the next day's baking.

"I don't know how I did it." She looked away from me, out the bedroom's window toward the floodlit yard and the darkness beyond. "I just ran, Eve, as hard as I could. I could hear them, you know, the others. At first I thought they were singing. It sounded like they were singing, but they were screaming."

"Shush," I told her. "We can talk about this later."

She shook her head, wiping her eyes with the back of her hand. "One of the men, he had me in his hands."

"It's okay," I said, feebly trying to reassure her.

"No," she insisted. "Listen." She hardened her face, as if this was something she had to get through, as if she couldn't rest until she did. "They were looking for something, someone. The American, he said."

I straightened slightly, the hairs along the back of my neck bristling.

Heloise looked up at me. Her eyes were huge and dark. "They came for you, Eve."

THREE

Most amnesiacs are not nearly as lucky as I am. Of the scant number of people who suffer some kind of brain trauma and lose their memories, the overwhelming majority lose not only their grip on the past but their ability to form new memories as well. Put simply, their brains can no longer learn. Introduced to someone at a cocktail party, they will forget that person's name before the next sip of their martini. Give them a trivial task, like making tea, and they will need to be reminded five or six times of what they are doing. Most people like this live in constant terror, each moment groundless, independent of the one that came before.

Among the few with simple, retrograde amnesia, only a miraculous few, like me, can remember skills from the time before. Most have to be retaught the simplest things, how to fry an egg or flush a toilet. Many find that their talents and handicaps, likes and dislikes have changed drastically. I knew a man once, one of Dr. Delpay's patients, who had been a successful lawyer in his old life, and in his new one had taught himself to paint. He never set foot in a courtroom again, and had no desire to, but his paintings, beautiful, dark canvases, now sell for tens of thousands of euros.

In the first few days after the accident my memory was utterly lightless, black like the depths of the convent's wine cellar, that terrifying blindness of not being able to see your own hand in front of your face. Then, slowly, my knowledge of the world came back to me in dozens of daily discoveries, things I'd learned and forgotten I'd learned. My ease with several languages, passable French and German, a smattering of Spanish and Russian. The names of constellations. How to drive a car. These all resurfaced like the tattered relics of a shipwreck, tide-driven to the nearest shore. And though I was familiar with the mechanics of these things, the pattern of a gear shift, the conjugation of a verb, the shape of Orion, I could not tell you how I'd come to know them.

In the beginning I'd tried to piece together a life from these scant clues, women I would have liked to have been. A housewife separated from her group, a stray from a wine country tour. A travel writer. A teacher. But there was other, less comfortable evidence that just didn't fit, how when I took a seat for prayer I felt compelled to scan the chapel for the closest exit, how my eyes were always turning toward the woods, as if I expected something to come from them. Or how I knew from the day I arrived every place on the abbey grounds where a man might conceal himself.

Then one morning while Heloise and I made our way to the kitchen, I'd reeled at the distant crack of Monsieur Tane's old rifle, the sound ricocheting up from the farm below us.

"The fox," Heloise had explained, her hand on my arm, her voice calm. But her face had betrayed me, her eyes reflecting some deep and instinctive terror in my own.

For an instant I'd looked at her fragile body, the pale V of skin where her shirt opened around her neck, and I'd thought of my fingers on her throat, the heel of my palm against her breastbone, all the various ways in which I could hurt her with only my hands.

For a long time after that the only mysteries I'd wanted to understand were those of the kitchen, the secret properties of yeast, the alchemy of combining butter and flour to make air, the way Heloise marked the tops of the *bâtards* so that they split like overripe fruits in the oven.

I sat with the Tanes through dinner, trying unsuccessfully to force down a small plate of food. I should have been hungry, but I wasn't. I felt stretched thin, tired and edgy at the same time. I managed a glass of Monsieur Tane's homemade wine, then excused myself and went upstairs.

Careful not to wake Heloise, I let myself into the little guest room, kicked my shoes off, and stretched out on the free bed. I switched the bedside lamp off and let my eyes adjust to the semidarkness. The light from the yard below threw spidery shadows onto the dormered walls, the crooked outlines of tree branches, the narrow thread of a power line. I could hear Heloise breathing, and the sound of the cotton sheets rasping against each other when she moved.

They came for you, Eve, I heard her say, and once again goose bumps stippled the top of my spine. She'd been afraid, I reassured myself. She didn't know what she'd heard. And yet, whoever did this had to have wanted something.

Shuddering at the thought, I pulled the thick wool blanket up over my shoulders and rolled onto my side. Sleep seemed an impossibility, but somehow my exhaustion overtook me. I closed my eyes, and when I opened them again the moon was sitting high in the room's one window, a thin crescent like the pared tip of a fingernail.

I swung my legs off the bed and let my feet touch the cold floor. I'd been dreaming, running on legs that stubbornly refused to move with any speed. There was a child in my arms, a little girl with Heloise's face.

Resting my head in my hands, I took a deep breath and felt my pulse slow. Yes, I thought, the knowledge sudden and inexplicable, they had come for me. And they would be back.

It was beginning to snow when I set out up the dark road to the convent. A thin smattering of flakes whirled landward, settling in a downy film on the asphalt. The Tanes' retrievers were inside for the night, and the only sound was the almost imagined hush of snow collecting on the dry leaves and deadfall in the dark woods. When I'd passed through the Tanes' kitchen on my way out, the clock above the stove had read three-fifteen. I could only hope the inspector and the others had left for the night.

The abbey was still floodlit, the gray stone gleaming through the trees as I rounded the road's last curve. I stopped for a minute, straining against the quiet. Something moved in the woods, something small, an animal turning in its dreams, an owl on the hunt. Up ahead a car door closed, the sound muffled by distance, sharpened by the cold.

I stepped off into the underbrush and continued upward, picking my way through the darkness till I emerged at the edge of the grounds. The crowd that had been there earlier was gone, but there was still one car in the large drive that didn't belong to the convent. The motor was running, and I could see the orange coals of two cigarettes brightening and dimming through the windshield. An unlucky assignment on a night as cold as this.

Skirting the drive, I headed for the far end of the priory. I ducked through the woods, came around the back side of the building, and crossed the snow-covered yard toward the kitchen door. The chapel loomed behind me, the windows dark, the door slightly ajar. There was a dusting of snow on the threshold, like a sprinkling of confectioner's sugar, the final delicate touch of the maker.

I had my keys out, but I didn't need them. The door was unlocked and swung open at my touch. It was warm inside, the air heavy with the smell of yeast, of dough left too long. The lights from the yard shone in through the windows, bringing a sort of eerie false daylight to the inside of the priory. The loaves Heloise had set out the night before for their first rise had overrun their pans and were lying in shapeless mounds on the large wooden baking counter.

I headed through the kitchen, out into the dining room, and down the first-floor hallway to the stairwell and the upstairs quarters. Whoever the killers were, they'd gone through the priory, looking, it seemed, for something. The quarters had been turned inside out, the sisters' meager possessions scattered roughly about. To me this seemed almost the worst of violations. There had not been much privacy at the abbey, so what little there was had been treated with reverence.

My own room lay at the far end of the hallway, a small but comfortable cell like all the others. The door was open, and the room's few furnishings had been scoured. The desk drawers were ajar, the contents strewn across the floor: papers and books, old pantry inventories, letters from the U.S. consul, my Bible. My clothes had been dumped from the dresser and lay in a mound on the bed. The mattress lay askew on the narrow frame.

A tattered North Face rain jacket, ripped Levi's, a black turtleneck sweater from Old Navy, and a muddy pair of Nike running shoes—these were all the possessions with which I arrived in the world. I carried no purse, no wallet, no money or passport. The only clue to the mystery of myself, the only hint at where I'd come from or where I was headed, was a worn slip of paper tucked in an inside pocket of my jacket, a dog-eared receipt for the Tangier-Algeciras ferry. It wasn't much of a clue, but it was the only one I'd come with, and I'd kept it.

I picked up my Bible from the floor, then moved toward the window and peered down at the yard, the expanse of unblemished snow between the priory and the chapel. The two cops were on the other side of the building. I could chance a light. I flicked on the bedside lamp. Opening the book to the front cover, using the tip of my fingernail, I loosened the glue that held the lining in place and carefully peeled it back. There, taped securely to the inside of the cover, was the ferry ticket.

The ticket was printed in English and Spanish and Arabic. It was a one-way fare, used, the date marked as the thirtieth of October, just two days before I'd been shot and left for dead. Freeing the paper from its hiding place, I set the Bible down and held the ticket closer to the light. In the left-hand margin of the paper, in fading pencil, were five Arabic characters, sketched one above the other.

Sad. A'in. Ya. Ha. Kaf. And following the five letters, the number 21. One of the investigators assigned to my case, a young officer of Algerian descent, had translated for me, shaking his head when I'd asked what the writing meant. They're just letters, Mademoiselle, he'd said with a shrug, an acronym perhaps. A thorough search of Moroccan companies and organizations had turned up no matches, no possible answers to this strange riddle, this single fragment of my past, and deep down I'd been happy to let it lie, relieved to tuck the ticket, and whatever dubious past it had carried me from, under the faded overleaf of the Bible. Now, though, it seemed that past had come on its own. Wherever I stayed would no longer be safe, for me or for those who sheltered me.

Folding the ticket, I slipped it into my pocket and started next door to Sister Theresa's room. I needed a backpack, something more practical than the overnight bag I used for my trips to Lyon. On the top of Theresa's wardrobe I found an old rucksack, the leather aged and worn to a dark patina. Hauling the bag down, I went back to my own room and gathered a couple of changes of clothes and essentials.

Theresa and some of the other sisters had taken a trip to the Holy Land earlier that fall, and there were a few souvenirs still in the pack: postcards of Bethlehem and Jerusalem, a half-used tube of Israeli toothpaste, a ticket stub from the Church of the Holy Sepulchre. In the sack's little front pocket was Theresa's passport. I took it out, along with the mementos, and set everything aside on my bed.

A passport, I thought, stuffing my own clothes into the rucksack. I would need one if I was going to leave the European Union, and a real name, something more official than the one the sisters had given me. I ran through the sisters in my mind. Theresa was too old by several decades to be anything near a match. Heloise was too short, and brown-eyed, as well. Sister Marie was close to me in age and build. Her eyes were blue, and if I dyed my hair blond I might just be able to fake it.

Hooking the rucksack over my shoulders, I turned the light off and headed into the hallway. Marie's room was on the opposite side of the priory, and I had to search in semidarkness, but I finally found the passport in one of her desk drawers. Tucking it in my bag, I headed down to the kitchen and back out onto the snowy lawn.

It took me a moment to get my bearings. I stood for a second in the glare of the lights and watched my breath rise up and vanish. More than anything, I wanted to go back to the Tanes' and crawl into bed next to Heloise. I wanted Magda reading the morning prayer while the older sisters slept and the younger of us struggled to keep our eyes open. And the feel of Heloise's arm touching mine at the breadboard, the smells of flour and proofing yeast. I wanted to take back what had happened, as the snow had already reclaimed the last traces of the sisters' passages across the yard: heel prints in the mud, grain scattered on the way to feed the chickens. If they had not found me that day, I told myself, they would still be alive.

Conscious of my footsteps in the new snow, I crossed the lawn toward the chapel. I drew a pack of wooden matches from a niche in the stone church wall, lit one of the votives, and said a quick prayer. *Keep us safe, Lord. And keep them safe, Heloise and the thirty-four souls who had given me harbor for so long.* Then, following what little remained of my own faint trail, I headed for the woods and the road beyond.

FOUR

What can you really expect from a place? A homecoming welcome, banners in the streets, flags in the windows? Or the shuttered indifference of a town that's forgotten you, that maybe never knew you? After twenty-seven hours on trains and another thirteen waiting for connections, I probably expected too much from Algeciras.

It was after midnight when I finished the last leg of my journey and stepped onto the platform with Sister Theresa's rucksack, almost two days since I'd left the convent. I'd hitched a ride into Lyon and taken the train to Perpignan and on to Barcelona, Madrid, Seville, and finally, this port town on the far southern tip of Spain.

Aside from room and board, the sisters had paid me a small wage for my work at the priory. In the year I'd been with them I'd managed to save a few thousand euros. I'd cleaned out my bank account before leaving Lyon, and I figured if I lived on the cheap I could stretch what I had

for a month or maybe two. I could always get a job cooking once the money ran out.

The train from Bobadilla was crowded with young
tourists, dreadlocked backpackers on their way to Morocco. I followed the crush of bodies out of the station
and down toward the waterfront and the cheap hostels. If
I was going to do something with my hair, I told myself, I
needed a room of my own and a private bath.

I found what I was looking for in a little one-star hotel
just two blocks from the ferry terminal. Twenty euros
bought me a view of the crumbling apartment building
next door, a window that opened partway to let in the
piss-and-flotsam stink of the port, a bed, a sink, a toilet,
and a bathtub with a faint gray ring.

Kicking my shoes off, I set the rucksack on the bed
next to the pillow and lay down on top of the covers. I'd
slept some on the trip, but not enough. I stretched out on
my back and closed my eyes, my body rocking and swaying to the ghost motion of the train.

I woke early, my sleep still tuned to the Benedictine
schedule. It was raining, a dull and persistent drizzle. The
sky and the rooftops of Algeciras were all various shades
of the same dull gray, a monochrome broken here and
there by the tousled green of palms. I got up, put on some
fresh clothes, washed my face, and, taking the rucksack
with me, went out, hoping beyond hope to find whatever
it was I had come for, a person or place like a spark on dry
tinder, that one thing that would make everything else fall
into place.

I stopped for coffee, then wended my way to the train
station and back to the waterfront, detouring down side
streets. What had been unfamiliar in the dark remained so
in the wan morning light. There was nothing recognizable

about the bland tourist cafés and utilitarian port. The ferry terminal itself was absolutely foreign, a hulking modern structure made of glass and steel. If I had been here, I had no memory of it.

I went into the terminal and got a ticket on the afternoon boat to Tangier, then backtracked to a drugstore I'd passed earlier. I bought a hair-coloring kit, a pair of weak reading glasses, and an assortment of cheap makeup, then returned to my hotel.

Marie and I were by no means twins. Her lips were slightly fuller than mine, her face narrower, her nose rounder. There's a limit to what can be accomplished with eyeliner, a lip pencil, and a little bit of blush, but with the makeup and the glasses and my new hair, even I almost believed the picture in Marie's passport was me.

I left my hotel at two-thirty, and by two-forty-five I was at the terminal, a good forty-five minutes early for my boat. I'd checked out the Spanish passport controls when I'd bought my ticket. There were three lines, and I wanted to get a good look at the three officials manning them before I chose one.

At around three o'clock the ferry started boarding. The passengers were a strange hodgepodge, half tourist, half local. Djellabas and head scarves mingled with tie-dye and jeans. There were two men and one woman manning the glassed-in booths. I ruled out the woman right away. She was fast but thorough, carefully scanning each face that passed, her little pinched eyes glancing from passport to person and back before she pressed her stamp to paper.

In the middle booth was a young man. Too young, I thought, a twenty-year-old bully hiding behind acne scars. His shirt was stiffly ironed, his uniform neat as a pin. I watched him questioning an elderly Moroccan woman with plastic bags for luggage. When she was unable to understand, he shook his head and gave her a look of exasperation, then stamped her passport and waved her off impatiently.

The second man seemed to be my best bet. He was older than his colleagues and more relaxed. His tie was loose around his neck, his hat slightly askew. He smiled briefly at each passenger.

It was the height of the boarding crush, and I wanted to get on before the crowd thinned and things slowed down. My heart hammering in my chest, I fished out my passport, hooked the rucksack over my shoulders, and headed for the back of the older man's line.

I hadn't given much thought to the possibility of not getting through, but as I watched the man mark each passport for transit I began to wonder what would happen if they questioned my papers. How would I explain the fact that I was traveling under the identity of a dead nun?

The last of a group of young German girls in line in front of me stepped up to the booth, and my stomach fluttered into my throat. The man smiled and nodded. Have a nice trip, he said to the girl in Spanish, then waved me forward.

Smiling, I slid my passport through the slot at the bottom of the glass. The man opened the cover and looked down at the picture, his gray eyebrows furrowing slightly. I could see him squinting to read the information; then his eyes shifted upward to my face and back down toward the photograph.

"Just a moment," he said in pleasant but firm Spanish. Closing my passport, he stepped away from the window.

This is it, I thought, watching his back disappear through an unmarked door, the passport in his hand. Someone grumbled in the stalled line behind me. Should I run? I wondered, glancing back toward the stairs that led down to the main terminal. A pair of policemen lingered on the landing. Maybe I could just walk away, I told myself, slip out unnoticed. I was half turning to go when the door opened and the man reappeared.

"Is there a problem?" I asked, trying to force my rusty Spanish to sound relaxed.

He laid the passport on the little counter and slid it toward me. "No problem, *mi hermana,*" he said, shaking his head. "Just a mix-up."

A mix-up. I smiled and took the passport. "Thank you."

He smiled back. "*Bon voyage.*"

Steadying my legs, I forced myself to move forward. There were two swinging doors just beyond the immigration booths, and on the other side of the doors, a long glass walkway that led out to the ferry's gangplank. I made my way with the other passengers, my stomach slowly calming, my pulse easing down toward normal. Halfway there, I told myself, conscious of the fact that I still had to get past the Moroccan officials.

We boarded the boat on the deserted lower car deck, then climbed up to the passenger deck. It was raining still, the dark bay dotted with gleaming whitecaps. Out the salt-rimed windows I could see the rocky flanks of Gibraltar and the geometric lines of the Algeciras waterfront. I found a free chair and settled in for the ride.

I opened Marie's passport to the photo page and read down through the typed information: name, place and date of birth, identity number. No, there was nothing about a profession, nothing to give away the fact that Marie was a nun. Yet the man had known. *No problem, mi hermana,* I had heard him say. *No problem, my sister.* Somehow, he had known.

FIVE

Nothing can prepare you for Tangier. Nothing can ready you for the crush of men, the hands grabbing for your bags, the taxi drivers fistfighting for your fare, the poverty and hopelessness of the place. The city assaults you with the stench of desperation: the sweat of illegals from Senegal or the Ivory Coast waiting listlessly in cheap cafés for a night crossing to Spain, the wool-and-saffron reek of the black-market money changers outside the medina, the gunmetal tang of the soldiers in the Grand Socco. Everywhere, the pervasive stink of colonialism gone to rot.

It was just before sundown when we docked in Tangier. I'd gotten a visa on the boat, a rubber stamp from a young Moroccan official who hadn't even bothered to look at my passport photo. He'd added my transit slip to a growing heap of identical scraps of white paper, some littering the ground at his feet, then waved me on my way.

The passenger deck was thick with too much humanity in too small a space, damp clothes and diapers and fried food. I was grateful when news of our imminent arrival crackled over the intercom, and we could make our way down to the car deck to wait to offload. Someone opened the chain-link cage that served as a baggage hold, and the crowd rushed recklessly forward, scrambling over the open top of the cage, fighting their way to backpacks and battered suitcases.

After a few minutes the gangway door swung open. The gangplank was lowered into place, and one by one we funneled onto the African continent, passports once again out. I had a brief moment of anxiety before I handed mine over, but there was no reason to worry. With the hundreds of bodies pressed behind me, there was time for little more than a cursory glance and a nod.

When I emerged from the terminal onto the long crumbling pier, I was immediately surrounded by some dozen local men, some in long hooded burnooses and pointy-toed babouches, others wearing Calvin Klein knockoffs and dark sunglasses, all clamoring to be of service in one way or another. I shook my head and kept walking, hands tight on the straps of my rucksack, moving forward with the crowd.

Through all the shouting and confusion, the dullest ache of recognition was beginning to form in my mind. Some part of my consciousness knew this place, the shape of the port, the rhythm of the language. I looked ahead toward the distant end of the pier, and somehow I knew there was a large gate there, and a square. Northwest of the square, where the land sloped upward, lay the labyrinth of the medina. I was certain of it.

One of the would-be guides stepped in front of me, blocking my way, and put his hand on my arm.

"This way," he said forcefully in thickly accented English. "My taxi," he insisted, yanking my arm, pulling me after him.

I shook him off. "No. Leave me alone."

He stepped closer, his finger wagging in my face. "No need to be rude." He spat as he said the words, and a droplet of saliva landed on my cheek.

"I don't need a taxi," I said, trying to smooth things over, but it was too late. I'd offended him, and there was no getting around it.

I moved forward, trying to get past him, but he blocked my way again. "Why so rude?" he asked, aggressively.

Shaking my head, I tried to guess at the best answer. With the crowd of passengers flowing past us, I hardly imagined I could be in danger, but still, there seemed to be no way to shake the man, and I could feel a wave of panic moving up into my chest.

I opened my mouth to say something when a voice spoke up in Arabic behind me. Sneering, my harasser spat out a response.

"Leave her alone," the voice said, in French now.

I craned my head to see a funny little man in a long woolen overcoat and wraparound sunglasses with yellow lenses.

Reluctantly, the guide stepped aside.

"Thank you," I said to the overcoated man.

"Of course."

I started forward again, and my strange savior fell in step beside me.

"They're harmless," he said, "but a nuisance. Especially during Ramadan. I don't think it's the food they miss so much as the cigarettes. People tend to get a little cranky by this time of day. Is this your first trip to Tangier?"

I thought about the question for a moment. "Yes," I said, taking in the man's incongruous attire. The curved wooden handle of an umbrella was hooked over his right arm. His shoes were Nikes, bright orange with a metallic sheen. His features were Asian, but his English had an almost perfect British accent. "And you?"

The little man shook his head. "I live here," he said. "I've just been up to Spain for a few days." He nodded toward his suitcase, a battered leather bag. "Stocking up on paints."

"You're an artist?"

"Yes. I've come from Japan. It's my experiment, to find cultural isolation." He had a delicate way of speaking, an air of intense deliberation to everything he said and did.

I smiled. There was something childlike and vulnerable about the little man, something entirely unthreatening, amusing even. "Could you recommend a hotel?" I asked as we neared the port entrance. "Something relatively reasonable."

He thought for a moment. "There's the Continental, of course. Abdesselom will take extremely good care of you."

"Abdesselom?"

"The manager," the man explained. He looked down at his watch and furrowed his brow. "Of course the sun's about to set. There's not much to be done for the next hour or so."

"I can wait," I said. "If you just point me in the right direction."

"It's not far." He pointed toward the jumbled hillside of the Old City. "You see that pink building?"

"Yes," I said, picking out the rose-colored facade.

He wrinkled his nose and stopped walking for a moment. "I'm going for some dinner, if you'd like to join me. Then I can take you up there myself. I live just around the corner."

"Oh, no," I said. "I don't want to trouble you."

"It's no trouble." He smiled.

I hesitated a moment. I didn't relish the idea of making my way through the medina alone. Besides, the man seemed lonely, grateful for my company, and I was hungry. "Sure," I agreed.

He bowed stiffly at the waist, then held out his hand. "I'm Joshi."

"Marie," I said, taking the offered hand. It was cool and soft against my own.

We ate at the Café Africa, a well-lit establishment near the Grand Socco. The restaurant was clean and cheery, with a white-tiled floor, mirrored walls, and freshly laundered tablecloths, a slightly exotic copy of a French brasserie. The meal was like a strange dance. I had the uneasy feeling that despite his meticulous appearance Joshi had little enough money to be hungry, that the price of a meal was the unspoken fee for his guidance. Yet when I reached for the check at the end of the meal, I could sense the depth of his embarrassment.

It was raining when we left, turning the sidewalks slick with filth. We walked across the Grand Socco and in through the gates of the Old City, down the bustling Rue as-Siaghin, past the Great Mosque.

"My apartment," Joshi said, as we neared the eastern ramparts of the medina and turned into a narrow side street. "There. Do you see the flag?"

I looked up, following his finger. There was a series of low rooftops lit now by flickering streetlights and a slightly taller building beyond. In one of the dirt-smeared windows of the taller structure was a white flag with a simple red circle in the center. I nodded. "I see."

"And here is the Hotel Continental," Joshi announced,

directing my gaze to a plaster gate that lay just a few steps in front of us. "I'll take you in."

The Continental was a large colonial structure, a Western stronghold perched at the edge of the medina. Inside the gate, a stone courtyard led to a sweep of stairs. At the top of the stairs was a generous veranda with an unobscured view of the port. It was a terrace wide enough for the foregone days of cocktails and dancing and Dior dresses, though my best guess told me even in its prime the Continental had verged toward the seedy. Today, a few bedraggled tables and chairs sat empty, staring out toward the dark bay. The building's pinkish facade was cracked, the plaster flaking.

Inside, the hotel was like a movie set, the walls richly mosaicked, trimmed with carved plaster and wood. The few guests in the lobby were a strange mix, a new breed of Western traveler, more Lonely Planet than Paul Bowles. Several members of an American film crew loitered around the front desk, hassling a gray-haired clerk about the rooms they'd been given. Two young German women huddled around the public phone, each taking turns with the receiver. A middle-aged woman in sensible travel attire, lightweight pants, hiking boots, and fanny pack, sat on a sagging couch paging through an English-language travel guide.

I stood behind Joshi, eavesdropping on the disgruntled Americans, while the clerk listened patiently, then politely explained that the rooms were the best he had to offer. The men were not easily convinced, but in the end the clerk's implacable manner won out, and the crew retreated, grumbling, while the elderly clerk turned his attention to us.

Spend a year hoping for recognition, and you will come to know the intricacies of the human face, the delicacy of expression. In the first few months of my new life I lived in a state of constant anticipation, examining each person I passed on the street for some hint of familiarity, some clue to a shared past, however brief. And though what I saw was never the bewildered tic of the long-lost acquaintance, I saw every other possible countenance, love, despair, and even emptiness.

When the manager turned his face from Joshi's to mine, the ripple that passed across his features was almost imperceptible, slight as the barest breeze roughing the surface of a lake, slight as a minute's interval of light at sunset. His eyes paused for just longer than a second on mine, long enough for me to think we had met before, then he murmured something in English. "It is easy for me," I swore I heard him say.

"Excuse me?" I asked.

He shook his head, the look I'd taken for recognition passing on. "Nothing, Mademoiselle." Smiling genially, he turned to Joshi. "I see you've brought us a guest."

Joshi nodded. "Marie's just come in on the ferry. I promised her you'd have a room."

The man glanced at me once more, then slipped on a pair of reading glasses and peered down at his registry. "I believe I can find something."

I watched the side of his face, his hands sliding across the page in front of him. He was Moroccan, but not fully, his blue-gray eyes betraying whatever Frenchman or Brit lingered somewhere not far back on his family tree.

"I have a room for two hundred dirhams," he offered, finally. "With a shared bath down the hall."

I nodded, fishing fifty euros from my pack. "Can you change this for me?"

"Of course."

The clerk opened a cash box and counted out a stack

of dirhams, setting two hundred aside for himself, giving me the rest. He penciled something in the registry, then slid a piece of paper across the counter.

"If Mademoiselle wouldn't mind," he said.

I looked down at the blank registration form in front of me, the lines marked *Name* and *Passport number*. Sliding Marie's passport from my bag, I penned in what information I could, hesitating over my home address, finally scribbling down the street number of the chocolate shop in Lyon.

When I had finished, the old clerk reached over, grabbed a key from one of the many hooks that hung on the wall beside him, and set it on the counter.

"Room two-oh-five," he said.

I picked up the key and looked down at him, willing myself to remember if I could, my mind straining to see through the dark night of all I'd forgotten. "Do I know you?"

He shook his head. "I don't think so."

"Are you sure?" I pressed.

Abdesselom looked to Joshi and then again to me. "I would remember."

I thanked Joshi for all his help, then climbed the stairs to my room. A funny little man, I thought, opening the door, setting my rucksack down on the bed, so stiffly British and Asian at the same time, so awkward in his intentions. Though I couldn't say I hadn't been grateful for his guidance. Leaving the lights off, I stepped to the window and peered down at the waterlogged veranda and courtyard. The hotel's front door swung open, and a group of tourists filed out, heading for the medina. A few seconds later Joshi appeared, his orange shoes glowing unmistakably. He stopped, drew a pack of cigarettes from his coat and lit one, then opened the black circle of his umbrella. A lonely man, I told myself.

Headlights flickered outside the gate, and a little red taxi pulled into the courtyard. I watched as a figure climbed out, a man in a long raincoat. He said something to the driver, then climbed up the steps to where Joshi was standing. The taxi sat where it was, engine idling. I could see the man's face in the veranda lights. An American, I thought, squinting to see better. Yes, he had that look: blond hair, white teeth, and an unnatural healthiness. He and Joshi exchanged a few words; then he reached into his pocket, pulled out a brown envelope, handed it to Joshi, and headed back to the waiting cab.

I went to bed early and was awakened sometime around midnight by a barrage of off-key German drinking songs. There was a chorus of drunken footsteps in the hallway, several minutes of slamming doors and water running in the pipes; then the floor fell silent, and I drifted back to sleep.

Sometime later in the night I woke again, wrangled from sleep by the quiet shuffling of another body in the room. In my half-dreaming state my first thought was that it was Heloise, come to wake me for the morning prayer. I sank down deeper under the covers, thinking it was far too early to face the cold walk to the chapel, the drone of Magdalene's voice.

Then the person moved again, and the fog in my brain lifted. I snapped my eyes open and stared into the darkness, heart racing, body flush with adrenaline. Stiffening, I willed myself motionless.

The curtains were open, and in the bars of bluish light shining up from the veranda I could see the figure's silhouette. It was a man, broad shouldered and tall. In his hand was my rucksack. Carefully unbuckling the little front pocket, he pulled out my passport.

Should I yell? I wondered. Surely the noise would scare him off. All the money I had in the world was in that bag, not to mention the passport. I could afford to lose neither. Then I thought of the sisters, of Heloise's face tight with fear, and what she'd told me at the Tanes'. Was this one of the men? Had he come for me? Opening the passport, he pulled a long thin object from his clothes.

Would the Germans hear me in time? Or were they too groggy from their midnight drunk? There was a soft clicking noise, and a small circle of light sprang from the man's hand. The thin object was a flashlight. The man shined the beam on the passport, reading, it seemed; then he snuffed the light and returned the passport to its place in the rucksack.

He hesitated a moment, then took a step toward me and another. Slowly, silently, I drew my breath in and lowered my eyelids. Yes, I thought, he could kill me now before anyone heard a thing. In the morning there'd be only someone's sleep-warped memory of a short, thin scream. One thousand one, one thousand two. I counted out each second till, miraculously, I heard him turn.

Opening one eye, I watched him put his hand on the knob and noiselessly pull the door inward. Light blazed in from the hallway, briefly illuminating him as he slipped out of the room and closed the door behind him. He was only visible for a second, but it was time enough for me to recognize him. It was the American, the man I'd seen on the veranda with Joshi.

SIX

I lay still for a good half hour, body rigid, ears alert to the slightest sound, some part of me expecting the man to return. When I finally lifted my arm from under the covers and checked my watch, it was just before five. Swinging out of bed, I dressed, slipped the rucksack over my shoulders, and headed into the hallway.

I made my way down through the empty lobby and out onto the veranda, then crossed the courtyard. Outside the Continental's gates, the medina was bustling with people, alive as I might have imagined it to be at midday. The streets smelled of roasting meat and hot bread, preparations for the predawn feast and the day of fasting ahead.

Backtracking to the spot where Joshi and I had stopped the night before, I found the flag that marked his window. A good fifteen feet of smooth wall separated the little rectangular opening from the roof below it. If I wanted in, I'd have to find a way inside the building. A corner apartment, I told myself, counting up the floors, skirting toward the front of the structure. The heavy wooden door was locked tight, barred by a thick iron strap.

I stepped into the street, contemplating my options. Could there be a back door? A lower window somewhere? As I started back the way I'd come, I caught sight of a woman in a djellaba and a head scarf coming toward me. The crook of her left arm held a shopping bag. In her right hand was a ring of keys. I let her pass me, then turned and followed a few steps behind. Hugging the shadows on the far edge of the narrow street, I watched her turn into the front alcove of Joshi's building. I flattened myself against the wall and waited. Keys jangled in the lock; then I heard her step inside.

The door creaked closed behind her, and I leaped forward, my fingertips catching the smooth wood before the latch clicked into place. I ducked into the alcove and waited, listening to her footsteps, the opening and closing of an interior door. When I was certain she was in her apartment, I pushed my way inside.

From what little I had been able to discern from the jumbled rooftops and seemingly random placement of windows, my best guess put Joshi's apartment on the third floor. The woman had switched the timed hallway light on, and a dim bulb illuminated the stairwell. I hit the switch again, buying myself another few minutes of light, then started upward. When I reached the third-floor landing, I found the corner apartment and knocked.

The building was beginning to awaken. From behind the other closed doors came the sounds of children's voices, the clatter of crockery, the race to eat and drink before the sun came up. Only Joshi's apartment was quiet. I knocked again, louder this time, and waited.

Finally, something moved in the apartment, bedclothes rustling, feet on bare tiles. I knocked once more, and the door cracked open. Two bleary eyes stared out at me. Jamming my shoulder against the door, I forced my way inside. The little man reeled backward, knocked off balance, and slammed into the wall.

"Who is he?" I demanded, closing the door behind me.

Joshi recovered himself and backed away. He had on striped cotton pajamas, blue bed slippers, and a blue robe. A pink sleep crease ran across the side of his face. "I don't know," he stammered. "I don't know what you're talking about."

I stepped closer to him and grabbed the front of the pajamas, pulling him toward me. He was smaller than I was, his face collapsing now like a scared child's. He made a little noise, a weak attempt at a scream.

"I saw you together on the veranda at the Continental," I said. "How much did he give you?"

Joshi squirmed in my hands. "I don't know this man," he insisted. "I only asked him for a light."

"Bullshit. He paid you to follow me from the beginning." I raised one fist as if I was going to hit him, and he shrunk back, his eyes pinched shut, his arm flying to protect his face.

"Don't hurt me," he whimpered.

"Who is he?" I asked again.

"Just an expat, an American," the little man said. "His name is Brian; that's all I know."

"How do you know him?"

Joshi shrugged. "The Continental, the Pub. I've seen him around. There aren't many of us. I ran into him on the ferry. He asked me to keep an eye on you."

I loosed my grip, and he straightened himself, smoothing the wrinkles from his pajama top. "Where does he live?" I asked.

"I don't know. Somewhere in the Ville Nouvelle, probably."

"Where can I find him?" I moved toward him again, and he cringed.

"It's Wednesday, right?"

I thought for a minute, then nodded.

"The Pub," Joshi said, "across from the Hotel Ritz. Wednesday's dart night. Things usually get started early, around the cocktail hour. If he's not there, you can try the piano bar at the El Minzah later."

I turned for the door, stopping briefly to look back. Joshi pulled his robe tight around him, and I could see for the first time that the blue cotton had been mended and remended. The hem was frayed with wear.

"I'm sorry," he said.

With one exception, the rooms at the priory were simple and unadorned. Decades, even centuries, of the same off-white paint covered the hallways, the kitchen, and the sisters' quarters. But at some point in the long history of the building, someone had decided to distinguish the library with wallpaper. And in the years after, other sisters had added more layers.

The library was a beautiful room and well used, airy and high-ceilinged with a stone fireplace and a view of the priory's garden. But at the time of my stay it had obviously seen some years of neglect. There were places where the paper had begun to peel away, ragged holes that revealed the old patterns underneath. A form of time travel, Heloise had called it, and sometimes the two of us would contemplate this backward record and its makers.

The upper layer was young enough for Magda to remember its having been hung, though the sister who hung it had long resided in the little cemetery next to the chapel. It was green, faded now, with a pattern of darker green leaves. Beneath the green were other prints, gaudy flowers, gold fleurs-de-lis, and simple stripes. My favorite paper was printed over and over with a Chinese village scene. It was a tiny world of fishermen and farmers, of pagodas and bridges, and a solitary oxen driver on a winding mountain road.

I often wondered at the sister who had picked it. Did she sit in the evenings and contemplate an escape to this strange place? Did she wonder at those static lives, the woman forever fanning herself, the fisherman still without a fish?

Once, when we were sitting in the library, I asked Heloise what it was like to remember, and she said it was like the library walls, the present faded green leaves, the past poking through here and there, and always, farther down, another mystery.

When I left Joshi's that morning and headed back through the Continental's gates, I felt as if a piece of my own present had begun to peel away. Somewhere beneath the glue-stiff layers lay this city. I was certain of it now. And beneath the faded print of Tangier lay the tattered edges of a far darker pattern, a part of myself I had long expected to find.

I climbed the stairs to the veranda and stood for a moment looking out at the harbor. The sky was an impossible predawn blue, glowing like a jewel above the bay. I knew this place, I thought. It was familiar to me in some deep-down way. But more familiar than Tangier, than the smells of the medina, than the cloaked shapes swaying under djellabas and burnooses, was the risen power of my own anger.

I thought of Joshi in his worn pajamas, his little arm moving to protect his face, and suddenly I was afraid. I would have beaten it out of him, I thought. I would have gotten the information no matter what. I knew how to do that kind of thing.

. . .

I slept late, then spent the afternoon wandering the city. It was just before five when I stepped into the Pub, and already the place was packed with expatriates. Bare-shouldered English girls and sunburned Australians flirted with each other over shandies and pints of porter. I ordered a lager and wandered back toward the dartboards and pool table.

Except for the small slice of Tangier that was visible through the front window, I could have been on any London corner. A large television over the bar broadcast Premier League soccer. A blackboard beside it listed the daily specials: scampi and chips, ploughman's lunch, and kidney pie. Save for a framed operating license, there was not one scrap of Arabic in the establishment. The man Joshi had called Brian was nowhere to be found, so I grabbed a free seat in a back corner of the bar, ordered some scampi and chips, and settled in to wait.

I didn't have to wait long. I was tucking away the last of my greasy french fries when the front door opened and a group of girls stumbled inside. Pulling off long-sleeved shirts and jackets to reveal half T-shirts and navel rings, shedding their outerwear like crabs ready for mating, they headed for the bar. I was watching them with fascination when the door opened again and a man stepped inside.

He had traded his raincoat for faded jeans, a gray cotton sweater, and running shoes, but it was the same man I'd seen on the Continental's veranda and in my hotel room early that morning. Yes, I thought, watching him make his way to the bar, he was definitely an American. He ordered a beer and started in my direction, evidently heading for the dartboards. I leaned my elbows on the table and watched him. He was handsome up close, his hair slightly mussed as if he'd just woken from a nap. He passed right by me, his eyes skimming my face, then moved on.

I ordered another pint and let him play a game of darts. When he made his second trip to the bar, I elbowed my way in beside him.

"Do I know you?" I asked.

He signaled for the bartender, then looked over at me nonchalantly. "I don't think so."

"No. I'm sure I know you. It's Brian, right?"

He shrugged. "I've got that kind of look."

"Maybe this'll jog your memory," I told him. "Four o'clock this morning. Hotel Continental. Room two-oh-five."

The bartender came over. Brian ordered another pint and slid a twenty-dirham note across the bar.

"Who the fuck are you?" I demanded. "And what do you want?"

He picked up his glass, took his change, and turned to move away. "Listen, I really think you've got the wrong guy."

I watched him walk back to the dartboards, exchanging brief hellos as he went. Most of the Pub's patrons seemed to know each other, and Brian was no exception.

A young woman with dreadlocks muscled her way in next to me.

"You a regular?" I asked.

She smiled. "Regular as I can be."

"You know that guy over there?" I pointed to Brian.

"Sure."

"His name's Brian, right?"

"Cute, huh?" She nodded.

"You know anything about him?"

The woman lit a cigarette and waved the smoke away. "American," she said. "From California, I think. Poor guy."

"Why do you say that?"

"He's down here looking for his brother," she explained. "Disappeared about a year ago."

"Did you know him? The brother, I mean."

She shook her head. "Before my time."

"What happened?"

"That's the problem, isn't it? No one knows."

The bartender appeared, and the woman ordered a vodka tonic.

"He was some kind of do-gooder," she offered. "You know, trying to modernize the medina, bring the Internet to the carpet dealers."

I watched Brian put his beer down and start for the men's room.

"Don't get any ideas," the dreadlocked woman said wistfully as her drink arrived. "He's single as they come, and appears to like it that way. Believe me, we've all tried."

I smiled. "Well, then, wish me luck."

"Good luck," I heard her say as I started toward the rear of the bar.

The rest rooms were tucked in a small hallway behind the pool table. I set my beer down next to Brian's, slipped into the little corridor, and leaned against the wall next to the men's-room door, listening to the sound of the faucets running. Something was wrong. No one took that long to wash his hands. Moving my ear to the door, I knocked lightly and got no answer.

I put my hand on the knob and pushed. The bathroom and its single doorless stall were empty. The one small window was too small and too high to have provided an exit. Stepping back into the hallway, I surveyed my surroundings. Next to the men's room was the women's. Across the corridor was a door marked *Office* and a second, unmarked door. I tried the blank door and felt the knob give way in my hand. The door swung outward to reveal the dank and putrid alley beyond.

Something moved in the darkness. I craned my head out to see a knot of rats swarming on the Pub's garbage, a tangle of teeth and furless tails. Farther away, near where the alley opened onto the street, a shapeless beggar coughed, the sound hoarse and hollow as a death rattle. There was no sign of Brian.

SEVEN

Figuring I'd try the El Minzah later, I took a taxi back to the Continental. I was doubtful I'd find Brian at the piano bar that night, more doubtful still that he'd tell me anything if I did, but Joshi's tip was the only trail I had to follow and I planned on pursuing it to its end.

Abdesselom had evidently quit for the night, and a middle-aged Moroccan woman with a bad orange dye-job and too much makeup had taken his place behind the desk. When I asked her what time things usually got started at the El Minzah, she folded her arms across her chest and eyed me skeptically.

"You are going to Caid's?" she asked.

I gave her a look of confusion.

"Caid's. The piano bar," she elaborated.

I nodded.

"Ten, ten-thirty." The woman shrugged. "But you can't go like that. Caid's is very fancy, very fancy."

I looked down at myself, at my convent work boots, faded canvas shirt, and patched jeans. The change of clothes in my pack wasn't much better, and certainly less clean. "It'll have to do," I told her.

Making my way up to my room, I locked the door and rummaged in my pack. I pulled out a rumpled black sweater and laid it on the bed, smoothing the wrinkles with the back of my hand, dabbing it clean with a damp washcloth before putting it on. I ran a brush through my hair and pulled it back off my face. With a little luck I hoped I could pull off the slumming-rich-girl look.

Yes, I thought, giving myself a good once-over in the mirror, it would have to do. I tucked a stray wisp of hair behind one ear, turned, and headed for the door. That's when I noticed the little book that lay open on my night-stand. I stopped short and stepped toward it. It had not been there before, of that I was certain. The maid must have left it, I told myself, glancing at the two open pages, the Arabic script. And yet if a maid had come while I'd been out, she had not stayed long enough to fold the two towels I'd tucked haphazardly over the chrome bar next to the sink.

I picked up the book. The text was divided into short, numbered sections, verses, it seemed. A religious book, but not the Bible, the Koran most likely. I closed the cover and, taking the book with me, picked up my ruck-sack. No doubt it wasn't appropriate attire for the El Min-zah, but I couldn't leave it, not now, knowing someone had been in my room. Hoisting the pack onto my shoulder, I stepped into the hallway and headed down to the lobby.

"Is this the hotel's?" I asked the clerk. I set the Koran down on the counter in front of her.

The woman scowled up at me. "Where did you find that?"

"Someone left it in my room," I told her. "Do you know who it belongs to?"

She slid the book protectively toward herself, then set it on the desk next to her computer. "I will see that it gets back to its owner. Good night, Mademoiselle."

It was just after ten-thirty when I pulled up in front of the sandstone portal and heavy, iron-studded wooden door that marked the El Minzah's front entrance. I paid my taxi driver, climbed out, and made my way inside. If the Hotel Continental was the geriatric specter of French colonialism, then the El Minzah was its teenage reincarnation, the Versace-clad, cell phone–carrying spirit of the unstoppable empire of twenty-first-century globalism.

Inside the plush lobby, potbellied oil money mingled with B-list celebrity. American English predominated; a variety of well-crafted accents wafted through the potted palms and up toward the blue-and-white zillij mosaics. The air smelled of Cuban cigars and eucalyptus.

Conscious of my convent clothes and work-blunted fingernails, I followed one of the doormen's directions down a flight of stairs, past the rambling Andalusian courtyard at the heart of the hotel to the piano bar. Scanning the sea of faces for Brian, I stepped into the elegant room, found an empty table, and settled in to wait. The piano bar was more British than French or Moroccan, dark and richly paneled like the library in some English gentleman's country estate. A large oil portrait of a serious-looking Scot in full military dress dominated the room, staring down on a crowd tinged with the shabby, desperate whiff of exile.

From down in the dank and tangled streets of the medina it would be hard to imagine the existence of such a place as Caid's. It would be difficult to conceive of such blind and easy luxury, the thin rattling of ice in a crystal glass, the fizz of champagne, a woman's bare shoulders rising like a frail white flower from the black sheath of her dress. There were no beggars in Caid's, no dirt-smeared children grappling for change, only the pervasive stink of orchids and tobacco, and a nauseating blend of expensive perfumes. Here, I thought, was the fantasy money can buy, the Victorian illusion of a separation between this world and the savage one, these few dozen bodies clustered under the pale archways and dark pleated drapes like exotic orchids in a winter hothouse.

The staff was all Moroccan and male, as was the piano player, a small round man with a smile as white as his dinner jacket. He was singing a maudlin rendition of "Ne Me Quitte Pas" while several couples pawed each other on the dance floor. One of the waiters, a handsome young man in a neatly tailored red vest and black pants, started over to me, his face brightening as he neared.

"Ms. Boyle," he said warmly when he had reached my table. Tucking his tray under his arm, he leaned in closer, beaming, shaking his head in evident disbelief. "I almost didn't recognize you."

Boyle, I thought, Ms. Boyle. I looked up at the man's delicate, caramel-colored face, searching in vain for something familiar.

"Nadim," he said, motioning to himself.

I smiled. "Yes, of course, Nadim."

He stood there for a moment, an awkward silence passing between us, then made a slight stiff bow. "Your drink," he said, turning. "I will be right back."

I watched him walk to the bar. He said something to the bartender, and they both glanced back at me and nodded; then the bartender pulled a clear bottle from the shelf behind him. I had been here, I thought, shifting my gaze to the piano player and the dark bank of windows beyond him, the panes reflecting the bar's dim faces. I had been here, and yet I could not remember. The waiter came back carrying a martini glass and laid a small linen bar napkin on the table in front of me.

"When was I here last?" I asked.

Nadim set the glass on the napkin, then straightened up. "It has been a while," he said, scowling, trying to remember. "A year. Maybe longer. You stayed with us."

I looked down at the drink. A single delicate sliver of lemon rested at the bottom of the glass. "Was I alone?"

"Yes."

"And I was here before that?"

The waiter drew back now, puzzled. "Of course. Ms. Boyle, is everything all right?"

"Alone?"

"Why no, with Mr. Haverman."

I took a sip of the martini. It was vodka, cold and citrusy, studded with tiny shards of ice. "A friend?" I asked.

"Of course, Madame."

"What does he do, this Mr. Haverman?"

"Do?" Nadim asked, perplexed.

"For a job."

"He's an American," the waiter said, as if being an American were a profession in itself. "Like you. A nice man."

"And what does he look like?"

Nadim shuffled his feet nervously. "Young, like yourself."

"Brown hair? Blond?"

"Brown," Nadim said, growing more and more wary of this game by the second.

A customer several tables away signaled for service, and the waiter gratefully excused himself. I put the drink down and reached up and grasped his wrist. "What else,

Nadim?" I asked, desperate to keep him there. "What else do you know?"

The waiter looked down, fear flashing across his face. "You are a patron of the hotel, Ms. Boyle," he said, trying to compose himself. "And a lovely lady. You drink vodka martinis with a twist. This is all I know."

"And Mr. Haverman?"

"A friend," he said, repeating his previous answer, "a customer like yourself. This is all I know."

Nadim had made no attempt to remove his wrist from my grip; now his arm was beginning to tremble. The man at the other table waved again, and I loosed my grasp. "I'm sorry," I told him as he hurried away, obviously embarrassed by what had just happened.

I finished my drink, ordered another, and watched the crowd revolve. Toward the end of the evening the American film crew from the Continental showed up. They were loud and underdressed, as Americans almost always are, throwing dollars around and ordering overpriced Scotch.

It didn't seem possible that this had been my life, and suddenly I didn't want it to be. I wanted my old clothes back, and if not the convent, some place like it, a small plain room and a little garden on a hill, a bell ringing the hours.

The piano player tapped out the first few lines of "As Time Goes By," and a smattering of applause rose from the tables. Giving up on Brian, I downed the last of my drink, stood, and made my way out of the bar. It was late enough that the rest of the hotel was nearly deserted. Out in the courtyard the only sound was the splash and gurgle of a fountain, and a woman's quiet laughter that drifted down from an open window somewhere above. The stars were out, a carpet of faraway sun catchers. The black shape of a bat cruised silently overhead.

I climbed up into the empty lobby and headed for the

front desk, where a young woman in a blue suit was bent over a computer keyboard. She looked up when she saw me coming and straightened, fixing some unseen crease in her jacket. I watched her face for some expression of recognition but saw none.

"May I help you?" she asked.

I nodded, thinking of the form I'd filled out when I'd checked in at the Continental. Surely a hotel as nice as the El Minzah would require just as much information from its clients, if not more. If I had been a guest here, there might be some record in the computer.

"How long have you worked here?" I asked, stepping forward, propping my elbows on the marble counter.

"Six months," the woman said. She was meticulously made up, her lips stained the same dark red as the drapes in the piano bar. Her name tag read *Ashia*.

I smiled. "I stayed here about a year ago," I explained. "I'm trying to pin down the dates. I just can't seem to remember. Do you keep a record of your guests on file?"

Ashia nodded. She looked at me expectantly and when I didn't answer, cleared her throat. "Your name, Madame?"

"Boyle," I said.

"*B-o-y-l-e?*" she asked, already typing the name into her computer.

"Yes," I said, hoping it was the right answer.

She hit ENTER and squinted down at the screen, her brow furrowing as she manipulated her mouse. "Hannah?" she asked without looking up.

"Sorry?"

"Your first name, Madame."

"Oh. Yes." I nodded. "Hannah."

"Here it is. Fall of last year. You spent eight days with us. September twenty-eighth to October fifth." She glanced up and smiled, appreciative of her own efficiency, then tapped at the keyboard again and frowned.

"Is there a registration form you have guests fill out?" I asked, pushing my luck and not caring. "You know, address, passport number, credit card?"

She nodded, half preoccupied by whatever she saw on the monitor. "Normally, yes, but I can't seem to find the information here." I watched her click her mouse again, her dark eyes roving the screen. "Look at that," she murmured to herself, then to me. "It looks like you left something with us, in the safe."

She looked up at me, suddenly skeptical, and I felt the skin along my arms flush with goose bumps.

"Oh, yes," I said easily, feigning irritation and surprise at my own thoughtlessness. "I had almost forgotten. How stupid of me. It's just something I picked up in the medina. I can't believe you've held on to it all this time."

"Of course," the clerk said, offended that I would question the hotel's reliability.

I took a step back from the counter and casually adjusted a stray lock of hair. Just a forgotten trinket, I told myself, trying to quell the desperate surge in my heart. "Could you get it for me?"

The woman nodded. "If I could just see your passport, Madame."

"Yes." I smiled. "Of course." I set my pack down and reached into the front pocket, brushing aside Marie's passport, pulling a one-hundred-euro note from my savings. I thought for a second, contemplating the plush lobby, the woman's blue suit. No, I didn't want to get this wrong. Reluctantly, I pulled out a second note.

"Will this do?" I asked, straightening up, sliding the two bills across the counter.

The woman hesitated a moment, and I felt my heart still. Then she put her hand out and carefully considered the sum before her.

"Yes, Ms. Boyle," she said, finally. "This will do."

Hannah Boyle. I said the name to myself, running my tongue along each syllable, hoping to feel the familiar pattern in the sounds, the words worn to fit like the ledge just below the altar at the convent's chapel, the stone cupped from all the knees it had received. All those months with the sisters I had imagined some kind of epiphany, a flash of self-recognition. I would stumble on something, I thought, a place, a name, and the past would spring open like a rusty gate newly oiled.

And yet, there in the lobby of the El Minzah, nothing had changed. The Tangier Hannah had moved in was still a mystery, the woman herself only a gaunt shadow, someone with a taste for vodka martinis, someone a waiter might remember fondly, even after a year. As I watched the desk clerk emerge from the door she'd disappeared through earlier, I remembered something Dr. Delpay had once told me. We all struggle to know ourselves, he had said, our whole lives.

The woman had a small black case in her hands, a little smaller than a shoebox. She came out from behind the desk, crossed to where I was sitting, and set the case on the low table in front of me. It was fastened by a lock, a metal circle with a narrow slit for a key.

"Thank you," I told her.

She nodded, her duty discharged, and turned away.

I sat for a moment, staring down at the relic, remembering how I'd acted with Joshi, more uncertain than ever of just how much I wanted to know. Just a trinket, I reminded myself, and perhaps it was nothing more than a forgotten bauble, a dead end.

There was laughter out on the patio. A group I'd seen earlier at the piano bar stumbled into the lobby and out the front door. The desk clerk raised her head as they passed, then looked back down, deeply engaged in some task. I needed privacy, I thought, glancing around the room, my eyes lighting on a row of wooden phone booths in the back of the lobby and beyond them an alcove marked *WC*. Taking the box with me, I stood and made my way to the ladies' room.

Ducking into one of the stalls, I sat down on the toilet and set the box on my knees. I fished two bobby pins from my pack, bent them slightly, slipped them into the lock, one on top of the other, and jiggled them gently. Yes, I knew how to do this. When I heard the latch click softly free, I set my thumbs on the box's lid and eased it open.

This was not a trinket, I thought, as the top fell back on its hinges and my heart stopped momentarily. Sitting on the very top of the box's contents, wrapped in a thin velvet cloth, was a bulky L-shaped object. There was no mistaking what the cloth covered, and when I finally unwrapped it I was not surprised to see the burnished black body of a handgun staring up at me. I picked it up and read the writing etched into the barrel: PIETRO BERETTA, GARDONE V.T.—MADE IN ITALY. And below, in smaller letters: MOD. 84 F—CAL. 9 SHORT.

There was a clip in the barrel. I released it, and it fell into my lap, fresh and full, the ten bullets it was meant to hold still neatly packed. I put my hand around the stock, and my hand knew the feel and weight of it. My palm knew the gun's contours, the pattern of ridges and the circular stamp of the maker, just as it had come to know the smooth texture of perfectly kneaded bread dough.

Setting the gun aside, I turned my attention back to the case. Beneath the cloth was a thick stack of dull green American dollars, the top bill a hundred. I picked up the stack and flipped through it. My best guess said there were at least five thousand dollars in all. A nice nest egg, enough for several rainy days, I thought, setting the bills in my lap, turning my attention to what lay under them.

At the bottom of the case were some half dozen passports, seven, to be exact, once I'd counted them. The covers and countries of origin varied. Among the seven were two American, one Canadian, one French, one British, one Swiss, and one Australian passport. I opened each little book and paged through the contents, studying the names and birth dates, studying the glossy face that graced each document. Here was Sylvie Allain, a brunette, with close-cropped hair and a pale face. Here was Michelle Harding, her face tanned, her hair bleached by the Australian sun. Here was Meegan McCallister, a redhead, born on an April day in Toronto. Here was Leila Brightman, a severe-looking Brit. But the one passport I'd expected to find was not in the bunch. Among the faces, shocking in their familiarness, the features my own, the noses and mouths and slightly asymmetrical eyes, was no Hannah Boyle.

Each passport was imprinted with a variety of visas and exit and entry stamps. Whoever these women were, they were a well-traveled bunch. The smudged stamps showed trips to everywhere from Hong Kong and the Chinese mainland to Argentina, South Africa, and a number of former Soviet Bloc countries. Not pleasure trips, I assumed, unless the beaches of the Black Sea were your idea of a tropical vacation. It was a disparate set of destinations, with little to tie them together other than the fact that of the dozens of trips each woman had taken, none, according to the dates on the imprints, had been made within the last five years. Not a single one.

The bathroom door opened, and I heard heels on the polished floor. Leaning forward, I peered through the crack where the door met the stall and watched the newcomer make her way to the sinks. Familiar, I thought, and then I realized that beneath the makeup and simple black sheath was the fanny-packed woman from the Continental's lobby. She set her purse on the marble counter and leaned in toward the mirror, surveying her face.

Hesitating a moment, I stuffed everything back into the case and closed the lid. Then I stood, reached back, flushed the toilet, slid the case into my pack, and let myself out of the stall. I glanced up at the woman when I emerged. She'd taken a lipstick from her bag, and the red tip was poised against her mouth. Her eyes were intent on her task, focused on the double arch of her upper lip, but as I turned for the door I saw them move slightly, taking note of me as I went.

As my taxi headed past the Jewish cemetery and the walls of the Old City toward the Continental, I tried in vain to fit the pieces of the newly formed puzzle together. The case rested heavily in my lap, its implications weighing even heavier on my mind. I had come to Tangier for answers, but what I'd found was an ever-growing snarl of questions.

The little red taxi veered to the left, and we rattled upward through the low, arched gate that marked the southeast entrance to the medina. I had to find the American, Brian, and no doubt he'd be keeping a low profile now that he knew I was looking. As we passed by the Great Mosque, I looked up to see Joshi's Japanese flag glowing in the window of his apartment, the electric lights blazing brightly behind it.

"Left here, please," I told the driver, directing him away from the Continental and toward Joshi's building. Maybe Joshi did know where the man lived after all. At the very least, it was worth a try. Faced with the Beretta, the little man might find his memory greatly improved.

The street to the building's front door was far too narrow for the car to pass. The driver stopped at the entrance to the little alley, turned back, and eyed me skeptically.

"It's not safe, Miss," he said in French, shaking his head, and then in English to make sure I'd understood, "Not safe." He was an older man with a neat nap of gray hair. A thick wool scarf was wrapped around his neck.

I paid him and opened the door. "It's okay," I told him, but he didn't seem reassured.

He sat with his engine idling while I navigated the cobbled street, his lights casting the alley in sharp relief. I wasn't sure how I was going to get past the locked wooden door, and I waved the driver away, knowing whatever I did to get in wasn't going to look right to the old man. But the little taxi stayed stubbornly in place, the sound of its motor rattling through the medina.

I ran through my options as I approached the shallow alcove, but as the door slid into view I could see that it was sitting slightly ajar, open just barely an inch, but open. Stepping into the entryway, I grasped the handle and let myself inside, out of the glare of the alley and into the darkness of the building's foyer.

Feeling the wall, I located the light switch I'd used on my earlier visit. The overhead bulb clicked on, the light flat and garish, the walls of the stairwell mottled and scarred where the paint had peeled away. I started upward.

I found Joshi's door closed, and knocked softly. There was no answer, and no sound from inside. The building around me was quiet as a tomb. I knocked again, louder this time, and pressed my ear to the door. Nothing. There was a soft click in the stairwell, and the overhead bulb switched off, plunging me into a darkness interrupted only by the thin bright bar of light that seeped out from under Joshi's door. Sweeping downward with my palm, I found the knob and twisted. It was unlocked, and the door swung open at my touch.

I stood on the landing for a moment and peered into the little apartment. From where I stood I could see straight down the narrow front hallway to what I guessed was the living room beyond. Just a part of the room was visible, one arm of a settee, a small wooden table and two chairs, Joshi's Japanese flag in the window. And there, at the very edge of my view, lying motionless on the rug, were four pallid fingers, the hand they belonged to hidden behind the plaster doorjamb.

"Joshi?" I called quietly, not quite sure what to do. My first and fairly certain guess was that the little man was dead. But it also occurred to me that he could be sick, or hurt, and in need of help. I thought of the taxi driver's words. *It's not safe.*

Stepping into the hallway, I set my pack down, took the case from it, and pulled out the Beretta. I jammed the clip up into the stock and heard it engage; then, flattening my back against the wall, I started forward.

The apartment was neat as a pin. Several feet down the front hall a tiny galley kitchen opened off to the left, its open shelves revealing a sparse but orderly collection of dishes and pans, an English teapot, a handful of chopsticks upright in a water glass like blossomless flowers. Farther along, to the right, was the tiny bathroom, no tub or shower, just a rust-stained sink and a toilet.

Aside from these two rooms, there was just the living room, which evidently served as bedroom and dining room and office as well. In one corner was a simple sleeping mat, its pillows and blankets neatly arranged. A Macintosh PowerBook sat open on the little table by the window.

Some part of me had expected to see Joshi as he'd been that morning, in his proper pajamas and robe. But he was fully dressed, in wool pants, a knit vest, a white oxford shirt, and a tie. Except for the lack of sunglasses, he looked much the same as he had when I'd met him on the street. On his feet were the familiar orange running shoes with their glittery laces. His right hand, the hand I'd seen from the hallway, was extended above his head, as if he was doing the backstroke across the carpet. He lay face-up, his eyes staring at the ceiling, one knee bent at an unnatural angle. On his neck was a thin dark line, a crease where someone had taken a cord or a wire and pulled it hard enough to stop his breathing.

When I had first arrived at the convent, one of the older sisters, a nun named Ruth, had died in her sleep. As far as I could remember, this had been my only experience with death. Sister Ruth had been old and frail, in the twilight of her nineties, and she had been heard in the chapel sometimes, praying for the end. When she finally did go, there was an earnest peacefulness to her corpse, an illusion, almost, of joy in passing.

There was nothing peaceful about Joshi. My first full glimpse of him repulsed me; I could smell the violence of his death. But I was fascinated as well, momentarily rooted in place by the grim sight, caught between my own curiosity and the urge to flee. Run, I told myself. It took a moment for me to obey my own command, but I finally turned and started back down the hall.

I had left the apartment's door ajar when I entered, and as I passed the kitchen I saw the light in the stairwell come on. I stopped short and strained my ears. Down at the bottom of the stairs a body shifted, clothes rustling as

it started upward, the sound of feet on the steps magnified
by the stairwell's hard walls and tall ceiling.

I took a breath and caught it, then ducked into the little
kitchen. A European woman stood out in this part of
Tangier, and the last thing I wanted was to be seen leaving
the apartment of a dead man. Placing myself just inside
the kitchen's doorway, I counted the person's steps. If
whoever it was stopped on the second floor, I'd be okay.

But the steps kept coming, leather soles shuffling
across the gritty tiles of the floor. The safety, I thought instinctively, fumbling with the gun, my thumb finding the
little lever. I heard the person reach the third-floor landing and stop, then continue cautiously forward. A hand
brushed the open door, and it swung inward, its hinges
sighing.

It wasn't warm in the apartment; December reached
Tangier with an almost autumnal chill, and the temperature inside the building was the same as the temperature
outside, but I was sweating. You can do this, I told myself,
pressing my back to the wall, steadying my breath. There
was no doubt in my mind I had fired the gun before. Just
like riding a bike, Dr. Delpay had said, and he'd been
right. Skills had come back to me, and so would this, just
like the delicate and miraculously unforgettable feat of
balancing on two narrow tires.

The intruder stepped into the hallway, moving so quietly that my knowledge of his presence was almost purely
intuition. No doubt he saw what I had seen by now, the
pale fingers on the rug.

Steady, I told myself, steady. The person took a step
closer, and I whirled around the jamb, Beretta at eye
level, wrists straight, forearms tensed.

"Don't move," I said, slamming the barrel of my gun
against the man's left temple.

EIGHT

The American stopped, frozen except for one muscle in his jaw that flexed and released like a misplaced heartbeat.

Keeping the Beretta steady with his head, I stepped behind him, caught the edge of the open door with my toe, and nudged it closed. "You ran out on me earlier," I said. "Very impolite."

He was wearing the raincoat in which I'd first seen him and, beneath it, a sweatshirt and jeans. I ran my free hand up inside the coat, then down along his legs.

"You won't find anything," he said, and he was right.

"It's Brian, isn't it?" I asked, standing. "I'm not sure I caught your name at the Pub."

He nodded carefully.

"Well, Brian," I told him, helping him forward with the barrel of the Beretta. "Why don't we chat in the living room?"

"Is he dead?" the American asked as we started forward.

"I'm afraid so."

We crossed into the living room, and I directed him toward the settee. He sat down and looked over at Joshi. "Did you kill him?"

I didn't answer. If Brian hadn't killed the little man, I figured any allusion to my own violent tendencies might give me some leverage.

"What were you doing in my room?" I asked.

"It *is* you, isn't it?" he said, ignoring my question. "When I first saw you at the terminal, I wasn't sure, and then in your room that night I thought I was wrong, but I wasn't."

I took a step toward him with the Beretta. "Cut the bullshit," I said, "or you'll join our little friend here."

Brian crossed his legs and stretched his arms out along the back of the sofa. He had the body of a swimmer, tall and fluid. "You won't kill me," he said, leaning back into the pillows.

"Who are you?" I demanded. "Joshi told me you paid him to keep tabs on me."

"Who are *you*?" he retorted. "Marie Lenoir? Hannah Boyle?"

I leaned over him, laying the tip of the Beretta's barrel just behind his ear. "Who's Hannah Boyle?"

He moved his head to look up at me. His eyes were as blue as mine, clear and flawless, cold with contempt. "I was hoping you could tell me that," he said. He made a movement with his right hand as if reaching for something in his coat.

Shaking my head, I nudged him with the Beretta's barrel.

"My wallet," he said, glancing toward his chest. "It's in the left breast pocket."

"I'll get it," I told him. Reaching into his coat with my left hand, I pulled out a worn leather billfold.

"Open it," he said.

Keeping my eyes and the gun on Brian, I stepped back, pulled one of the wooden chairs out from the little table, and sat down. If he had wanted to kill me, I thought, he could have done it that night in my room at the Continental. And yet, it struck me, death was not the only danger to be aware of.

"Open it," he repeated.

I laid the wallet on the table and opened it. A handful of dirham notes peered out from the top of the billfold. A half dozen plastic cards were tucked neatly in the leather slots. In the centermost panel, secured behind a piece of clear plastic, was a California driver's license with Brian's face on it. Brian Haverman, the license said; 1010 Bridgeway, Sausalito, California.

"There's a picture," he told me. "In the fold behind the license."

I reached in with my left index finger, slid the photograph out, and unfolded it. The print was color, the edges of the paper worn from being handled too much, the image creased where it had been folded to fit into the wallet. It was not risqué, but it was an intimate picture, meant to be tucked away as it was, meant for the person who had taken it. It had been taken on a train; that much was clear. The woman in the photograph had a travel-weary tiredness to her. Her hair was mussed; her eyes were still sleep-swollen. She had her hand out as if to ward off the photographer, but she was smiling nonetheless, a smile I could not remember smiling, though I must have, on a train somewhere, on a trip I could not remember taking.

She was me, and she was not. She was my face, my body, my clothes even. The same North Face jacket I'd been found in was draped over her like a blanket. And yet, whatever had happened to this woman had not happened to me; whatever experiences had shaped that drowsy smile were hers alone.

"I found it in my brother's apartment," Brian said. "He wrote me about you, before he disappeared."

"What did he say?"

"He said that you were the girl of his dreams."

"What else?"

"Not much. Only that you were an American, that he met you at the pool at the Hotel Ziryab. He used to go there sometimes for a cheap swim."

"How long had we known each other?"

He hesitated, puzzling over the question, over why I would have to ask.

"How long?" I repeated.

"A month or so."

I looked down at the picture again, at this ghost of myself. Was this the same woman who'd drunk vodka martinis at Caid's, who'd left a Beretta and a wad of cash in the safe at the El Minzah? The girl of someone's dreams?

"And your brother?" I asked. "Do you have a picture of him?"

Brian nodded, and this time I handed him the wallet. He pulled a second photo from the billfold and gave it to me. It showed two men in ties and dress shirts, arms hooked over each other's shoulders, smiling widely. Their affection for each other was obvious.

"It was taken two years ago. At our sister's wedding," Brian explained.

Stifling a shudder, I looked down at the worn photograph, at the darker of the two brothers. Here was a face I knew and knew well. Here were the same pale lids I'd seen closing over and over on themselves, the one blood-stained relic my shattered mind had preserved. The man on the rooftop. The man of my dreams.

"Why did you run from me at the Pub?" I asked.

"I'm not sure. I was scared, I guess." He nodded toward my gun. "Not without reason, it seems."

I glanced down at Joshi's body sprawled out on the carpet. I didn't think Brian had killed him. If he had, it made little sense for him to come back to the apartment. Standing, I backed across the room, pulled the coverlet off the bed, and laid it over Joshi.

"Thank you," Brian said.

"I didn't kill him," I told him.

Brian smiled. "I know."

I sat down again. "Tell me about your brother."

"Why?"

"Because I'm the one with the gun," I said. "What was he doing in Morocco?"

Brian sighed. "He was working for All Join Hands."

I gave him a blank look. "Humor me," I said. "I know less than you think."

"They're a nonprofit group," he explained. "They work to bring technology to the emerging world."

"Computers?" I asked, remembering what the English girl at the Pub had said.

He nodded. "You can't belong to the global marketplace without belonging to the World Wide Web."

"You seem to know a lot about it," I remarked.

"I'm in the business, too," Brian said.

"Another altruist?"

He shrugged.

"Do you think he's dead?" I asked. It was a terrible question, and as soon as I spoke I wished I hadn't.

Brian looked at me as if I'd just slapped him. "Did you kill him?"

"I don't remember," I said. I relaxed my grip on the Beretta and lowered my hand and the gun till they were resting on my thigh.

"What's that supposed to mean?"

"It means I don't remember," I said. Handing the picture back to Brian, I turned my head slightly and pulled the hair just above my temple aside, revealing the pale scalp beneath. My fingers brushed the raised edge of my scar, the neat circle of the healed wound. "Can you see it?" I asked.

Out of the corner of my eye I saw Brian lean forward. "What happened?"

"I was shot," I said.

"Why?"

"That's the big mystery, isn't it? I woke up a year ago in a field in France with a bullet in my head and nothing else. Before that, I don't remember."

"Amnesia?" Brian asked, skeptically.

"I wouldn't believe me either."

"But you knew Pat. You remember Pat."

It took me a moment to answer, and when I did it was with a lie. "No," I told him. "I don't remember your brother either."

"What are you doing in Tangier?"

"There was a used ticket stub in my pocket for the Tangier-Algeciras ferry. I thought I might remember something, that someone might know me."

"Why now? After a year."

I thought about what to say, how much to trust this person. "It wasn't safe to stay where I was."

He shook his head, still disbelieving.

"When's the last time anyone saw your brother?" I asked.

"The end of October, a year ago."

"Do you know the date?"

"The twentieth. He was a regular at the Pub. They had a darts tournament that night. A bunch of people saw him there."

"Alone?"

Brian nodded.

"Then what?"

"According to All Join Hands, he had a meeting in Marrakech on the twenty-fourth, then headed down to Ourzazate. He was supposed to check in again on his way back, but he never showed up. They called my mom and dad in the States about a week later asking if they knew where Pat was. That's the first we knew something was wrong."

"Where's Ourzazate?" I asked.

"South of Marrakech, on the other side of the Atlas Mountains."

"What was he doing there?"

"Work stuff. Evidently he was looking into starting a project with some of the date plantations down there. All Join Hands doesn't know much more. Pat was pretty much on his own."

"Did anyone see him in Ourzazate?"

"Not as far as I've been able to tell."

"Did you go to the police?"

"Of course."

"And?"

"And, you know how many Africans disappear into the Strait of Gibraltar each year? There's a limit to the amount of time the police here can or want to spend on some wide-eyed American who took a wrong turn in the medina."

"What about the consulate?"

"There's no American consulate in Tangier, but I've made at least a dozen trips to the embassy in Rabat. There's not much they can do. They figure nine times out of ten when someone disappears like this, they don't want to be found."

"And what do you think?"

"I don't know. You see these old men in the cafés in the Petit Socco sometimes. White guys in burnooses drinking mint tea. At first I used to think maybe that's what happened to Pat, that he read too much Paul Bowles and decided to go native. But that's just not him. Don't get me wrong; he wanted to do this. But he wanted to come home someday, too. Get married, have a couple of kids."

"With the girl of his dreams," I said.

"Yeah," Brian agreed.

We stood there for a moment, each of us silent as the corpse at our feet.

"Where do we go from here?" Brian asked finally.

"I don't know," I admitted. "Right now, I'd say anywhere but this place."

I took one last look at Joshi. The coverlet had failed to cloak his outstretched hand, and it lay there, pale and disembodied, still reaching for something.

"There's something wrong with his finger," I said.

Brian stepped toward the body and took the hand in his own. The dead man's pinky flopped downward at an unnatural angle. "It's broken."

I winced, thinking of my own encounter with Joshi the night before. The barest hint of violence had been more than enough to get the little man to talk, and yet someone had hurt him. What had that person wanted? What kind of information had Joshi had to give? The same information he'd sold to Brian? My room number at the Continental?

"Let's get out of here," Brian said.

I nodded in agreement. "I can't go back to the hotel."

"You can stay at my place."

"No," I told him.

"Whatever you want." He shrugged, then glanced back toward where Joshi lay, as if for emphasis. "It just seemed to me that you and I might be after a lot of the same answers."

"It's not safe," I said. "You're not safe with me."

He turned away and started for the door. "I'll take my chances."

NINE

"It was Pat's apartment," Brian explained as we pulled up in front of a nondescript residential building not far from the tourist office. We had walked through the medina to the port entrance, then taken a *petit taxi* to the Ville Nouvelle.

Brian paid the driver, then unlocked the building's front door and motioned for me to step inside.

"How long have you been here?" I asked as we started up the stairs.

"Eight months."

"And you never thought of giving up?"

"Every day," Brian admitted. "But when I really thought about it, thought about what it would mean to make that decision, to decide to leave . . ." He stopped and looked at me. "If I was the one in trouble and Pat was the one looking for me, he wouldn't give up."

We started upward again in silence. The apartment

was on the fifth floor, at the front of the building. It was nicer than Joshi's place, but blander, more utilitarian, all square angles and white paint. An L-shaped front hall led to a galley kitchen and a good-sized living room with a small balcony. Two partially closed doors revealed a bathroom and bedroom.

That it was the apartment of a transplant was obvious. Many of the furnishings were tastefully Moroccan, but the accessories hinted at a life left behind. A bulletin board over the computer desk in the living room was crammed with photographs: well-groomed girls in summer dresses, distinctly un-African gardens in full bloom, a picnic on a beach somewhere. An open cabinet next to the television held several dozen videotapes, the handwritten black-and-white labels marked *Yankees/Red Sox* or *NHL East Finals*. A football rested on an end table.

"Can I get you something?" Brian asked, laying his coat across the back of a chair. "Tea? Something to eat? I've even got good old American peanut butter."

"No thanks," I told him. It was well past three by now, and all I wanted was a good night's sleep.

"There are some women's clothes in the dresser in the bedroom," Brian said. "Hannah's, I've always assumed. And you're welcome to anything of mine or Pat's as well. There's just the one bed, but it's a big one, if you don't mind sharing. I can always sleep out here."

"No," I said. "Sharing's fine with me."

Brian nodded toward the bedroom door. "I'll let you change."

Hannah's wardrobe was that of a traveler, just a few simple pieces, modest and practical. October fifth, I thought, remembering the last date of Hannah's stay at the El Minzah. It hadn't taken her long to move out of the hotel and in with Pat. I set my pack down, stripped out of my grungy clothes, and pulled on an oversized T-shirt.

Brian was waiting for me just outside the door when I emerged from the bedroom. "Thank my mom," he said, handing me a brand-new toothbrush. "She sends a care package every couple of weeks. She's big on oral hygiene."

"Thanks, Mom," I said.

"There's a clean towel in the bathroom," he told me. "Do you need anything else?"

I shook my head.

When I came out of the bathroom, Brian was already in bed. I slid in beside him and pulled the covers up over my shoulders. The bed felt good, the sheets clean and soft.

"Did you grow up in California?" I asked.

"Massachusetts," he said. "A little town outside of Boston."

Massachusetts, I thought, a collegiate place, all brick and ivy and old maple trees. Cape Cod was there, and Harvard.

"What do your parents do?"

"My father teaches history at a private high school. My mom's an artist, a sculptor." He reached over and turned the light off, then settled back into his pillow. "What's it like?" he asked. "Not being able to remember."

I thought for a minute, my eyes accustoming themselves to the darkness so that I could just barely make out the contours of his body beside me. "It's hard to explain. I do remember a lot: facts, languages, how to do things. It's myself I've forgotten." I paused, frustrated at my own inability to express myself. "It's like a jigsaw puzzle, only half the pieces are lost." But no, that wasn't quite right either.

Brian didn't say anything. I could hear him breathing, deep and evenly. I was almost asleep when I heard his voice in the darkness.

"What should I call you?" he asked.

"Eve," I told him, without hesitation. "My name is Eve."

I opened my eyes, and I could see his face just a few inches from mine, his own eyes wide, alert, and shining in the darkness, almost as if he were watching me.

I didn't go to Dr. Delpay right away, didn't want to. He'd come each day while I was in the hospital, and we'd talked mostly about trivial things, his garden, that year's lingering autumn, the price of persimmons in the Croix Rousse market. I had not minded his visits, had taken a certain comfort in the plight of his climbing roses, the codling moths in his apple trees. He sat in the cushioned visitor's chair in my room and cracked walnuts or pistachios and handed me the meat. Not once did he ask me about what I'd lost. But on the day I was discharged to the abbey, he brought me a bag of figs with his business card tucked inside, and I knew without him saying that if I called or came to him now, it would be for answers.

I've said that in the beginning I craved forgetfulness. I wanted anything but the black wounds of memory that came and went as stealthily as the fox, his red coat slipping in and out of the brambles at the edge of the wood. Mostly there was just a feeling, fear or discomfort, the shove of adrenaline when I walked into the butcher's shop in Mâcon and the smell of fresh blood hit me.

Then, one afternoon in the spring, on a trip to the ruins of the old Cluny abbey, I'd seen a little girl in a yellow dress dart across what, some thousand years earlier, had been the narthex of the vast church. She was maybe four years old, in white sandals and a cream-colored sweater, the bodice of her dress dotted with yellow-and-white daisies. Her hair was pulled into two pigtails, her part slightly lopsided, her face bruised by a smudge of what looked to have been chocolate ice cream.

She was at least twenty feet away, and I saw her for

only an instant, but I had a sensation of her as if she were an extension of my own flesh. I closed my eyes, and I could smell her hair, that unwashed child's tang. I could smell the ice cream on her cheek, the sticky sourness of her breath. She was a disheveled little ghost, hands gummed with sugar and saliva, knees darkened by a thin patina of dirt from when she'd knelt to examine some small stone. When I looked again, she had slipped away, and I felt her absence like the bone-deep ache of an old injury before a storm.

That was early May, and by the end of June, the Feast of the Nativity of St. John the Baptist, I'd come to trust in the child, and in some other, more innocent version of myself. I'd come to believe it the way the sisters believed in God, this great and unknowable specter, a house somewhere, a family, a job, even love, like a suit of clothes hanging forgotten in some dusty closet, waiting to be rediscovered and worn.

It had not occurred to me that the person I feared and the one I longed to recall might have been one and the same, that the woman whose eyes moved warily through a crowd and the one who woke in the middle of the night to the ghostly ache of milk-heavy breasts might inhabit the same person. It did not seem possible to combine such anger and such love in one human being. And so I'd believed I could find one without the other.

When I phoned Delpay, it was if he'd been expecting the call, as if my readiness were as predictable as the first hard green fruits on his apple trees.

"The child," I stammered.

"Yes," he said. "I understand."

No, I thought, though I didn't say it, you don't understand. What I wanted was only the child. Nothing more. As if I could assemble a past from the few bright memories I'd gleaned, the smell of pancakes, the lazy sound of a screen door closing on itself. As if I could choose.

Even when we'd succeeded only in resurrecting the worst of my past, I'd convinced myself that the answers I wanted lay elsewhere, in the strange country of my origin. And now here I was, as far from the celluloid streets of America as I could imagine, looking for the one person I didn't want to find.

It was daylight when I woke, the flat Maghreb sunshine streaming in through a crack in the bedroom's shuttered window. I felt drugged, groggy from my first good night's sleep in what seemed like forever. I stretched out in the bed and rolled over. Brian was gone.

Swinging my legs off the bed, I found a pair of sweatpants in one of Brian's drawers and headed out of the bedroom. There was a fresh pot of coffee on, and a note on the kitchen table that read, *Gone for breakfast supplies, back soon.*

I helped myself to some coffee; then, for lack of anything better to do, I sat down at Pat's desk. A computer geek, I thought, looking at his PC's blank monitor, the jumble of electronic toys, a much more sophisticated setup than the convent's outdated Mac. I thought about switching on the computer, then decided against it. For now, best to keep my snooping as subtle as possible.

Turning my attention to the less high-tech aspects of what Pat had left behind, I opened the topmost desk drawer and perused the contents. Brian had been living in the apartment long enough that most of what I found was his. There was a bundle of letters from the consulate in Rabat, written in the maddeningly patronizing tone so common to any interaction with the mechanisms of bu-

reaucracy, repeated requests for Pat's Social Security and
passport numbers, a half dozen letters from various consular officials telling Brian he would have to contact their
superior for more help. From the letters' dates, I could see
it had taken Brian almost six months to get through all the
consular red tape. And at the end of this infuriating line
of correspondence, confirmation that they could do nothing to help.

There were other letters as well, neat envelopes with
the return address of a Linda Haverman in Andover,
Massachusetts. From Mom, I thought, pushing aside a
Peanuts birthday card.

There wasn't much on paper about All Join Hands or
any of Pat's projects. I figured most of his work had been
done on the computer. The only item of real interest in the
desk was a leather-bound address book, a strangely ar-
cane system, I thought, for a techie like Pat. On the inside
of the front cover was a brief inscription. *For Pat,* it said,
*so you'll always be able to find the ones you love. Love,
Mom.* The entries were a mix of old U.S. acquaintances
and Moroccan addresses. Kimberly Abbott of Green-
wich, Connecticut, shared a page with Hassan Alfani of
Rabat.

I turned to the *B*'s and then the *H*'s, scanning the
names, finding no entry for Hannah Boyle in either place,
only Borak, Brown, Hamidi, Hassan, and a single, seemingly misplaced item penciled in at the end of the *H*'s.
Mustapha, Pharmacie Rafa, it said, followed by a phone
number and a Marrakech address.

A key rattled in the apartment's front door, and I
quickly slid the book back into its drawer and stood up.
Brian appeared from around the corner of the front hall, a
plastic shopping bag in one hand.

"Good morning," he said, smiling.

"Thanks for the coffee," I told him.

"Did you sleep well?"

I nodded. "Better than I have in a long time."

He walked to the little kitchen table, set the bag down, and pulled out a loaf of bread, some eggs, and a package of dates. "Scrambled or fried?" he asked.

"Fried," I said, enthusiastically. It had been a long time since my grease-logged meal at the Pub.

He put the dates in a bowl on the table and pulled a frying pan from one of the kitchen cabinets. "Find anything interesting?" he asked, lighting the gas stove.

"I shouldn't have been prying," I apologized. "Sorry."

"Don't be," he said, pouring a generous amount of olive oil into the frying pan. "I'd be overjoyed if you could find something I haven't, though I doubt you will. I've been through the computer at least a dozen times."

"And the address book?"

"A lot of dead ends," he said, reaching for the eggs. He cracked one into the skillet, and it popped in the hot grease.

I took one of the dates from the bowl and watched him cook. "I thought I'd go down to Marrakech," I said. "Pay a visit to the folks at All Join Hands. Any idea when the next train is?"

Brian flipped the eggs, then looked at his watch. "There's a train at one in the afternoon, and a red-eye that leaves after midnight. But if you're going to Marrakech, I'm going with you."

I shook my head. "I'm going alone."

"No arguments," he said, sliding the eggs onto two plates, setting the plates on the table.

No arguments, I thought. I crossed my fingers behind my back, a gesture from childhood, the motion instinctual. "We'll take the red-eye."

• • •

There's a part of me, a part of all amnesiacs, that operates purely on blind faith. Take away memory, and you're left with little more than intuition, a sense of people and their motives that's as precise and mysterious as a bat's knowledge of the space it inhabits. Despite the peanut butter and the Super Bowl tapes, despite the photographs, my faith told me that something about Brian wasn't quite right.

Besides, if I had come to know one thing about myself in the days since my drive back from Lyon, it was that I was a danger to those around me. The sisters were dead because of me, and there was no doubt in my mind Joshi was dead because of me. I liked Brian Haverman, and the last thing I wanted was his blood on my hands, too. We'd both be better off, I told myself, if I went to Marrakech alone.

I worked on an exit strategy over breakfast. A trip to the bank? No, a return to the Continental for something I'd forgotten. Though I wasn't sure how I'd explain having to take my bag. Then, over the dishes, Brian announced he was going to the post office, and I gratefully declined his invitation to accompany him.

I waited till he was out the door, then set to work outfitting myself with Hannah Boyle's castoffs, exchanging my own dirty travel clothes for her clean ones. I put enough money for the train trip and some incidentals in my pocket, then stuffed everything else, including the black box's contents and the Beretta, in my pack.

It was just past twelve when I checked my watch. Brian would figure out where I'd gone sooner or later, but I hoped to at least buy myself enough time to get on the one o'clock train alone. I copied the address of the All Join Hands offices out of Pat's address book and left a hastily scrawled note on the kitchen table: *Back soon, Eve.* Then I slung the pack over one shoulder and let myself out the door.

TEN

Imagine spending ten hours in a paint mixer stuffed with humans, and you will come close to the experience of taking the train from Tangier to Marrakech. In spite of a well-spent extra thirty-five dirhams for a first-class seat, I knew my body would be cursing me for days.

The first five hours, from Tangier to Rabat, I shared a compartment with three loud Australians, college friends off for a winter-break adventure, who'd just come from a week on the Costa del Sol. Despite their penchant for off-key drinking songs, I was happy for the company, grateful for their enthusiastic bad jokes and stories of their drunken misadventures. When we rolled into the now-dark outskirts of Rabat, I was sorry to see them collecting their things to go.

The passengers who boarded in Rabat were different from the ones at the station in Tangier. There were fewer tourists here, for one thing, and the Moroccan travelers were well dressed, stylish, and cosmopolitan. The women wore business suits and French high heels, and the men's ties matched their shirts. The train filled up quickly, and five men crowded into the compartment with me, stowing their briefcases and bags, claiming their seats, as we pulled away from the city.

The man directly across from me, an older business-man in an elegant gray suit and shiny black shoes, snapped open a fresh copy of *Le Monde* and buried his head behind the paper. Next to him was a pair of slightly shabbier urbanites, salesmen of some kind, I figured, from the mammoth proportions of the leather cases they'd hauled on board. In the middle seat, next to me, was a younger man in a leather jacket and slacks. He was good-looking, though in a dangerous kind of way, his nose slightly aslant as if it had been broken once. The fifth passenger sat next to the door on my side of the com-partment, his eyes hidden behind mirrored sunglasses, his long slim legs crossed delicately over each other. More than one of my fellow passengers was wearing too much cologne, and the compartment reeked of dueling fragrances.

There was an air of sated lethargy to the travelers, the long day's fast broken not long before. People lingered in the corridor, smoking leisurely, faces turned toward the train's open windows. One of the salesmen in my com-partment unwrapped a sugar-dusted pigeon pie, cut thick wedges, and offered them around. I took my piece and thanked him, grateful for the food.

As we passed the outskirts of the city and headed into the countryside, the man next to me, the one with the crooked nose, turned in my direction. "American?" he asked.

I shook my head. "*Française.*"

He looked me over, unconvinced, then shrugged.

What was it, I wondered, that was so unmistakably American about me? What was it that told even this man that I was not really what I claimed to be?

"You are alone?" he queried, in heavily accented French.

"I'm meeting my boyfriend in Marrakech," I told him, hoping to head off any unwanted attention, but the man was undaunted.

"Salim," he said, pointing to himself. "I am a student. You are a student as well?"

I shook my head and yawned. "Sleepy," I said, though I wasn't. I leaned my head against the window and feigned fatigue. No doubt he was harmless, but it was going to be a long trip south if I had to fend him off the whole way.

"Why are you alone?" Salim prodded.

"I'm meeting my boyfriend," I repeated.

Salim opened his mouth to say something else, and the man in the sunglasses clicked his tongue disapprovingly. I gratefully watched my interrogator sink dejectedly back into his seat, scowling like a scolded child.

About an hour after we'd left Rabat the train slowed again for the Casablanca stop, and the two salesmen and the man with the newspaper gathered their things and let themselves out into the passageway. The man named Salim got up and took one of the now-empty seats on the opposite banquette.

There were fewer passengers to get on in Casablanca, and as the train started southward again the three of us had the compartment to ourselves. The man with the sunglasses and the long legs dozed, but Salim, evidently still holding a grudge, fixed his eyes on me and stared unabashedly. Four hours to go, I told myself, trying to concentrate on the dark landscape. Outside the window the countryside was black, pocked and dimpled here and

there by a lone electric light or a pair of headlights where
the train tracks ran close to the road. Ten hours, I thought,
to carve through this tiny slice of Africa. And yet people
had imagined they could conquer this continent.

Some two hours out of Casablanca a conductor appeared, checking our tickets before heading on to the next
compartment. Except for the tongue clicking earlier, my
fellow travelers had not spoken, and I had taken them for
strangers. But as soon as the conductor had left us, they
nodded to each other, briefly exchanging words. Their
manner was disconcertingly businesslike. The man in
the sunglasses peered out into the passageway, evidently
watching the conductor. After a few minutes, he reached
up and pulled down the privacy shade on his side of the
compartment. The man named Salim did the same, completely obscuring the view from the passageway. Then,
quickly and efficiently, he flipped the door lock.

I sat up, my skin prickling with fear and adrenaline.
The Beretta, I told myself, but there was no time to retrieve
it. Salim had already grabbed my pack. In another second
the man with the sunglasses was on top of me, his hand on
my shoulder, his legs straddling mine. Salim set the pack
down on the seat opposite me and undid the top flap.

I shrank back into the seat and stilled myself, my mind
considering the possibilities. There was no point in calling for help. The noise of the train would drown out any
sound I could make, and in the end I'd just wear myself
out. I took a deep breath and brought my knee up into the
man's groin. My bones connected perfectly with the soft
flesh, and the man doubled over. He swore in Arabic, then
staggered, thrust off balance by the rocking of the train.

I brought my leg up again, and this time the sole of my
shoe found his chest. He reeled backward, knocking into
the wall, and sank to his knees, retching.

Leaving the pack, Salim reached into his pocket and

produced a little bone-handled knife. "I see you haven't forgotten how to be a bitch, Leila," he sneered, his English perfect now, British public school. Planting his feet firmly on the floor of the compartment, he brandished the knife in front of him.

We stood for a moment like that, bodies balanced over the jerking and swaying carriage, eyes hard on each other. *You can do this,* I told myself, half of one eye on the crumpled figure in the corner of the compartment, the man still wheezing to catch his breath. *You can do this.*

Salim smiled slightly, the expression exaggerating the crook in his nose. He took a step toward me, and the train jerked violently to the left; the car careened wildly. I slid my foot around his ankle, my boot hooking the back of his calf, and threw my right fist against the front of his throat. The man tottered for an instant, hands gripping his windpipe; then he fell back into the banquette.

Grabbing my backpack, I opened the door and slipped out into the passageway. I hurried backward, passing from one car to the next, glancing over my shoulder as I went. What damage I had done would only be temporary; I knew my pursuers could not be far behind. Faces peered out at me from the compartments, an old woman and a child, four young backpackers, a strange group of women in black chadors, only their dark eyes visible beneath the folds of fabric.

I paused outside the women's compartment, looking ahead toward the dark window that marked the end of the car and the train. Beyond, there were only the tracks falling dizzyingly away. And behind me, Salim and his long-legged friend.

Sliding the door of the compartment open, I stepped inside. The women turned to me in unison. There were four of them, two older than the others, the skin around their eyes delicately puckered. Even in Morocco, a Muslim country, it was not usual to see the chador, and there was something otherworldly about the foursome, something almost perverse about these silent and shadowy women.

"Help me!" I pleaded in French, my breathing labored.

The women remained silent. One of them shifted slightly under her cloak, then blinked up at me.

"Help me!" I repeated my request in English, stepping deeper into the compartment.

One of the older women pressed her head to the window and peered down the passageway. Turning back, she barked something to the other three; then she and the woman opposite her pulled down the privacy shades. In an instant the women were up. One of them grabbed my rucksack and stuffed it in the overhead storage rack while another pulled down one of her own bags. Unzipping it, she removed a wad of black fabric. It took no more than twenty seconds for the eight hands to cover me. There was a knock on the door, and someone pushed me down into a seat.

The knock came again, and the same woman who'd first spoken lifted her shade. My pursuers peered into the compartment, Salim's crooked nose almost touching the glass. The older woman opened the door a crack and said something to the two men, her tone severe, reproving. The man in the sunglasses smiled at her and made a little bow, a show of mocking respect. She slammed the door in his face and turned away.

The two men hesitated a moment, their eyes ranging across each of us; then the man with the sunglasses said something to Salim, and they moved off toward the rear of the train. I took a deep breath and exhaled. A minute passed, and another. Finally, the men reappeared, heading in the direction they'd come from, hurrying now. The woman next to me reached over and grasped my hand through her cloak. Her grip was tight, her hand cool and smooth.

"Thank you," I said, and the four veiled heads nodded together.

The silence broke, and there was a relieved rush of conversation. Until that moment, I realized, I had not really heard Arabic spoken by women. It was entirely different from the language spoken by men, softer and rounder, more like a song. One of the women gesticulated, and her chador unfurled like a great black bird, like a wing opening to take me in, like the walls of the convent, the community of women they enwombed.

They spoke animatedly, as if to cleanse themselves of the earlier tension, and as they did, I began to see how different they each were. Here was the joker, and here the bossy one, and next to me, the serious one of the group, the one who had squeezed my hand. Each one was unique, as each of the sisters had been. The sisters. I shuddered under my chador, thinking of that night at the convent, Heloise's pale face. Pushing back the folds of fabric, I glanced at my watch. Two hours to Marrakech and no stops.

The train slowed slightly, and I got up and went to the window. Up ahead, some dozen small lamps flickered along the berm of the rail bed, the lights like fireflies, arcing and bobbing in the darkness. The train slowed further, crawling to a stop. In the glow of each lamp I could see a small boy, a cluster of dark faces and white teeth. The boys approached the cars close to the front of the train, holding up pottery and trinkets, pleading with the unseen passengers. Several hands thrust bills or coins out in exchange for the meager goods.

Two hours for Salim and his friend to find me, I

thought, glancing at the women. I stood and unwrapped myself, folding the chador, laying it on the seat.

"Thank you," I said again to the women. "*Shukran*." The Arabic word came easily to my tongue.

"You're welcome," the woman next to me said. She stood, helping me with my rucksack, then took my hand once more before I slipped out into the corridor. "Be safe."

Moving quickly, I headed for the rear of the train, opened the door, and stepped out onto the little apron that jutted off the back of the last car. Making sure the backpack was secure on my shoulders, I grasped the handrail, swung myself free of the car, and dropped down onto the berm. I hit the ground with a thud and rolled once. The train clattered forward, slowly picking up speed.

I stood up and dusted myself off, watching the lights of the rearmost car move away. Several of the boys had seen me jump from the train, and the whole group was heading toward me now, running along the berm like some ragtag Lilliputian army running into battle. I reached into my pocket, pulled out a wad of dirhams, and held them above my head, waving the bills like a white flag of surrender.

"Here," the oldest of the boys insisted, pointing toward a squat, near-windowless structure.

"The bus," I said, repeating the request for the dozenth time. "To Marrakech."

"Yes, yes." He nodded, grasping my wrist, pulling me while the other boys followed behind. "No bus now."

Besides being the eldest of the group, he spoke a kind of fractured urban American English, the language of the new colonialism, of movies and music and satellite TV.

"Relax, lady," he reassured me. "First you eat something." He said something to the other boys, and they fell away, scattering into the darkness with their lanterns. I allowed myself to be led into the little building, dragged along like some exotic creature he'd discovered, some long-awaited messiah or prisoner.

"My crib," the boy explained as we stepped inside.

From somewhere inside the house I could hear laughter and music, the sounds of revelry. The boy slipped his shoes off, and I followed his lead, tagging along as he led the way down a short hallway and into a plush room lined with wool rugs. Some dozen adults were crowded into the small space, women in bright robes and men in typical brown burnooses.

We had evidently interrupted some kind of dinner party. A carpet in the center of the room was set with dishes and cups, with half-eaten platters of lamb, vegetables, couscous, and a fowl pie similar to the one I'd eaten on the train. The crowd went silent when I entered, all faces turning to me.

The boy pointed to me and spoke, as if I were a lost puppy. Whatever he said, the mood lightened considerably. At the end of the short speech, one of the women smiled graciously in my direction and motioned for me to take a seat. Another woman disappeared through a curtained doorway.

"Sit," the boy directed, settling himself on the floor, and I did as I was told.

"In the morning," he explained, as I crossed my legs and offered my biggest smile to the diners. "The bus goes in the morning. My uncle will take you there on his machine. Tonight you stay here."

He said this firmly, not offering, merely stating what was fact. There seemed little point in arguing with him.

The woman who had disappeared returned with a small copper decanter, a bowl, and a towel. I washed my hands as shown. When I was done, a cup and a plate were placed in front of me, and I was poured a frothy cup of mint tea.

"You will please eat," the boy said.

I nodded, following his lead as he helped himself to the food. "What's your name?" I asked, between bites of lamb. The meat tasted faintly of lemons.

"Mohammed," he said. "And your name?"

"Eve," I told him.

"Eve." He repeated the name to himself, acquainting his mouth with the strange syllable.

"How old are you?" I asked.

"Twelve."

"You speak excellent English," I told him. "Did you learn in school?"

He beamed, shaking his head, and pointed to a large television that occupied one corner of the room. "American programs," he explained. "You are American?"

"French," I said.

Mohammed shook his head. "American," he insisted. "I know America."

I smiled. "I used to live in America."

"Then you are American." He said this matter-of-factly, as if teaching me the rules and rigors of nationality.

"You are married?" he asked after some time.

I shook my head.

"Kids?"

I thought for a second, and when I finally said no, he seemed saddened by my response. I must have seemed old to him, an impossibly old maid.

"Why not?" Mohammed asked.

I shrugged and took a sip of tea.

I slept in a small chamber at the back of the house, the bedroom, Mohammed explained, of his newly married older sister. There was one small window in the room, a square opening high up on one wall, through which I could briefly see the moon. Before I went to bed, I took the black case from my pack and flipped through the passports until I found the one I was looking for, the British one. The photo inside was the darkest of the bunch, my hair in it long and square at the ends, the skin around my eyes gray. Leila Brightman, the name said. What had Salim told me on the train? *I see you haven't forgotten how to be a bitch, Leila.* I put the passport back in the box and closed the lid.

ELEVEN

It was midmorning when I said good-bye to Mohammed and his friends. I traded my dirhams for a dozen beaded bracelets and a head scarf, then climbed on the back of Mohammed's uncle's dilapidated Honda.

"Good-bye, sister," the boy called as his uncle kicked the starter. He was standing in the thin shade of an acacia, surrounded by his mute and dark-eyed friends. I watched him over my shoulder as we drove away, the Honda's dust-and-exhaust wake slowly shrouding his up-stretched limbs, his hand waving an enthusiastic farewell.

Twelve years old, I thought, as we headed out of the village and onto the open road. I could have a child that age, tanned and gangly and full of questions. Or younger, like the littlest of the lamp-lit salesmen. It seemed impossible, and yet it was not.

• • •

After an hour's wait at the CTM stop in Mechra Bennabou, I boarded the bus to Marrakech. Some two hours later, deafened by the nonstop wail of Moroccan pop music, suffocating in the overheated cabin, I arrived at the ramparts of the great red city. Following the advice of my seatmate, a young Marrakechi on his way home from the university in Rabat, I hailed a *petit taxi* and headed for the grid of streets just south of the Djemaa el-Fna, in search of one of the many cheap tourist hotels the young man had promised I would find there.

I wasn't looking for the Ritz, just somewhere clean and safe, and I found it in the Hotel Ali, a bright little establishment on the Rue de Moulay Ismail, tucked between the post office and the Pâtisserie Mik Mak. The proprietor, Ilham, a sturdy, meticulous woman in a pink djellaba and careful makeup, showed me to a room on the second floor, indicating the shared bathroom and showers as we passed them. There was something about the woman, an air of unquestionable competence, a no-nonsense solidity, that reminded me of Madame Tane, and I felt a sudden flash of nostalgia for the Frenchwoman's patter in my kitchen.

Once alone, I took a shower and put on some clean clothes, then emptied the rest of the clothes and incidentals from my pack. The Hotel Continental had left me skeptical of Moroccan hotel security, and I figured it was best to keep my pack and its more irreplaceable contents with me at all times. Hooking the lightened sack on my shoulders, I headed down to the front desk.

"May I bother you for directions?" I asked the proprietor, producing the piece of paper on which I'd scrawled the All Join Hands address.

She squinted down at my writing. "It's in the Ville

Nouvelle," she explained, "behind the post office, on the
Place du 16 Novembre. It's not far from here. Take a right
out the front door and another right on the Avenue Mohammed V. You'll run right into it."

If Tangier is the dying soul of French colonial Morocco,
then Marrakech is the country's Berber heart, an earthen
city tucked in the shadow of the High Atlas, washed by
clear African light. It was that light more than anything that
told me I knew the place. Even in December the sun shone
with a cool desert purity, clean, uncompromised, and familiar as my own voice. Yes, I thought, the two cities, new
and old, laying themselves out in my mind like a long-
stashed map finally unfolded, I had been to this place. I had
walked these streets before, the orderly grid of the Ville
Nouvelle, and the wild rambling alleys of the medina.

I left the hotel and headed up the Avenue Mohammed
V, past the towering minaret of the Koutoubia Mosque,
out the Bab Larissa, and into the twenty-first-century bus-
tle of the Ville Nouvelle. Even in the modern part of the
city, a lethargy permeated the air. There was an irritability
to people, dour looks on the street, the edgy ache of
hunger and thirst, a languor born of the long hours of
fasting. It reminded me of Lent at the convent, of the dark
Saturday-night vigil before the exaltation of Easter.

It was early afternoon when I reached the Place du 16
Novembre and the All Join Hands offices. A plaque on the
windowless door announced the company's well-
intentioned name in English, French, and Arabic. The
door itself was locked, the building's windows shuttered.
I knocked several times and got no reply. Closed for Fri-
day prayers, I thought, as was much of the city. I could
only hope there'd be someone working on Saturday.

Telling myself I'd come back first thing in the morn-

ing, I started back the way I'd come. But instead of going
to the hotel, I veered north at the Koutoubia Mosque and
made my way to the Djemaa el-Fna. Save for a few vendors who had stayed open to cater to tourists and those
too young for the fast, the square was empty. Foreigners
lingered in the outdoor cafés, Europeans, Americans, and
a few Japanese sipping mint tea and picking guiltily at
their lunches.

Figuring I had nothing better to do than to walk, I
passed through the square and kept going. I shook off the
ubiquitous crush of would-be guides and made my way
down the Rue Souq as-Smarrine, toward the covered market, the textile shops, and souvenir stands, toward the tangle of alleyways I could see in my mind.

To walk through the *souqs* of a Moroccan city is to
travel back through time, far back, and yet, at the same
time, to remain firmly grounded in the present day. In the
hivelike labyrinth of the market, donkeys navigate streets
far too narrow for cars, their stout backs laden with buckets of flour, piles of blue jeans, or stacks of still-bloody
goatskins bound for the tannery. In the coppersmiths'
souq workmen toil over open fires, their faces blackened
and sweaty, while in the textile stalls, men in hooded
burnooses do business on cell phones, their counters plastered with the bright emblems of Visa and MasterCard.

There's a persistent odor to the *souqs,* the sour stench
of the tannery mixed with the musky smell of saffron, the
tang of curing meat, and the smothering sweetness of
diesel fuel. Where the main arteries of the market inter-
sect, the wave of bodies surges like a swollen river
through a narrow canyon. Irritated cries of *Zid!* from donkey drivers mingle with the monotone chants of little boys
in the *madrassas* and the tubercular coughs of beggars.

I wandered without direction, following the crowd
through the bloody stench of the meat *souq,* through the

sparkling jewelers' *souq,* along a street of leather slippers, till I finally found myself in the pungent lanes of the spice market. The streets were at their narrowest here, the markets spilling their bounty out onto the cobbles. Waist-high burlap sacks bulged with cumin and cayenne, with various curries and garam masala. Baskets held the dried and brittle bones of small animals, desiccated skins, bird beaks. I inhaled and smelled the familiar, the sweetness of cloves and mace and ginger, the last few weeks of Advent at the abbey, and something older than that, not the convent but this place, so utterly foreign and yet so completely familiar at the same time.

"Miss!" A man fell in step beside me, a young guide in a leather jacket and slacks. "You want to visit the Berber pharmacy?" he asked.

I shook my head and kept walking.

"*La pharmacie Berbère,*" he tried in French, then motioned to himself. "I can show you."

I turned, ready to tell him no, then stopped for a moment. "Do you know the Pharmacie Rafa?" I asked, thinking of the strange entry in Pat's address book, the one he'd filed under *H.*

The young man nodded vigorously. "Yes, of course. This way."

It was not far to the pharmacy, not much more than a European city block down the *souq*'s main thoroughfare. I paid my guide for his help, then paid him again to leave me to my own devices, thanking him profusely before stepping inside the cramped little establishment.

I don't know exactly what I had expected, lip balm and laxatives perhaps, a woman in a white coat, but the room I had entered was nothing like the pharmacies I knew. The walls were lined with shelves, the shelves crammed with hundreds of glass jars. Most of what the jars held was powder, but in some were parts of plants or animals, more exotic versions of what the outdoor displays contained. English, French, and German translations, done with Western customers in mind, identified some of the remedies. *Ashes of crow,* one label read.

The front of the store was narrow, but the back opened up to form a small seating area. A group of middle-aged tourists, northern Europeans from the looks of them, were crowded into the space listening to a large man in a burnoose and a fez tout the merits of saffron.

"It is the most expensive of spices," he explained, holding the jar of reddish orange filaments aloft for all to see. "Does anyone know where it comes from?"

"From a flower," a woman in the crowd offered.

The salesman nodded. "Madame is correct. It is the stigma of the crocus flower. Imagine the care in harvesting."

The tourists nodded appreciatively.

"Tell me, Madame," the man in the burnoose said, "in your market at home, how much does saffron cost?"

The woman shrugged noncommittally. "It's very expensive."

"And for what?" the salesman demanded. His English was almost perfect, American in its intonations. I was sure his French was just as good. He took a step forward, and his burnoose opened slightly. Under the brown robe he wore suit pants and black leather wing tips. Even from the brief glimpse I'd gotten, I could tell the pants and shoes had not been cheap.

"For red powder, floor sweepings," he went on. "You don't really know what you're getting." Opening the lid, he offered the jar around. "Smell," he exhorted. "This is the real thing. One hundred percent pure."

It was true: even from where I stood the odor was overpowering.

"For you," the man said, closing the jar's lid, "a special

price today. A mere quarter, no, less than a quarter of what you would pay at home for this precious spice."

He quoted a figure in dirhams, and a murmur swept through the group. A Moroccan woman in the back, evidently their guide, nodded her awe at the price.

I did a quick calculation in my head. I'd ordered saffron for the priory, and the deal he offered was barely less than what I'd paid in France. Nonetheless, the crowd seemed eager to buy. There was a flurry of activity as the tourists pulled their credit cards from the money pouches they wore around their necks.

The salesman lifted his hand theatrically, as if to stem the flood of demand. "One at a time," he said, taking in the full sweep of paying customers, his eyes ranging greedily across the store.

He was good, this salesman, an accomplished deceiver, as most salesmen are, but when he saw me in the back his gaze lingered for just an instant too long. Who did he see? I wondered. Leila Brightman? Hannah Boyle? Or someone else, another of my incarnations? He blinked once, then, skipping only the briefest beat, turned back to the throng and clapped his hands.

A young boy, his left leg slightly crippled, appeared from behind a curtained doorway. Silently, he installed himself behind a glass-topped counter and began weighing out bags of the saffron.

I lingered in the front of the store till the group left, herded along by their guide to whatever rug vendor or coppersmith was their next stop.

When the last of the customers was gone, the salesman looked in my direction. "May I help you, Madame?" he said coolly. He snapped his fingers at the boy, and his little helper scuttled away, disappearing behind the curtain he'd emerged from earlier.

"Are you Mustapha?" I asked, moving toward the counter.

Nodding, he unzipped his burnoose so that I could see the fine suit and starched white shirt beneath it. On a shelf behind the counter was a cell phone and a ring of keys with a Mercedes-Benz emblem. Rich accessories for a Berber pharmacist, even considering the price he was charging for saffron. A photograph next to the cash register showed a younger, svelter Mustapha, standing almost exactly where he stood at that moment, shaking the hand of an American movie star. A second picture was of Mustapha and a former first lady.

"I know you," I said.

"I don't think so, Madame." He smiled when he said this, but there was nothing light about his tone.

"No," I said. "I'm certain of it. I've met you before. You're a friend of Patrick Haverman's."

Mustapha shrugged. "Again, Madame, I think you are mistaken. I know no one by that name. And now, if you don't mind, we are closing for the day." He came out from behind the counter and stepped toward me, his bulky frame a physical invitation to leave.

I stood there for a moment, certain he was lying, unsure of what to do. "Of course," I said, finally. "Sorry to have taken up your time." Then I turned for the door.

He was just behind me when I reached the threshold, and I turned back to look at him.

"Good evening, Madame," he said. There was menace in his voice, an unspoken warning. He put his hand on the door and pushed it closed, turning the locks behind me.

The sun had already set by the time I found my way back to the Rue Souq as-Smarrine. The call to prayer had rung out, echoing from the city's minarets and down through the dark alleys of the medina. The only business now was to eat and drink. Those without homes to go to clustered in cafés or crouched on the sidewalk with bowls of thick *harira*. There was something comforting to me about the ritual of Ramadan, the cycle of fasting and prayers. In my year at the convent I'd grown accustomed to the daily cadence of worship, and I could not see much difference between the call of the muezzin and the chapel's bell ringing the Benedictine hours. Only here an entire country lived by the rhythm of devotion.

When I reached the Djemaa el-Fna, the square was jammed with tourists and locals alike. Acrobats, storytellers, snake charmers, and herbalists hawked their talents and wares. Henna artists circled the outer edges of the crowd. The food stalls teemed with bodies.

As I worked my way through the melee, I felt someone tugging at the hem of my shirt and, turning, saw a little boy in sandals and jeans and an Adidas T-shirt.

"Miss," he said in English. "Please, Miss. Come here."

I shook my head and tried to pull away, but he held on tight.

"Here, please," he insisted, motioning to an old Berber woman in a blue djellaba and head scarf. "My auntie please to speak you."

"No, thank you," I said, but the boy was not going to be put off.

"Your fortune," he explained, batting his dark eyelashes like a houri temptress. "You like."

"How much?" I asked reluctantly, thinking I might get a kick out of whatever the old woman had to say. Besides, the boy reminded me of Mohammed.

The boy shrugged. "For you we make gift."

I shook my head. "Five dirhams," I told him, knowing

if I didn't set a price now, my "gift" could prove expensive.

"Five for my auntie, five for me."

"Sorry," I said, turning to walk away, but the boy leaped in front of me.

He smiled and held up his fingers. "Five dirhams."

I nodded, fishing a five-dirham note from my pocket. Then, following the boy's instructions, I took my place at a low wooden stool facing the old woman.

She leaned forward and peered at me. Her left eye was milky, clouded by a cataract, but her right eye flickered, alert and alive. When she opened her mouth, I could see that what teeth she had were worn, speckled with decay. She spoke to me in Berber, repeating the same words over and over. Her tone and her hand on my arm were insistent, irritated even, as if I should understand her but didn't.

The boy listened, then turned to me. "She says you are ghost."

I smiled. "Does that mean I don't have to pay?" I asked, but the boy had turned his attention back to the old woman, who was speaking again.

"She says she knows you," he translated. "You come looking something."

The woman reached forward and took my hands in hers while the boy spoke. Her fingers were rough as sandpaper, the skin on her palms hard and thick.

"Will I find it?" I asked, thinking her guess was a rather safe one. Wasn't every Westerner who came to Marrakech looking for something?

The boy repeated my question, and the old woman shook her head.

"She talks to the ghost," the boy explained.

She mumbled in Berber, gripping me tighter, her good

eye hard on my face. It was a stunning piece of choreography, a dance the old woman and the boy must have perfected over time. By the time I caught on, it was too late. I saw the knife out of the corner of my eye, the steel blade flashing in the torchlight. Then I felt my pack slip from my shoulders, the straps sliding away, cut cleanly and neatly. The boy ducked into the crowd.

Regaining my bearings, I wrenched my hands from the old woman's grasp and plunged after the thief. The crowd closed around me, and for an instant I was certain I had lost him; then I caught a glimpse of my pack speeding past the food stalls. I elbowed my way forward, struggling to keep track of the boy as he dodged through the sea of djellabas and jeans, toward the far edge of the square.

He was fast, but the weight of the pack and his child's legs gave me the advantage in speed. He slipped from the square into the ill-lit snarl of streets, and I careened after him, following the slap-slap of his cheap plastic sandals, the dim beacon of my pack. I was gaining on the little robber, slowly but steadily. Then he rounded a tight corner, and his sandals momentarily lost their grip on the street. His free arm windmilled, struggling to balance his body's weight against that of my backpack, and he slid sideways, his bare leg touching the street.

I leaped toward him, grabbing first for the pack, getting a good grip on one of the straps. Then, with my free hand, I reached for the boy's arm. I had his wrist for a moment, but he wrenched himself free and slid deftly from my grip, wriggling away like a fish off the hook. He scrambled into the darkness, his footsteps rounding a corner, receding into the distance.

I stood there, gratefully clutching the backpack, and listened to him go. First the men on the train, and now this, I thought. Something told me there was more than just petty thievery at work. But why? *You come looking something,* I heard the boy say as I started back to the Hotel Ali. Apparently, I wasn't the only one.

TWELVE

Choosing to believe Ilham's assurances that the storage lockers were safe, I left my pack at the hotel before starting on my way to the All Join Hands offices the next morning. It was the lesser of two evils, but the proprietor exuded extreme trustworthiness, and in truth, I didn't have much choice. I said a brief prayer as I stowed all my worldly possessions in one of the wire mesh lockers and watched Ilham close the lock and pocket the key. Then I left the Hotel Ali and started for the Ville Nouvelle.

It being Saturday, and still fairly early, I had only the slimmest expectation of finding anyone at the All Join Hands offices. When I finally reached the Place du 16 Novembre, I found the building's windows shuttered as they had been the afternoon before. The door, with its logo of multiracial hands conjoined to form an unbroken circle, was closed and locked. Two days, I thought, displeased at the idea of having to wait out the weekend, mad at myself for not having come earlier the afternoon before. I told myself I'd check back later. With any luck, I'd catch some ambitious soul burning the weekend oil.

My only other plan for the day was to head back to the Djemaa el-Fna to try and find my little thief and his Berber auntie. I had a hunch they were regulars at the square, and I figured if I waited long enough they'd show up there to ply their skills. A bad feeling in my gut told me someone had put the kid up to his crime, the same someone who'd enlisted Salim and his friend on the train. Perhaps the same someone who'd had the sisters killed.

It was late morning when I passed the landmark of the Koutoubia Mosque and turned up toward the Djemaa el-Fna. There were several dozen vendors out, and a school of djellabaed henna artists and fortune-tellers prowling the crowds of tourists like sharks looking for a meal. With their hair covered and their bodies draped in fabric, it was difficult to tell the women apart, but after a good fifteen minutes of looking, I was fairly certain the boy and his aunt were not among them.

When a young woman in a blue robe approached and offered in competent French to henna my hands, I agreed. Like the old auntie, she had a young boy with her, a gangly child who produced two squat stools for us to sit on. I took my place opposite the woman and offered her my hands. She pulled a paste-filled syringe from beneath her robe and, with the deftness of a surgeon, began an intricate pattern on my index finger.

"There's a fortune-teller," I said, as she progressed to the back of my right hand. "An old woman with one bad eye. Do you know her?"

The woman didn't reply. She made the petals of a flower, then lifted the syringe and drew a curling stalk down toward my wrist. The henna paste was cool and damp. Where it was starting to harden and dry, the skin puckered beneath it.

"She had a boy with her," I elaborated. "She was here yesterday. She read my palm, and I'd like to see her again."

The woman shook her head, her eyes still intent on her task. "Ten dirhams," she said. "I tell your fortune."

"No, thank you," I told her.

"Eight dirhams," she countered.

I shook my head. "Twenty dirhams if you can tell me where to find the old woman."

Making no comment on my offer, she finished her design and tucked the syringe back in her robe. "Finished," she said. "Five dirhams."

Standing, I reached into my pocket and pulled out a five-dirham note.

She took the money, secreting it into one of the many fabric folds that draped her body, then turned and, with the boy in tow, disappeared into the crowd.

I watched her go, then glanced around the square, surveying my options. A host of cheap cafés lined the Djemaa el-Fna on either side, each with a terrace overlooking the action. From where I stood, the best of these looked to be the Café Glacier, a large establishment next to the Hotel CTM, with a big second-floor balcony. I'd be in for a long day of coffee drinking, but if I got a table outside, I figured I'd have a good view of the square, and the comings and goings of the Berber ladies. Picking my way through the crowd, I made my way to the lobby of the Hotel CTM, bought a copy of *Le Monde,* then headed next door to the Café Glacier.

It was deep into the day's fast, and the café's clientele was made up exclusively of non-Moroccans. Hungry-looking waiters in blacks and whites circulated through the tables serving forbidden glasses of Ricard and *pain au chocolate*. The decor was French: caned chairs, marble-topped tables, white tiles, and airy café curtains.

I found a table on the terrace, a corner spot right next to the railing from which I could easily see the area of the square where most of the Berber ladies gathered. The woman who'd hennaed my hands had found a new client, and the two of them were hunched together on their little stools. The boy was nowhere to be seen. Gone off for a piece of candy, I figured, or some dates, like the other children too young to take part in the fast. I ordered a coffee and settled in for the duration.

In the chapel at the abbey were two very different depictions of Christ. One, of course, was the Christ we all know, the Christ on the cross, the gruesome sufferer, hollow-eyed and gaunt, each corporeal misery carefully sculpted and shadowed, wounds fresh and red, thorns so sharp they'd cut through leather. It was this Christ the sisters faced during worship, this Christ toward whom they prayed each prayer, toward whom each head bent in almost erotic supplication. The other Christ loitered in the back of the chapel, tucked high up in a dark alcove, a baby, an innocent, pink-cheeked and half-naked, riding his mother's hip.

"He gave His only son," Sister Magdalene used to say, to remind us of the magnitude of the sacrifice. But which son? I would wonder. Which Christ? My own gaze was drawn to the fat little boy, to the hand reaching toward Mary's breasts, the two nipples tight and round beneath the pleated scrim of her dress. It seemed this was what a parent would remember, that Mary, there on Golgotha, would have looked up and seen her milk-breathed baby on the cross.

Here was the sacrifice, I had thought, not God's but Mary's. For how would you not offer your own flesh to the executioner instead?

A cruel God, I'd once said to Heloise. It was August, just after the feast of St. Mary the Virgin. We'd gotten up in the moonlit hours of the morning to begin the long, steamy process of canning the garden's overabundance of green beans. Even with our early start it was sweltering in the kitchen, what was left of the morning's cool defeated by the dozen large pots on the boil.

Heloise didn't say anything at first. She finished loading the pot in front of her, carefully lowering each glass jar into the scalding water. When she turned away, her face and hair were damp with steam, her skin red and flushed. I'd expected her to disagree with me, to say something about the Light and the Salvation, but she didn't.

"Yes," she said, instead, "cruel." Pushing her sleeves up above her elbows, she wiped her hands on her apron and pulled a crumpled pack of Gauloises from her pocket. Then she leaned back against the counter, put a cigarette to her mouth, and lit it.

"And yet here I am," she said. She closed her eyes and took a long, slow drag off the Gauloise, savoring the taste, this brief moment of rest. The only sound in the kitchen was the clink-clink of the canning jars as they nudged one another in their baths.

My coffee came in a chipped cup, the little spoon dulled by dishwater, but it was a good French roast, thick and frothy. I sunk two cubes of sugar in the demitasse and took a sip, letting the sweet liquid linger in my mouth.

Down in the Djemaa el-Fna two young boys stumbled past the fruit vendors, lips rimed with silver paint, faces flushed, dizzy on fumes and poverty. On the far side of the square, near the snake charmers and herbalists, a little Berber girl posed for a photograph, her hand reaching for the offered coin before the shutter closed.

Yes, I thought, here was the sacrifice. And my own capacity for love? How would I know it? Would I put my hands to the rough wood, or would I give the boy instead? How would I know my own courage, my own cowardice? How would I know my own child?

From somewhere in the distance came the long slow call to midday prayer. *Allahu akbar, Allahu akbar ... Ashhadu an la Ilah ila Allah ... Ashhadu an Mohammedan rasul Allah ... Haya ala as-sala ... Haya ala as-sala.* In the name of Allah, Lord of the Worlds, the Beneficent, the Merciful. There is no God but the one God, and Mohammed is his messenger.

Would I feel it, I wondered, love, like a wound?

Down in the square a group of men had gathered around a common spigot and were drawing buckets of water to wash their hands and feet for their prayers. And in the desert, when there was no water, you washed yourself with sand. And when there was no sand, you went through the motions of ablution. How did I know that?

There was a commotion inside the café, a scuffle of some kind, and I turned my head in time to see three waiters converge on a small figure. It was a child, a beggar, it looked like, up from the square to use the bathroom. The men surrounded it as if it were a rat at a royal wedding banquet, hands grasping the frail limbs, and hustled it toward the stairs.

I peered over the railing and down toward the front door. After a few minutes the men emerged, half carrying, half pushing the boy in front of them. They shoved him out into the square, each spouting fierce Arabic, then headed back inside.

The boy paused a moment before turning his face up toward where I sat. It was the little Berber boy, the child of the woman who had hennaed my hands earlier. He made a motion toward me with one hand, then put the other hand to his eye, as if covering it deliberately with a patch. I stared down at him, and he went through his pantomime again. The woman with the bad eye, I thought. Had they taken me up on the twenty-dirham offer?

Nodding my understanding, I hastily paid my waiter, then headed down the stairs. The boy was waiting for me just outside the front door. He stepped forward when I emerged, holding up four dirty fingers. "Forty dirhams," he said in thick French.

I shook my head. It wasn't even four euros, but still, I felt like I was being played for a sucker.

"I take you to the woman with the broken eye," he said.

"Twenty," I insisted, "and it's the boy I want to find."

"Thirty," he countered. "I take you now."

I reached into my pocket, pulled out ten dirhams, and handed the money to him. "You can have the rest when we find him," I said.

He looked petulantly at the money, then shoved it into the pocket of his pants and motioned for me to follow him.

It was cool in the medina. The thick honeycomb of walls held the morning's air and kept the day's heat at bay. The boy ducked around a corner like a rabbit going down a hole, and I plunged after him, deeper into the warren of alleys. Only a thin strip of blue sky was visible above our heads. I was lost now, and I knew it. Doubtless the boy knew as well. If he left me, I could wander here all day and night before I found my way out. I glanced down a covered side street and caught sight of a pile of filthy rags and a dirt-smeared face. Too sick or weak to speak, the person lifted a gaunt hand to us as we passed. I reached into my pocket for a coin, but the boy dashed on ahead. Afraid of losing my guide, I gave up on the coin and sped after him.

As we made our way farther into the Old City, my own foolishness became more and more apparent to me. I was entirely at the mercy of the child, and for all I knew, he meant to rob me, or worse. No doubt there was a much nastier surprise than the little thief waiting at the end of our journey. I'd left the Beretta in my locker at the hotel, thinking it the safest place for it, but I was beginning to wish I had it with me.

We turned down another alleyway, and the boy stopped abruptly, the sound of his plastic sandals on the cobbles falling silent. "Thirty dirhams," he said, holding out his hand.

Catching my breath, I took a good look at my surroundings. The houses that faced the street were windowless, their facades stark except for their heavy wooden doors. There was not another person in sight.

"There," the boy insisted, pointing toward the mouth of an even narrower alley. "My money now."

I shook my head. "You bring me to the boy first."

My guide sighed, exasperated. He crept forward to the mouth of the alley, and I trailed close behind. "There," he said, pointing.

I followed his finger down along the canyonlike passageway. At the end of the little street was a knot of small bodies. "The boy," he said.

I reached into my pocket and pulled out the promised payment. "There's ten more if you take me back."

Not a chance in hell, I thought, watching him smile and nod.

He reached out and snatched the money. Then, quick as a cat, he turned and darted away, disappearing around a corner.

Leaning my back up against the cool plaster, I peered down the alley toward the group of children. They were playing a game, craps, or some version of it. I could hear the rattle of dice bouncing off the cobbles. There were six children in all, all boys, all close to the same age, poised between childhood and adolescence. And all, I reminded myself, with an intimate knowledge of this labyrinth.

But despite our uneven levels of expertise, and the advantage given them by their youth, I had a few things going for me. From where I stood, the alley the boys were playing in appeared to have no outlets: they'd have to come right by me on their way out. And there was the simple matter of size as well: I far outweighed even the largest member of the group. Picking my little thief from the crowd, I made a rough plan of action, took a deep breath, and started forward.

Engrossed as they were in their game, the boys didn't notice me at first. I was just a few meters away when the first of the group looked in my direction, regarding me with some confusion. I smiled broadly, turning on the charm, but he wasn't having any of it. Nudging the boy next to him, he said something in Berber, and all heads turned my way. The pickpocket peered up at me, recognition clicking in.

He yelled, and the boys scattered, rushing past me like cockroaches trying to escape the sudden glare of light.

Keeping my eyes on the pickpocket, I stood my ground. As narrow as the alley was, I could almost touch the walls on either side. The boy came forward, ducking and lunging to avoid my grasp. I reached out and locked my hand on his wrist.

He cried out for help, but his friends were already

gone. Working to free himself, he kicked me hard in the shins, then sank his teeth into my arm.

Wincing against the pain, I yanked my arm away and shifted my grip so that I had both of his wrists behind his back. "I'll call for the police," I warned.

A shadow passed across his face, the unmistakable look of sheer terror. He stopped struggling and glared up at me.

"My pack," I said. "Who asked you to take it?"

He shook his head vehemently. "No one." I could tell the way I held his arms was hurting him, but he wouldn't give me the satisfaction of showing it. "I take for me," he insisted.

As good a thief as he was, he was an equally poor liar. "I won't hurt you," I said, loosening my grip just slightly. "But I know someone paid you to steal it. Who was it?"

He looked up at me, his eyes beginning to fill with water, but said nothing.

Hoping he wouldn't call my bluff, I mumbled something about the police station and started forward, pushing him in front of me.

"Please," the boy pleaded. "It was *l'allemand*."

As thick as his accent was, it took me a moment to understand what he meant. *L'allemand.* The German.

"His name," I prompted.

The boy shrugged.

"He found you in the Djemaa el-Fna?"

"No," the boy said, shaking his head, frustrated by my adult ignorance. "He has a great house in the Ville Nouvelle. My mother's sister works there."

"Where in the Ville Nouvelle?"

The boy shrugged again. "Near the Jardin Majorelle."

I paused a moment. "You'll take me there," I said.

"Please, Madame," he entreated. "No police."

"No police," I told him. "I promise."

Because the streets in much of the Old City are too narrow for vehicles of any kind, all goods are transported either by human or by donkey. When people die, their bodies are wrapped in white cloth and carried through the medina on the heads of their relatives, floating along above the fray like leaves washed from stream to river to sea.

It was this same current that swept us toward the Bab Doukkala. Once the boy and I left the empty side alleys and found one of the medina's main arteries, we didn't walk so much as ride, buoyed by the crush of the crowd. It was midafternoon when we emerged from behind the medina's red walls into the twenty-first-century rush of the Ville Nouvelle. I hailed a *petit taxi,* and we rode the rest of the way, the boy snapping directions to the driver.

As is so often the case in Moroccan cities, where what faces the street provides little clue to the character of the homes, the windowless facades of the neighborhood we finally stopped in revealed almost nothing of what lay behind them. Only the occasional glimpse of well-tended foliage, old poinsettia bushes and towering palms, and the preponderance of well-dressed Europeans and mirror-black Mercedeses, hinted at just how far from the *souqs* we had come.

The taxi pulled to the curb, and the boy started to get out. "Which house is it?" I asked, holding him inside.

He pointed to a large gate. "There."

I reached into my pocket, pulled out what cash I had with me, forty dirhams and some change, far more than what the cab would cost, and handed it to the boy. "Take him back to the medina," I told the driver. Then I opened the door and stepped out onto the sidewalk.

THIRTEEN

Among Holocaust survivors, periods of retrograde amnesia are not uncommon. I once spoke to an old woman, another of Dr. Delpay's patients, who had been to Bergen-Belsen as a child and was still haunted by the fact that she could remember nothing of the eighteen months she had spent there. It's tempting to think of this as a blessing, the brain's way of saving itself. But to her, for whom bearing witness was the greatest salvation, for whom dozens of loved ones could be known only through memory, the loss was unspeakably painful.

"We were always hungry," she told me, pulling a chocolate bar from her pocket, proof of her compulsion. Some sixty years later she still could not leave her house without food. "My sister says we were," she said guiltily, "but I don't remember it."

"Your past is not a *bouchon* menu," Dr. Delpay had

said when I'd first told him of my plan to go to América. "It all comes together on one big plate: *quenelles, andouillette, tablier de sapeur*. You can't pick and choose."

"Yes." I'd nodded, but Delpay could see I didn't believe him.

"He'll find you, you know," he'd insisted. "Your friend from the rooftop. He doesn't care that you don't want to be found."

I'd told myself he was wrong, but even then I'd thought of the woman with her chocolate, the way her speckled hand had reached for it in her pocket.

Now, as I watched the taxi make a U-turn and head back to the Bab Doukkala, I thought of her again, and of that morning in the kitchen with Heloise, her cruel God. Yes, I told myself, there was no picking and choosing, no answers but all the answers, and the certainty that knowledge, even the worst kind, is worth the risks.

I headed across the street, trying to make like a tourist out for a stroll. The large iron-and-wood gate, the villa's only visible entrance, was closed and, I assumed by the keypad and intercom on the outer wall, locked. A tall, thick, pisé wall, topped with jagged shards of broken glass, ran the length of the grounds. A porcelain plaque on the gate gave a street address but no name. Short of ringing the bell and asking, there seemed to be little I could do to get any more information about the house or its owner.

Ringing the bell, I thought, was a crazy idea, though not so crazy as it might at first seem. Stepping closer to the gate, I pushed the little round button below the intercom.

There were a few seconds of silence, then the speaker crackled on and a static-garbled yet polite female voice asked me to identify myself.

"It's Chris Jones," I said in English, choosing the most

generic American name I could think of, ignoring the fact that my unseen inquisitor had spoken French. "I'm here to see Mr. Thompson."

There was a confused pause on the other end, then, in impeccable English, "I'm sorry, Madame. Did you say Thompson?"

"Yeah, Fred Thompson."

"There is no Mr. Thompson here," came the reply.

"Sure there is," I said. "We met last winter in Chamonix. He gave me this address."

"There is no one here by that name," the voice repeated.

"Just tell him it's Chris," I persisted, "from Dallas. He'll remember."

"I'm sorry, Madame," the woman apologized again, her tone showing exasperation this time. "This is the Werner residence."

"Well, where does Fred live, then?" I asked, incredulously.

"I don't know, Madame," she said, curtly. "Good day." Then she clicked off, and the intercom went dead.

I lingered by the gate for a moment longer, then cut back across the street. The Werner residence, I thought. Werner. Walking the length of the wall, I shadowed the perimeter of the property. The villa was on a corner, and two sides of the enclosed grounds came right up to the street. The house's remaining boundaries bordered the equally imposing villas on either side. Besides the main gate, a large wooden door near the rear of the property, which I assumed was a service entrance, was the only opening in the unbroken plaster wall. The whole place looked as if it had been built to withstand a siege, from prying eyes or angry rabble or both.

I did a tour of the neighboring homes, making a loop around the large block the Werner villa was situated on, sticking to the far side of the street. Each of the properties showed evidence of at least some kind of security system. A discreet army of surveillance cameras studded the walls and rooftops. The sound of barking dogs could be heard from inside one of the compounds. Here was the price of wealth, the penalty of privilege in a place of such abundant poverty.

Finishing my tour, I turned back onto the street where the taxi had let me out and stopped several yards from Werner's main gate. There was a limit to the amount of loitering even a dumb blond playgirl could do in a neighborhood like this, and I figured any more snooping would have to be done at night.

As I took in the villa and its walls one last time, I heard the electric gate beep in warning. The latch unlocked, and the two iron doors swung slowly outward. The black prow of a Mercedes appeared, sun blazing off its chrome bumper and hood ornament. The car paused for a moment in the driveway; then the wheels turned in my direction, and the hulking sedan moved out into the street. I ducked back around the corner, flattening myself against the wall.

I heard the car roll forward, its German engine speaking the language of engineering perfection. The hood appeared, then the front windows, and I caught a glimpse of the driver. He was a North African, with powerful shoulders and a heavy jaw. In the seat next to him was another man, a familiar face, his eyes hidden behind dark sunglasses. One of the men from the train, I thought, though I couldn't be sure. Then the rear windows slid into view, and I knew I was not mistaken. Through the window closest to me I could see another man, this one a European, middle-aged, with salt-and-pepper hair. Next to him was a young Moroccan, his features unmistakable as those of an old friend. But he wasn't a friend. It was my other fellow passenger, the one who had called himself Salim.

He glanced in my direction, and I held my breath, as if by not breathing I could keep from being seen. But Salim must not have noticed me. The Mercedes kept going, toward the Boulevard de Safi and the heart of the Ville Nouvelle.

The trip through the medina and the subsequent taxi ride had left me somewhat disoriented, but I had a vague idea of my location in the Ville Nouvelle. I knew the Jardin Majorelle lay almost dead north of the Place de la Liberté. And from there, it was just a short walk through the Bab Larissa and down the Avenue Mohammed V to the Koutoubia Mosque and the Hotel Ali. A brief detour would take me to the Place du 16 Novembre and the All Join Hands offices. I'd give it one more try, I told myself, heading in what I hoped was a southerly direction, wending my way finally to the dusty axis of the Ville Nouvelle.

I found the door to the All Join Hands offices still locked, but one of the windows on the second floor of the building was open, the shutters thrown ajar to let in the afternoon breeze. I knocked hard and took a step back, peering up at the window. Someone moved inside, a white-shirted figure rising, then flitting out of sight. I heard footsteps on the stairs and the deadbolt rattling; then the door opened, and a sunburned face appeared.

"Can I help you?" the man asked. He was short and stocky, uncomfortably pink, with the flaccid, overfed look of so many Americans. He wore a badly wrinkled white dress shirt, the sleeves rolled above his elbows, and his dirty-blond hair was coarse and unruly.

I had not prepared myself for the question, so it took me a moment to answer. "I'm an old friend of Pat Haverman's," I said finally.

The man squinted at me, his face nearly swallowing his eyes. "Hannah, right?"

I nodded.

"Sorry," he apologized. "We only met that once, at the pool at the Ziryab, I think. I didn't recognize you with your clothes on."

"Of course," I told him. "I'm afraid I've forgotten your name."

"Charlie," he said, "Charlie Phillips." He motioned for me to enter, and I stepped into the foyer. "We thought you'd come by," he said. Closing the door behind me, he started up the narrow flight of stairs. He was breathing heavily from the exertion of climbing the stairs, and when we reached the second-floor landing Charlie paused a moment to catch his breath.

"Look who I found," he called out, before stepping through an open doorway into a space crammed with a vast array of electronics.

In the far corner of the room was a sitting area furnished with some old chairs, a coffee table, a badly scarred dartboard, a small refrigerator, and a TV. And there, sprawled on a sagging couch, his long, athletic legs stretched out before him, a bottle of Flag Spéciale in his hand, a copy of the *Herald Tribune* in his lap, was Brian Haverman.

"I had a hunch you'd show up here," he said, smiling. He set the paper down, swung his feet to the floor, and stood. Something about the ease with which he moved unnerved me.

"You shouldn't have followed me," I told him, lingering in the doorway.

"You shouldn't have run out on me," he countered, taking a swig of his beer.

I glanced quickly around the cluttered space that seemed to serve both as office and as meeting place for the homesick Americans' club. Some shelves above the refrigerator held a selection of U.S. supplies, most of which I had only seen in movies. There were several boxes of Pop-Tarts, an unopened bag of Doritos, and a healthy supply of Jack Daniel's.

"You want a beer?" Charlie asked, his face flushing a deeper red. He was clearly working on an early drunk and didn't want to have to go it alone. "We've got a stash of Budweiser, though Brian here prefers the local stuff."

I shook my head. "No, thanks."

Charlie shrugged, already heading for the fridge. "So where'd you disappear to?" he called over his shoulder. "Brian says you just came back to Morocco a few days ago."

"I've been in France," I said, looking at Brian as I spoke, wondering what else he'd told the man.

My answer seemed to satisfy Charlie; he didn't ask for details. I was just another expatriate drifter, like how many others who'd stopped here for beer and satellite baseball games, just another girl from the pool at the Hotel Ziryab. A displaced American with a little money and a lack of ambition. What had he said? *I didn't recognize you with your clothes on.*

Charlie grabbed a Budweiser and popped the top. "I guess this blows my theory out of the water."

"What theory is that?" I asked, stepping toward the two men.

"That he ran off with you." He winked at me, then threw his full weight onto the sagging couch.

"Any other theories?"

Charlie looked philosophically at his beer. "None that make any sense."

"Did you see him when he came through here on his way to Ourzazate?"

"We had a drink that night, at the Mamounia."

"What did you talk about?"

He shrugged. "The date plantations. You."

"What about me?"

"That boy had it bad," he said. "Head over heels." He took a long pull off his beer, then motioned to the shelf of foodstuffs behind him. "You sure you don't want anything?"

"No, thanks," I told him. In truth, I wanted to try everything—the strangely unfoodlike food, the shelf-stable pastries and corn chips, the box of neon macaroni and cheese—but I shook my head. I had the odd feeling that if I stayed too much longer, or ate what was offered, I'd be trapped, like some unfortunate fairy-tale princess.

"What about this project with the date plantations?" I asked. "What did he say about that?"

"Just the same Pat Haverman bullshit. Save the world and all." Charlie waved his beer toward me as if it was an important visual aid. "He wasn't like the rest of us fucks, come down here to get laid. It's summer camp for most of us, you know, but not Pat. He was going to go down there and convince those farmers they needed his help."

I glanced over at Brian and saw him looking back at me, both of us thinking the same thing. Whatever All Join Hands did have to offer, today wasn't the day to find it. Charlie's drunk had taken a turn for the maudlin, and if we didn't leave soon we'd be here for the long haul.

"I should get going," Brian said. "Got some things to take care of."

Charlie winced, a quick, bitter smile. Drunk, but not stupid, he knew when he was being pushed off.

"I guess it's just you and me," he said, slightly sarcastic, his tone saying he knew full well I was on my way out, too.

I shook my head. "Sorry."

"I don't like being followed," I said, as we emerged from the dim stairwell into the bright daylight.

"Well, I don't like being lied to." Brian closed the door behind us and started for the Place du 16 Novembre.

"I told you," I said, keeping pace with him. "You're not safe with me."

"Thanks for the warning, but like I told you, I'll take my chances."

I put my hand on his arm and stopped walking, pulling him up short alongside me. "Someone wants me dead."

"Then you need my help."

"I don't need anyone's help," I told him, but in truth I wasn't so sure. I was tired of being alone and afraid.

We walked in silence for a while, down the Avenue Mohammed V and in through the red walls of the Old City. The familiar late-afternoon torpor had settled on the town. Most shops were closed already, and the few people on the streets walked slowly, dragging themselves along.

If you've never lived by the cycles of prayer, it might be difficult to imagine the effect of such a schedule. The sisters at the abbey, like Muslims, prayed five times a day. Though I rarely even made three services, and was not expected to, still there was the quintuple ringing of bells to remind me of the divine. Because it's nearly impossible to forget God in the three or four hours between devotions, you live almost constantly with some sense of His presence. That's not to say all people who pray like this are particularly holy; some are more afflicted than blessed, while others, misconstruing God's intentions from the beginning, become even more deeply confused.

To live in the convent had been powerful enough, but even I had difficulty understanding what it would mean to live in a larger society governed by the rhythm of prayer. It would be, I thought, a kind of profound surrender. Wasn't that the meaning of *Islam*? Surrender. Submission.

"You want to go get something to eat?" Brian asked, as we passed the Koutoubia Mosque.

I nodded, realizing just how hungry and tired I was.

"There's a place I like near the Djemaa el-Fna," he said. "Local food."

"Sounds fine," I told him.

It was just before sunset when we arrived at the Restaurant El Bahja, a clean, simple place just south of the square. Save for a Senegalese waiter and a German couple, the little café was deserted.

"It might be quite a wait," Brian warned. "I think everyone's gone to pray."

"It's okay," I said.

The server hustled over to greet us, arms outstretched, his face one wide smile. He and Brian exchanged pleasantries. It was the first time I'd heard Brian speak French, and his accent was nearly flawless.

"This is Eve," he said, motioning in my direction, and then to me, "Eve, meet Michel."

The man reached out his hand. "Pleased to meet you, Mademoiselle."

"And you," I said, returning the handshake.

"The cooks are gone," Michel explained as he led us to a table, "but they'll be back shortly. I'll bring you something to snack on."

"Thanks," Brian said. "And could you bring a bottle of Valpierre, if you have it?"

"Of course." Michel beamed.

"Your French is good," I said when the man had gone.

"I took it in college," Brian explained, shrugging off my compliment. "You should have heard me when I first got here."

"Where did you go to school?" I asked.

"Brown," he said.

"That's in Rhode Island, right?" Another piece of knowledge I hadn't realized was tucked away in my brain.

Brian nodded. "Providence."

"No graduate school?"

"It's a wonder I finished my undergrad. I moved out to California when I graduated and started my own company. I was one of the lucky few who got in on the ground floor and got out before the tech market took a nosedive."

"Retired at thirty," I commented.

"Thirty-two," he corrected me.

Michel reappeared with a bowl of olives, a chunk of bread, some pistachios, and a bottle of white wine.

"Thank you," Brian said, as the waiter opened the bottle and poured out two glasses. Taking a sip of his wine, Brian picked up our two unopened menus from the table and handed them to Michel. "Tell Jamal to make whatever he thinks is best today."

Michel nodded, then left.

I watched Brian crack open a pistachio. He wasn't a pretty man, but he was handsome in the best kind of way, his face softened by its imperfections. There was a scar on his chin, a single cut that was almost hidden by the crease below his lip.

Sliding an olive into my mouth, I separated the flesh from the pit. The meat was perfectly rich and briny, flecked with bits of fiery *harissa*. Eight months, I thought, of dead ends and cold leads, and nothing was getting any warmer. It seemed to me his sojourn here had long outlasted any hope of finding his brother.

"It's not just Pat that keeps you here, is it?" I asked, watching him dismantle another nut. He seemed to have mastered this strange place and all its nuances. He was one of those people who were profoundly at home in their voluntary exile.

He looked up at me but said nothing.

"Would you go back if you found him?"

Pausing a moment, he shook his head. "I don't know." There was nothing false about his statement, not a single hint of trickery, just the uncomfortable truth.

"So," I said, changing the subject, "you don't think this thing with the date plantations had anything to do with Pat's disappearing?"

"No. I mean, I don't know. It wasn't even really a project yet. As far as I can tell, that was his first trip down there. He was just scouting things out."

"And the other projects he was working on? Can you think of any reason why he might have pissed someone off?"

"All Join Hands helps a lot of people down here. And I'm sure they step on some toes in the process, but there's nothing that really jumps out at me."

"You ever run across the name Werner?" I asked.

Brian took one of the olives, spitting the pit discreetly into his hand, then depositing it on a little white plate that had been put on the table for exactly that purpose. "Not that I can remember. Why?"

"It's probably nothing," I told him, taking a sip of my wine, watching his face through the glass. "Just a name I thought I remembered."

I wanted to tell him everything, but something inside me wouldn't let me do it. I told myself it was out of concern, that he'd be better off not knowing, but the truth was that there was something about him I didn't trust. Maybe it was just the effortless grace of American privilege, or the ease with which he slipped into the colonial culture. Maybe it was my memory of him in my dark room at the Continental, or the fact that he'd followed me to Marrakech. Whatever the reason, I discarded the subject of Werner as quickly as Brian had set aside the scoured olive pit. Maybe tomorrow, I told myself, setting the wine glass down, watching him crack another pistachio.

FOURTEEN

Dinner was slow in coming, and by the time we'd finished the four courses the cook at the El Bahja had fashioned for us, we'd gone through half of a second bottle of Valpierre. I was tipsy from the wine, not drunk, but more fearless than I'd been in a long time, loosened up enough to say yes to Brian's suggestion that we head over to the casino at the Mamounia Hotel. It had been one of Pat's favorite haunts, Brian explained, and I told myself there was a chance I might have been a patron as well, that someone might recognize me, just as the waiter at the El Minzah had.

The hotel was a short walk from the restaurant, just inside the Bab el-Jedid, on the southwestern edge of the Old City. It was an imposing French colonial structure, with costumed doormen to keep out the rabble, and a towering triple-arched entryway. I followed Brian up the outside steps and into the sumptuous lobby.

To compare the Mamounia to the El Minzah would be to do the old Marrakech hotel a great disservice. There was nothing grade B about the clientele or the surroundings. Hand-polished surfaces lined the interior, marble and mirrors, brass and wood. Here everything, from the money to the acres of hand-knotted rugs, was old but not tired. Easy wealth circulated through the public rooms. And on the periphery of it all, darting down back passageways, whispering so as not to disturb the masters of privilege, was a discreet army of servants.

"Your brother had an expensive habit," I remarked as I followed Brian through the art deco maze of the hotel. I had a hunch the Mamounia's casino didn't offer quarter slots.

"There's not much else to spend your money on down here," he answered.

Could that have been the problem? I wondered. Could an unpaid debt have gotten the American killed? Or maybe he just owed enough that he needed to skip town. Still, neither of these theories made much sense. If he had left, why not just head back to the States? Surely a local shylock would stop at the border. And if he'd been killed, I doubted it would have been done in secret. There's nothing to be gained by murdering someone who owes you money, except that it serves as a warning to others. Pat's death, if he was dead, was hardly public enough to have been a statement. And where did I fit into all of this? For I was certain I fit into it somewhere.

A tuxedoed bouncer stopped us at the door to the casino, his eyes ranging across my body, no doubt taking in the shabbiness of my attire. Brian grabbed my hand, pulling me toward him.

"Wait over there, will you?" he said, nodding to indicate a nearby sitting area.

I did as I was told, keeping one eye on Brian and the

man as I walked away. A couple came out of the door of the casino. The man was Asian, fat and fiftyish, in a dark suit. The woman, though making a valiant attempt to look twenty years his junior, showed the hard-edged wear of an aging film star, too much makeup on too brittle a palette. She had squeezed herself into a floor-length pink gown and sequined shoes. Her breasts were a good three cup sizes too big for her frame, some plastic surgeon's over-the-top idea of beauty. Her hair formed a stiff blond halo around her head. They turned and headed past me, moving down the hall together like a bad impersonation of Ginger Rogers and Fred Astaire.

Brian said something to the bouncer, and the man pulled a tiny cell phone from his pocket and made a call. He had a brief conversation with whoever was on the other end; then he looked at Brian and at me. I saw Brian reach into his pocket, pull out a neatly folded dollar note, and slip it into the man's tuxedo. Then he looked in my direction, motioning for me to join him.

"Enjoy your evening, sir," the bouncer said as I approached.

"Thank you." Taking my hand, pulling me after him, Brian stepped in through the doors of the casino.

"How did you do that?" I asked as we navigated our way to the cashier.

"Let's just say it's guest privileges," he answered.

"You're staying here?"

Nodding, he pulled out his wallet and laid down a thick wad of cash for chips. "What do you want to play? Roulette? Craps? Baccarat?"

"I think I'll just watch, thanks."

Brian smiled. "What are you worried about? It's not your money. Besides, haven't you ever heard of beginner's luck?"

I eyed him skeptically.

"C'mon," he urged, starting across the room.

It was still early in the evening, and there was only a smattering of guests in the casino. All the patrons were non-Arabs, and with one or two exceptions, all the players were men. The women who were there mostly just sat and watched.

"It's dead this time of year," Brian said, as if reading my thoughts. "Ramadan keeps most of the Muslim clientele away. It's a shame, too, because it's the Saudis who've got the real money to throw around."

We found a table, and Brian directed me to a seat, then took one himself. "Baccarat," he said. "You know the rules?"

I looked at the green felt, the white lines radiating out from two half rings, one marked *Banker's,* the other, *Player's.* "You bet on either the banker's or player's hand," I said. "Nine wins, and if the hand adds up to a double digit, you drop the first number."

Brian looked over at me. "I thought you spent the last year in a convent."

"Things come back to me," I told him, smiling. "I must have done this before."

I played the first hand and lost, then won the next two. Brian was right; it was easy to play with someone else's money. I might have remembered the rules, but my skills were rusty, and I lost quickly, running through most of Brian's chips in the first half hour.

"Let me have a hand or two," he asked when I'd whittled his cache down to almost nothing.

"Sorry," I said sheepishly.

He smiled. "Don't be."

Relinquishing the game and the chips to Brian, I sat back and scanned the room. The Asian man and the woman in the pink gown were back, taking a turn at roulette. A group of loud Frenchmen were playing poker near the back of the casino.

Just a few tables away, engaged in what looked like a game of twenty-one, was a solitary figure, a man. He must have come in while I was concentrating on my baccarat, for I hadn't noticed him earlier. He was an Arab, Moroccan from the looks of him, though I couldn't quite see his face from where I sat. His play was businesslike, almost devoid of pleasure, dispassionate as a visit to a prostitute might be, as if he were simply taking care of some unpleasant need.

He peeled the cards back and looked furtively at them, then nodded to the dealer for another card. There was something about him, something about his gestures, that made me think I knew him. Sitting forward, I craned my head to get a better look. The dealer slid his third card out, and the man glanced quickly at the result, then flipped the cards over, obviously disgusted with himself. This way, I thought, willing him to turn in my direction, just a few inches. He reached into his pocket, pulled out a cigar, and cut off the tip. Then, as if obliging me, he turned his head and signaled a nearby waiter.

I was right. He was someone from my past, though not so distant a past as I might have expected. I'd seen him just the day before in the medina. It was Mustapha, the man at the Berber pharmacy, the spice seller from Pat's address book.

"Eve?" It was Brian.

I sat back and turned to face him.

"Recognize something?" he asked, looking past me to the twenty-one table.

I shook my head and glanced down at the table. "Are you out already?"

Brian nodded. "Not my lucky night. You ready to go?"

I nodded, getting up out of my seat. Why was I lying to him? I wondered.

"Look," Brian said. "It's Charlie."

Our flush-faced host from earlier that day had just stepped through the casino's entryway. He looked worse for wear, sweaty and disheveled. Brian waved, but Charlie didn't notice. His eyes were glued to the twenty-one table, to the pharmacist's bulky back. He lingered for a second inside the doorway, slightly unsteady on his feet; then the spice seller turned in his chair, his eyes flicking briefly in Charlie Phillips's direction. A peculiar look flashed across the American's face, a strange mixture of greed and shame. Blanching visibly, he ducked his head and turned, heading out of the casino.

"Poor, pathetic Charlie," Brian said.

It was, I thought, a generous description. "Who is he?" I asked. "The man playing twenty-one?"

Brian put his hand lightly on my back, guiding me to the door. "A local entrepreneur," he said. "Keeps the expat community in gambling money."

"It looks like Charlie has some unpaid debts," I remarked.

"Doesn't surprise me."

"And Pat?" I asked.

Brian didn't say anything. We had reached the door, and he lifted his hand from my back and gestured to the bouncer. "Where are you staying?" he asked, as if he hadn't heard my earlier question.

"The Hotel Ali," I told him, "just off the Djemaa el-Fna."

Brian nodded as if he knew the place. "You feel like taking a walk?"

"Back to my hotel?"

He shook his head. "Come on."

• • •

It was a perfectly cloudless night, the dark desert sky
brimming with stars. A chill breeze blew down from the
Atlas, making the white canvas pool umbrellas billow and
creak like the sails and riggings of a yacht. The pool was
light itself, casting a sea-blue blush on the hotel's plaster
walls, dancing like film glow on the water-misted over-
growth. Papery bougainvillea flowers stippled the patio,
bright as drops of newly spilled blood. Somewhere in the
garden an automatic sprinkler hissed on.

"Do you know why Marrakech is so red?" Brian asked
as we skirted the pool.

I shook my head.

"There's a Berber legend," he said, "that when the
Koutoubia Mosque was built, it stuck in the city's heart
like a giant sword. So much blood poured out that it
stained everything crimson."

He stopped walking and turned so that he was standing
just a few inches away. "You can almost believe it, can't
you?" he said, pointing through a gap in the trees to the
Koutoubia, the illuminated minaret thrust up into the
black sky, the stone gleaming like honed steel.

"We're not allowed inside it, as non-Muslims, are
we?" I asked.

"No," he answered. He lowered his hand, and his fingers brushed my arm, making my skin pucker with goose
bumps. "Too bad, isn't it? It must be beautiful."

"Yes," I agreed.

In the summer at the abbey we had a little outdoor
chapel, a garden house made of bamboo and old boards
one of the sisters had salvaged from an old chicken coop.
Instead of a crucifix there was a small rock fountain in the
back of the structure, and a tiny pool that caught the glim-
mer of whatever votive candles had been brought out for

prayer. The structure was built behind the larger stone chapel, on the far lip of the grounds, overlooking the farms in the valley below. It had been my greatest pleasure to sit on one of the rough-hewn benches, listening to the splash and bubble of the fountain, watching the fields succumb to evening.

Brian started forward again, deeper into the garden, and I followed silently behind, letting the great monolith of the mosque slip from view. What was it about these holy places? Where did the stillness come from? I had not prayed, I realized, since I'd lit that last candle at the convent, and even that had been in anger.

"You must miss him," I said as we emerged onto a wide path bordered by orange trees. "Your brother, I mean."

"He was always the better person," Brian remarked sadly.

"I'm sorry I don't remember him."

"He wrote poetry. We used to give him shit about it. He was the kind of person who was always falling in love."

I didn't say anything. I was thinking about Hannah smiling for the camera. Hannah, the girl of Pat Haverman's dreams. What lies, I wondered, had she told, and why? Surely Pat hadn't known about the box at the El Minzah. My guess was he hadn't known about Leila Brightman, either.

Brian stopped. "I'm sorry. I shouldn't have said that."

"Said what?"

"About Pat being the kind of person who was always falling in love."

"It's okay," I assured him.

He shook his head. "If I'd met Hannah Boyle at the Ziryab, I would have fallen in love with her, too."

I reached out and put my hand on Brian's wrist. "And Eve?" I asked.

There are certain advantages to not being able to remember, certain experiences that, when lived again for
the first time, are miraculous gifts. Like my first snowfall
at the abbey, a sudden blanketing of white that came early
one morning during matins, so that when we stepped out
into the bitter November morning the world had been
transformed. Or the first fresh egg I ever tasted, the yolk a
deep orange, the white lacy, the edges crisped in butter.

"I would have fallen in love with her, too," Brian said.

Remember this, I told myself, as I moved through the
darkness. Beneath my fingers I could feel Brian's pulse,
the slow stride and rhythm of his heart. I opened my
mouth just slightly and put my lips on his lips. Wasn't this
the way to do it? Somewhere deep, deep in my memory
the old sensations of pleasure stirred, the unassailable desire for touch.

Kissing him made me forget everything for a moment,
Joshi, Pat and Hannah, the men at the convent, Salim and
his friend on the train. We followed the orange trees to the
far back of the garden, hands and mouths grappling as we
went. When we reached the great earthen wall that
marked the edge of the Old City, I leaned my back up
against the plaster and pulled Brian toward me.

The wall was warm on my back, the thick pisé releas-
ing all the heat it had gathered and held during the day. I
looked up, searching the sky for the minaret, but it was
nowhere to be seen.

"I don't remember," I said, reaching for his face in the
darkness.

"Don't worry," Brian whispered, his mouth on my ear.
"You will."

Then, suddenly, laughter sounded, someone coming
down the walk, and I drew back. It was only the woman
from the casino, the one in the pink gown, a benign figure
if ever I'd seen one, but still she reminded me of all the

hazards I'd forgotten. She stepped into the glow of one of the garden lamps, and for an instant I thought I knew her, had seen her somewhere before. One of us was in danger, I thought, shivering slightly, perhaps both of us.

Brian squeezed my hand. "Come on," he whispered, pulling me after him. "Let's go to my room."

I nodded, agreeing despite my better judgment.

"What's out there?" I asked. From the balcony of Brian's room I could see the pool and the dark gardens we'd come from. Beyond the gardens, past the unseen city wall, was more darkness, the immensity of it broken here and there by the lights of a lone car.

"The mountains," he said. "You'll be able to see them in the morning." He came and stood behind me, his body fitting perfectly against mine. Then he brushed my hair aside and pressed his lips to my neck.

The mountains, I thought, and beyond them, Ourzazate and the date plantations. "I want to go down to Ourzazate," I said.

Brian stepped away from me and went inside. "We could rent a car in the morning," he offered. "It's just a couple hours' drive."

"Who knows?" I told him. "I might remember something."

"Yes," he said. "You might." Crouching, he opened the minibar and pulled out a tiny bottle of bourbon. His shirt was untucked, the sleeves rolled up, the buttons one hole askew. He had taken his shoes off, and there was something about the nakedness of his bare feet that made him seem delicate and vulnerable. I wanted to take the rest of his clothes off and make love to him, slowly and carefully.

More than anything, though, I wanted to tell him about

Werner, about the men from the train, and the little thief in the Djemaa el-Fna. Lying seemed pointless now, worse than pointless. It seemed somehow perverse, and dangerous.

Brian straightened up, looking for a drinking glass. Finding one on top of the bar, he opened the ice bucket, plucked out three half-melted cubes, and tossed them into the glass.

"So," Brian called, disappearing into the bathroom. "This Bruns Werner, you think he knew Pat?"

Bruns Werner. I froze, my heart hesitating while my mind frantically rewound our dinner conversation, the way Brian had taken the olive into his mouth when I'd asked him if he'd ever heard the name Werner. And then the pit falling into the little white plate. *Not that I can remember,* he'd said.

Fighting back a wave of nausea, I stepped inside. Werner, I'd said. I hadn't used the name Bruns, hadn't even known the name. I was certain of it. Instinctively, I scanned the room for a weapon, something sharp and substantial. Letter opener? Nail scissors? On the top of the minibar was a stainless steel wine key. It was no Beretta, but it would do in a pinch.

I heard Brian turn the tap off and crack the seal on the bourbon bottle. "Eve?" he called, appearing in the doorway, the glass of bourbon in his hand.

He handed me the whiskey, and I took a sip. "What did you say?" I asked casually.

"Bruns Werner," he said. "You mentioned the name at dinner. Do you think he had something to do with Pat?"

He was a good liar, almost good enough to make me doubt myself. I took another drink and shrugged. "I can't remember. Like I said, it's probably nothing."

Kissing me on the top of the head, he reached up and

unbuttoned his shirt, then pulled it and his pants off and laid them neatly on the back of a chair. "I think I'll jump in the shower. You want to join me?"

"You go ahead."

"If you change your mind..."

I smiled, stifling a shiver. "I know where you are."

He ducked back into the bathroom, and I heard him turn the shower on and pull the curtain closed.

How did he know? I wondered. Setting the whiskey down, I crossed toward the minibar and grabbed the wine opener. Part of me just wanted to run, but another part needed to hear what he had to say. I opened the wine key and surveyed my options. There was a little knife on one end, but it was dulled from use. No, the corkscrew was my best bet. Making my way back to the open bathroom door, I flattened myself against the wall, took a deep breath, and started a slow count back from one hundred.

What else had he lied to me about? I wondered. Over the sound of the shower I could hear Brian humming, the tune too faint to be recognized. And what if he had lied? Hadn't I lied to him, too? Hadn't I been lying all along? The water ebbed and subsided, and Brian stepped out of the tub. I heard him grab a towel and rub himself dry. "I feel like a new man," he called. "This place is worth the price of admission for the shower alone."

Tensing my grip on the wine key, I widened my stance and braced myself. Brian's feet sounded on the tiles, the muted slap of bare skin on cold ceramic. His face appeared in the doorway, chin and nose first, hair still dripping water.

"Werner," I said. Wrapping my left forearm around his neck, I jammed the metal tip of the corkscrew into the berm of his carotid artery. "I called him Werner. I never said Bruns."

Brian's jaw flexed, the muscle tensing and contracting like something alive under his skin.

"How did you know?" I demanded.

He turned his head to look at me, and the steel pressed farther into his skin. "I'm sorry, Eve."

"Who are you?"

He didn't answer.

"Did I know you?" I asked. His skin was warm from the shower. I could smell the shampoo in his hair. "Did you know me before?"

He shook his head. "No."

"Who am I?" I demanded.

"I don't know."

"Who are you?"

He didn't say anything. I couldn't hurt him, and he knew it.

I lifted the corkscrew from his neck and took a step backward. The steel had left a red mark on his skin, a single welt like a bee sting.

"I'm sorry," he said again.

"Me, too," I told him, starting for the door.

"Be careful, Eve," I heard him say, as I stepped out into the hallway.

Too agitated to ride, I shook off the half dozen taxi drivers camped outside the Mamounia's gates and started up the Avenue Houmane el-Fetouaki toward the Hotel Ali. It was late, too late to be walking, but I needed to get my thoughts together. Still gripping the wine key, I put my head down and marched forward. A car pulled up next to me, and I looked over to see one of the taxi drivers beckoning through the open window.

"Get in!" he called.

I shook my head and waved him off.

"It's dangerous," he warned.

"Go away," I said, rudely.

"Crazy," the man snarled in French, rolling his window up, speeding away.

I *was* crazy, I thought, crazy to have trusted Brian in the first place, crazy to have come to Marrakech. And yet, this was where the thread of my past ran out.

A car engine slowed behind me, and wheels pulled to the curb. Another taxi, I thought, keeping my eyes on the sidewalk. Jeezus, why couldn't they leave me alone? Out of the corner of my eye I caught a glimpse of a black hood, a dark window. No, it wasn't a *petit taxi*. The door opened, and a man jumped out. My friend from the train. Salim.

I leaped forward, my hand tight on the corkscrew, and broke into a dead run. Behind me, a second door popped open, and a man's voice shouted in Arabic. Go, I told myself, powering ahead, but I wasn't fast enough. A hand grabbed my waist, and I went down on the sidewalk, my shoulder cracking against the pavement, the pain knocking the breath out of my lungs.

I rolled over, swinging the corkscrew, catching a piece of Salim's jacket, drawing a long red welt on his forearm. Then the second man was on me, his fingers hard on my wrist. He wrenched the wine key from my grasp, then grabbed my hair and pulled me up. There was more shouting in Arabic. The car rolled forward, and the second man shoved me inside, then climbed in after me. *This is it,* I thought, *they're going to kill me,* and the last thing I saw before they slipped a sack over my head was the Koutoubia's minaret against the black sky.

FIFTEEN

I'm with Patrick Haverman, on the other side of the mountains, in a casbah on the road to Ourzazate. Behind us is the moonscape of the Atlas, a jagged silhouette of treeless peaks. On one of the nearby parched foothills someone has written a message to God in white stones. *Allahu akbar,* it says, the letters several stories high, the script flowing across the rocky terrain as gracefully as if it had flowed from the tip of a giant ink pen.

There's a dry wind blowing, a desert wind, clean as sand. It has a left a film of fine grit in my hair and on my skin. We're on the roof, and above us is the most perfectly blue sky I've ever seen, a great placid lake of blue, stretching all the way to the northern tip of the Sahara. In my right hand I'm holding the Beretta.

It's a familiar scene, this old and uncomfortable memory. Pat is hurt, bleeding badly.

"I'm sorry," I tell him. "God, I'm sorry."

He's trying to tell me it's okay, but I don't believe him. This is my fault, I think. I'm the one who has done this.

"You have to go," he says, and I know he's right, but my legs won't move. Now I'm down on my knees beside him.

"Go," he tells me. "I'll be all right. They're coming."

From far off down the valley comes the sound of beating wings, something powerful slicing through the air.

"I'm sorry," I say for the last time. I lean down and kiss him, putting my hand against his chest.

"Stand up," he demands, and I do. For the first time I notice a huge stork's nest on one of the corner ramparts of the old Casbah, an engineering feat of sticks and mud large enough to cradle a grown man.

They're coming, I think, there's nowhere to go, and then I'm plunging down into the blackness of the Casbah, down into the earthy smell of it, the jumble of rooms and stairwells, this place that seems to have risen from the land itself.

I'm on a sailboat, on a lake somewhere, no, on an ocean. There's a gray mist coming off the water, and my face is wet with it, wet with the spray our hull makes as it carves through the dark water. We are in a narrow passage, a channel closed on either side by two rocky islands. There's an overwhelming sense of the primeval to this place, to the moss and ferns and rambling green brambles, and the little rain-wet beaches spilling down to the water, as if they are completely secret, untouched by humans. The water is so clear that I can see the giant rocks far below, the islands' craggy foundations. The channel is dotted with rafts of kelp and white sea froth.

There are four of us on the boat, two women, a man, and me. We've brought a picnic: cold salmon, green beans, potato salad, strawberries, and chocolate cake. Everyone else is drinking champagne, but I am drinking sparkling grape juice. My mother poured it into a tall glass flute like the adults have, where it bubbles and fizzes just like the real thing.

"Look there," my grandmother shouts, and we all follow her finger to the mouth of the channel.

Sliding toward us through the mist, its giant bow cleaving the water into two perfect white combs, is the largest boat I think I've ever seen.

"The ferry," my grandfather says, leaning hard on the wheel, nudging us closer to land.

It's too big, I think, it's going to crush us, but I'm wrong. We skirt it easily, slipping along beside its rust-washed flanks.

"Come on," my mother says, standing, waving her arms.

I struggle to my feet beside her.

"Wave," she tells me, and I wave with her, to the several dozen brightly clothed passengers on the upper deck of the ferry, who are waving back.

Then the horn sounds, loud and low, sending a shiver down my spine, and the ferry turns, curving deftly around us, its prow just missing one of the green rock islands.

I'm in a stairwell, a narrow, garbage-strewn passageway that descends into near darkness. There's a man with me, and we're both running, careening downward, taking the steps two at a time. Below us, working their way up out of the gloom, are several dim figures, men in strange clothes, cotton shifts and loose pants. We emerge onto a landing, and my companion pulls me after him, off the stairs and into a large room, a vast, high-ceilinged industrial space bounded on one side by a long row of grime-streaked windows.

The warehouse, I think, and already I know what is to come. There is no way out, and we can hear the men, their feet pummeling the stairs. My friend looks at me, and his eyes are black with fear. He is sweating, his face glistening in the swampy light. It's okay, I want to tell him, but I know it's not. In an instant the men are upon us. The knife winks, flashing toward me like the ivory tooth of some giant predator. I feel it briefly on my neck, not pain, but something swifter and cleaner, and then I feel nothing at all.

It's hard to say how long I was out, a few hours, possibly more. It was just before dawn when I woke, cottonmouthed and nauseous, groping my way toward consciousness. Through the high window across from my bed I could see the first hint of the sun, the black sky draining to blue, the stars fading like spring snowflakes settling on a pond.

They'd given me vasopressin. I could taste its bitter reminder in the back of my throat. They'd given me something else, too, something that had knocked me out with the speed and precision of a heavyweight prizefighter. But whatever it was had quit working, and now, for the first time since I'd been stuffed into the black Mercedes, there was nothing to mask the throbbing in my shoulder. I rolled over, trying to sit up, and the pain caught me right in the pit of my stomach. I took a deep breath and lay back, running through the litany of my dreams, while the pain subsided to a dull ache.

To live with amnesia is to live with a suspect mind, a renegade piece of yourself that cannot be contained.

Dreams may be memories, memories may be dreams, and neither one is to be trusted. I had seen my mother before, or at least her shadowy incarnation, and I had long since learned to discount her appearances as wishful specters of my own desires.

In the beginning I had been deceived by the vivid conjurings of my imagination. The places in my dreams had seemed impossibly real, home interiors furnished down to the last tiny detail, china figurines on the end tables, a cluttered pot rack in the kitchen. I had come to believe in these places the way the sisters believed in the kingdom of heaven. Here was Christmas morning, a flocked fir tree in the living room, a fire in the fireplace, a new red bicycle with a bow on it. And here I was in a pair of blue-and-white pajamas.

And then, one night at the abbey, I'd recognized that pajamaed little girl in one of Sister Claire's videos. The house was a relic from another movie, a ghost story about a man who'd killed his mistress. How could I believe in anything after that?

And yet, try as I might, I couldn't shake the vision of Patrick Haverman, the Beretta in my hand. He was dead. I knew it now. Hadn't I dreamed this before? Hadn't I shuddered at the person in my piracetam nightmares, the same person who'd gone to Joshi's apartment that night, who'd left a gun in the safe of the El Minzah, who knew how to use it? There are some things we're better off not knowing, I thought. Like whatever had happened in that warehouse.

Somewhere in the distance, the muezzin started his call to morning prayer, and a handful of other, fainter voices joined in. We were still in the city, then. I sat up again, slowly this time, and surveyed my surroundings. The single, open window let in just enough light for me to make out the room's spare furnishings. Aside from my bed, there was a small dresser, a wardrobe, and a single chair.

The room had two doors, one on either side. I stood up, taking a moment to get my balance, and made my way toward the closest one. It was locked tight, dead-bolted from the outside, without an inner knob or latch to try. I swept my hand across the wall, feeling for a light switch, but found nothing.

The second door gave way easily at my touch, swinging inward. Finding a light switch on the inside wall, I flicked it on to reveal a small, utilitarian bathroom with a white porcelain toilet and sink. I caught a glimpse of myself in the mirrored medicine cabinet and winced. My hair was matted from sleep, my right cheek red and abraded from the fall. My lip was fat on one side, my right eye showing a darkening half-moon bruise that promised to blossom into a nasty shiner.

Working through the pain, I lifted my arm and made a small circle, loosening my shoulder joint. No, I didn't think it was broken, but the muscles would be sore and stiff for a while.

My arrival had evidently been expected. A shelf next to the sink held an array of basic toiletries, soap, tooth-paste, hairbrush, a new toothbrush still in its wrapper, and a plastic drinking cup. There were clean white towels on the back of the door.

I took a drink first, letting the tap run till the water came out cold. Vasopressin always made my mouth dry, but this was worse than any hangover the medication had ever left me with. It took three good cupfuls of water for me to wash down the cotton taste. When I'd drunk my fill, I brushed my teeth, then turned the tap to hot and washed my face, carefully scrubbing the crusted blood from my right cheek.

Where was I? I wondered, stepping back into the main

room, listening to the muezzin's voice fade to silence. Out the open window I could hear a bird singing and the faint rumble of a car engine. In the city, yes, but somewhere quiet. At Bruns Werner's villa, perhaps. Had Brian set me up? He must have known all along, from the moment he saw me on the ferry. No, he must have known before that. Someone at customs in Algeciras had known who I was. And Patrick Haverman? And Hannah Boyle? Had they been a lie as well? Some part of me deep down refused to believe it.

I crossed to the locked door and stretched myself out on the terra-cotta tiles, my eye to the inch-wide crack at the threshold. There was a light on in the corridor, but no sign of life. Standing, I crossed back to the bed, shoved the bedstead against the wall beneath the window, then positioned the chair on top of the mattress.

It was a precarious arrangement, but with careful climbing I managed to reach the window. Lifting myself on my tiptoes, I peered out. From where I stood I could see the walled gardens of several large properties, and not too far away, a slice of what looked like the Jardin Majorelle. Yes, I was definitely in Marrakech, at Werner's house in the Ville Nouvelle.

I stretched, craning my neck over the edge of the sill, looking for some way out, but there was none. Below me, the pisé wall dropped three long stories straight to the ground. Above, more smooth plaster rose to the roof. No way down. No way up. Somehow, I'd have to make my own way.

I had taken the top sheet from the bed and was tearing it into long, thin strips when I heard them, two men coming down the corridor. Working quickly, I tucked my project under the bedspread, then flattened out the wrinkles with my palm. It was Salim who entered first, followed by a man I hadn't seen before.

Salim leered at me, his eyes lingering on the scythe-shaped bruise that was his handiwork. He was wearing a short-sleeved shirt, and I could see the gash my corkscrew had made along his forearm. The wound was slightly infected, the skin around it flushed hot and tender.

"Good morning, Leila," he sneered, in a tone that confirmed what I had already guessed, that we'd met long before that day on the train, and that our acquaintance had not been a pleasant one. "How are you feeling?"

"Fuck you," I told him.

He nodded to his shadow, and the other man came over and grabbed my arm, yanking me up off the bed.

"Nice try," Salim said, pulling the covers back to reveal the strips of sheet. He said something in Arabic to his partner, and they both had a good laugh, apparently at my expense.

"What happened to your boyfriend?" I asked, motioning to my eyes to indicate the sunglasses of the second man on the train.

Salim reached forward and hit me hard in the jaw. My head snapped to the side, and I felt the warmth of blood on my tongue. No, whatever past we shared was not a happy one. He barked something to his partner, and the man pulled a hood over my face and hustled me toward the door.

I tried to keep my bearings as we navigated the villa, but somewhere in the curve of the stairwell I lost all sense of direction. By the time we reached our final destination, all I could be certain of was that we were still in Werner's house. A door was opened in front of me, and I was shoved forward; then I heard the lock click closed and Salim and the other man returning the way we'd come.

Freed of my guides, I reached up and lifted the hood from my face.

The room I was in was dark and masculine, furnished in the same ubiquitous colonial fashion I'd seen at both the El Minzah and the Mamounia, the hallmark of expatriate good taste. Leather and dark wood predominated; there were hand-worked ottomans, overstuffed chairs, a red Persian rug, and a mammoth desk inlaid with ebony and cedar. Three of the room's walls held a staggering collection of weapons, everything from samurai swords to eighteenth-century rifles to medieval maces. An intricately carved *mashrabiyya*, made to hide the faces of women from the street below, covered the only window, though I couldn't see what purpose the screen served here, in such an obviously Western place. Outside, heavy iron barred the glass.

On the wall behind the desk was a conglomeration of photographs, mostly black-and-white, mostly taken sometime earlier. Many of them were hunting scenes, shot all over the world. Some had obviously been taken in Africa, the images studded with white canvas tents, Land Rovers, and native guides, the trophies savanna animals. Others showed glimpses of the American West or Canada, a mountain goat, a grizzly bear with monstrous claws. Still others were unmistakably Asian, their backdrops rife with grass huts, the prey here more exotic: a tiger with a single dark hole in its temple, a half dozen wild boars, their stomachs slit to reveal a bloody tangle of viscera.

The non-hunting photographs had been taken in equally exotic locations. In one, a small figure stood next to a giant statue of Buddha. Another showed a man shaking hands with a camouflaged soldier, while behind them, the downdraft from a helicopter's propellers bent a giant cowlick in waist-high jungle grass.

Though the cast of supporting characters changed, there was one consistent face in almost all of the photographs. He had aged greatly during the years they chronicled, but the essence of his face, the gray eyes and square jaw, had not changed. He was the same man I'd seen in the car that day. Bruns Werner.

There was one photograph, more than any of the others, that caught my eye. It had been taken in black-and-white, in the full-sun blaze of afternoon, and showed three young people at an outdoor café. The setting was Asian. A rickshaw driver sat idle at the edge of the picture. Opposite him, a woman in a plain white cotton shift carried a basket of fruit. A French movie poster behind her showed a young Peter Fonda in *Easy Rider*. Over the heads of the three friends, a sign told the name of the establishment. *Les Trois Singes*. The three monkeys.

The figure on the far left was Werner. He held a glass in his hand, lifting it toward the camera as if to toast. On the far right was another man, more handsome than Werner, dark-haired and trim, with the well-muscled physique of a swimmer. The sleeves of his white cotton shirt were rolled up, and he was sitting slightly back in his chair, at perfect ease with the world around him. Between the two men was a woman. She was dressed plainly, in a dark T-shirt, khakis, a canvas jacket, and leather boots. Her head was in motion, her face blurred beyond recognition. Both men were turned toward the woman, as if waiting for something from her, as if enthralled by some electric presence, something I couldn't see.

There was movement in the corridor, and I turned in time to see the door swing open. Bruns Werner came forward into the room, the soles of his perfectly shined shoes tapping the inlaid floor. He stopped at the edge of the red wool carpet, his hands in the pockets of his suit coat, as if seeing me for the first time. My host regarded me for a moment, his gray eyes revealing nothing.

"Do you know who I am?" he asked, finally.

"Werner," I answered.

He nodded, then came forward and took a seat behind the desk. "Sit down."

I did as I was told, taking the chair Werner indicated.

"You must be hungry," he remarked.

"Yes," I agreed, my hunger winning out over my pride.

My host punched an intercom on his desk and rattled off a command in Arabic, then turned back to me. "Your breakfast will be here shortly," he said, sitting back in his chair, regarding my face. "I'm sorry about Salim," he apologized. "I understand there's some bad blood between you. Old times."

"I wouldn't know."

"No. I guess you wouldn't."

Werner lifted the lid of a small wooden case and took out a cigar. I could smell the tobacco from where I sat, the odor so rich it was almost unpleasant.

"Have we met before?" I asked.

"It must be difficult," he said, ignoring my question. "A tricky situation, really, not knowing one's past."

I shrugged. "What do you want from me?"

Werner produced a tiny hooked knife from the top drawer of the desk and snipped off the end of the cigar. "You really don't remember?" he asked, incredulous.

There was a knock on the door, and Werner called for the person to come in.

"Your breakfast," Werner observed. "I took the liberty of ordering coffee. You do drink coffee, don't you?"

An attractive Moroccan woman in a cream-colored suit and matching high heels came forward and set a tray on the table next to me.

"Will that be sufficient?" my host asked.

I looked at the offering. There was a bowl of yogurt, a plate of fresh green figs, a *pain au chocolat,* a glass of grapefruit juice, and a small pot of coffee. I nodded and gulped down the juice, then took one of the figs. Something told me to eat while I could, that this might be the last food I would see for some time.

Werner slid the little knife back into the drawer, pulled out a gold lighter, and carefully lit the cigar.

"I'd like to arrange a trade," he said, watching me take a bite of the *pain au chocolat* and a sip of coffee. "I can help you remember. But there's certain information I'll need in return."

I looked past him to the menagerie of dead animals, the wild boars with their stomachs so cleanly slit. The pictures made me think of the sisters, and what Heloise had said. *I thought they were singing*. The pastry suddenly tasted rancid in my mouth, the coffee bitter.

Werner exhaled a thick cloud of cigar smoke. "Of course you don't recall, but you've taken something of mine, something I would very much like to recover."

"Go to hell," I told him.

He looked at me with curiosity. "You think I killed your friends, don't you?"

I didn't answer.

"I'll take your silence as a yes," he said, "but I'm afraid you're wrong."

"Who, then?"

Werner shook his head. "That's the million-dollar question, isn't it, Miss Brightman? Or should I call you Eve?"

I shrugged.

"I will tell you what I know," Werner said. "But you'll have to help me first."

"And this thing you claim I took. It would help if I knew just what it was you wanted me to remember."

He leaned back in his chair and savored the cigar.

"That's the problem, my dear. You see, it's information you stole, something that can take many forms. I'm afraid you'll have to remember just which form you've given it."

"It's not that easy," I told him.

"Don't worry," Werner said. "I've arranged for you to have some help."

He took a long toke on the cigar and rang his intercom again, this time summoning Salim.

SIXTEEN

Though the hormone that is its main component is tied inextricably to the brain's ability to recall information and events, the use of vasopressin as a memory enhancer is strictly experimental. The approved medical application for the drug and its more potent counterpart, desmopressin, is as an antidiuretic. Normally, the two drugs are given to diabetics or chronic bed wetters, to cut down on the frequency with which they urinate. As a result, an unfortunate side effect of the medication is that it greatly, sometimes dangerously, reduces the outflow of bodily fluids.

In other words, a person who drinks too much while using vasopressin runs the risk of literally drowning from the inside out. I experienced this nasty aftereffect firsthand one night in Lyon, when I'd had one too many gulps of water from the cooler in Dr. Delpay's office and ended up on my hands and knees in the bathroom, racked by uncontrollable vomiting. I escaped the seizures that would have been the next result of the internal deluge, but the episode left an indelible impression on me and gave me a new respect for the drug's hidden powers.

So when Salim and his nameless cohort appeared with a syringe and an inhaler, my mind leaped immediately back to each drink I'd had that morning. Three cups of water, the grapefruit juice, at least half a cup of coffee.

I looked at Werner, unable to keep my panic from showing. "You can't give me that now. It could kill me."

Werner pushed the chair back from his desk and stood. "I'm afraid your comfort is not the top priority here," he said, then made his way to the door.

"Don't worry," Salim said when Werner was gone. He came forward and grasped my wrists in his hands, pressing my arms against the arms of the chair. "We've taken special care." He nodded to his accomplice. "Hassan here is a doctor."

Somehow the news was less than reassuring. "What's in there?" I asked, glancing at the syringe.

Hassan spoke for the first time. "Idebenone, pyritinol, piracetam," he said proudly, jabbing the needle into my arm. "I call it a memory cocktail."

Jesus, I thought, watching the plunger depress, I was in for a wild ride. I took a deep breath and closed my eyes.

Finished, the good doctor lifted the needle from my arm, set the syringe aside, reached back, and grabbed a handful of my hair. As he lifted the inhaler to my nose, I caught a glimpse of the label. *Desmopressin*, it said. With his free hand, Hassan primed the pump, then jammed the plastic tip into my right nostril, and I felt the sickening rush of the drug.

Keep us safe, Lord, I prayed, though I wasn't sure what help, if any, the prayer could bring me now.

• • •

The real downside to overdosing on nootropic drugs is that they leave you with an acute and lasting memory of each unpleasant detail of the experience. I will never forget that room at Bruns Werner's house in Marrakech, the gruesome photographs, the three figures at the café Les Trois Singes. Nor will I forget the trip that followed, the vertiginous ride across the mountains, the color of my bile on the roadside, or the smell of the car we rode in, a mixture of aftershave and body odor, and some unknown sweetness I have yet to put a name to. Nor, try as I might, will I ever forget the constant, shivering, bone-deep ache.

Hassan, Salim, and I left the villa shortly after my meeting with Werner and, with Salim driving, headed out of town and up into the green foothills of the Atlas. Before we crossed the Oued Zat, I had regurgitated the entirety of my breakfast and was retching up mucus. By the time we reached the High Atlas, I was incapacitated enough by convulsions that my two escorts felt safe leaving me in the Mercedes at the Tizi n'Tichka Pass while they rinsed their feet and hands, unrolled their mats, and performed their midday prayers. Then we were on our way again, plunging down into the austere southern mountains, toward Ourzazate and the desert.

In its own spiteful way, the noxious combination of drugs was working, though what I remembered on that trip was doubtless not what Werner had hoped I would. Later, I would be tempted to think my prayer had worked, but at the time I didn't have the strength to question the source of my luck.

Though it was the beginning of November when the sisters found me, I spent the first six weeks of what I remember as my life in the hospital in Lyon, vainly trying to retrieve myself. It wasn't till the middle of December that Dr. Delpay suggested I might think about a more permanent home, and the sisters offered to take me in. I arrived at the convent just in time for the last week of Advent.

That week before Christmas is a time for summoning Christ, and each night at vespers, before the Magnificat, the Benedictines sing a series of antiphons that literally call out to Him, each addressing the Savior by a different name. *O Wisdom*, they sing, *O Root of Jesse, O Adonai*. It's a primal kind of call, beautiful and mystical as a Buddhist chant, each yearning *O* resonating through the barren winter air.

On that trip to the desert it was my first night at the convent I relived, the singing of the antiphon. Heloise had been appointed my unofficial guardian, and it was she who took me to the chapel that evening. It was snowing, the flakes fine as sifted sugar, dusting us on the walk across the yard. We arrived at vespers glistening like candied almonds.

I had come from the hospital in Lyon that afternoon and had yet to meet many of the sisters. When we entered the chapel, each head turned briefly toward us, each pair of eyes falling on my own, then looking quickly away. I would later come to learn the delicate equilibrium it took to maintain such a community, the magnitude of the chance they'd taken by giving me a home. I'm sure they were eager to see what they'd gotten themselves into, eager to get a look at the strange American who would be living among them. Heloise must have known how scared I was. She reached out, took my hand in her own, and gave my fingers a tight squeeze.

We sat in the back, under the apple-cheeked statue of the Christ child and the adoring face of his mother. The chapel smelled of wet wool and frankincense, and of old age, of camphor and lavender soap and garlic. The antiphon that night was O Oriens.

"O Radiant Dawn," Heloise sang beside me, "brightness of light eternal, and sun of all justice; O come and illumine those who live in deep darkness, in the shadow of death."

I sat in the hard pew and watched my new friend, the snow melting in her dark hair. It was such a rich memory, so immediate, so lush with detail, each bead of water reflecting the altar candles. Heloise looked over at me and smiled, and her face brightened as if by magic. How lucky, I thought, how incredibly lucky I was to have been found by these women.

Heloise was with me all the way to Ourzazate and down into the oases of the Draa Valley, not an angel but an escort, a guide through the dark terrain of memory. She was with me when we arrived at the *palmeraie,* at my side as Salim and Hassan carried me in through the doors of the great red Casbah and down into the cool warren of dark rooms. She remained there through the first two nights of desmopressin and Hassan's foul concoction, a nightmare from which I thought I might never awaken. Sometimes she perched in the far corner of my cell, and sometimes she lay beside me in the narrow cot that served as my bed, her hips touching mine, her fingers stroking my hair.

It was dead silent in my small room, the thick mud walls and heavy door damping the sounds of the house. A tiny, grated window high up in one corner let in just enough light to allow me to differentiate between day and night. A single bare bulb, of which I thankfully had control, offered respite from the terrifying darkness.

I'd seen Werner's black Mercedes when we'd first arrived, and I had no doubt he was somewhere in the Casbah. In my more lucid moments I wondered if Brian was there as well, or if his betrayal had served an interest other than that of my host. I had a feeling Werner wasn't the only one with a stake in whatever treasure Leila Brightman had disappeared with.

I was left alone for some time after my arrival, and eventually the drugs wore off enough for me to relieve myself in the plastic bucket I'd been given for that purpose. Then, toward what my best instincts told me was late evening, there was a knock on the door, and Salim appeared with a tray of food and a bottle of mineral water.

"Eat!" he said, setting the tray down on the floor next to my cot. "We don't want you to die."

He was just a few inches from me. I worked up what little saliva was left in my mouth and spit in his face.

"Not yet, at least," he leered, wiping my spittle from his cheek.

I watched him go, then took a swig of the water and poured out the remainder of the bottle on the floor. As thirsty as I was, I didn't trust myself not to drink the whole thing. Of the food, I ate just enough to quell my hunger pangs, then scraped the rest into my rudimentary chamber pot.

I had no doubt Hassan would come to medicate me again, and I wanted to be as ready as possible this time. When he did come, there was no knock. I heard the door latch click; then Salim and the doctor stepped into my cell.

During my time at the abbey, I often wondered at the lives of the saints, so many of them martyred, tortured and killed for their faith. How did they do it? I wanted to know. How did they survive the searings, the drownings, the rapes, the stretching of their bodies, the slow disembowelments, the desolate years in some cramped hole not fit for a rat? When Hassan came for me again, I began to see how they withstood it all.

There's a certain bleak comfort in the familiar, an advantage in knowing exactly what has to be endured. As I watched Hassan come toward me with the needle and the inhaler, I had a fleeting memory of a beach somewhere, great blue curls of surf moving in to shore. *Here's how you do it,* I thought, *take a deep breath and duck your head to the wild tussle of the waves.* I could feel the water close on me, the sand scraping my legs, the inescapable pull of the sea. *Just ride, just ride,* I told myself, my lungs aching, my arms fighting to pull myself up. And then, when I thought I couldn't hold my breath for a second longer, I shot up and out. I would come out of this, too, I reminded myself, as Hassan's cocktail hurried to my heart, and the desmopressin rushed toward my brain.

Imagine the wind-scoured contents of a prairie tornado, a roll of barbed wire, a half dozen fence posts, a tire, a bale of hay, part of a roof, a single high-heeled shoe lifted from the bedroom of a trailer, each tumbling momentarily into view, then snatched back into the whirlwind. Or a garden spied through a picket fence, narrow glimpses of green grass, a rosebush, a white chaise lounge, seen, then unseen, then seen again.

That's how everything came to me that first night in the Casbah, a great tumult of places and things clicking in and out of focus. Here was an endless expanse of dry scrubland, the dark shards of mountains in the distance, the wind blowing sage and smoke. Here I was hurtling through Burgundy, past newly stripped vineyards, past a long stone wall and a field of milk cows. Here was the ditch, and the man beside me with the gun. Then there was a loud crack, the door swung open, and I tumbled forward onto the road.

For a brief moment I was on the train with Pat, smiling for the camera, trying to blink the sleep from my eyes. I was in the abbey kitchen, weighing dough. Then the melee turned again, and I was back at Werner's house in Marrakech, with the photograph of Les Trois Singes in my hands, the three young friends, the rickshaw driver waiting for a fare. Though even here my memory failed me: the woman in the white shift was missing.

For the most part, the things that came to me were trivial—a lake at dusk, a golden retriever chasing a stick, the smell of bread baking, a baby's fist on my breast—while what I most desired to remember still refused to reveal itself.

Of my three nights at the Casbah, the first was the best. When the desmopressin wave crested and started its slow downward slide, I figured I was invincible. I could do this. I could beat them, I thought.

A different man came in the morning with food and water and a clean bucket. He was older than my two regular visitors, his skin tanned and weathered beneath the hood of his brown burnoose. He set the tray on the floor and leaned in close to me.

"Eat, Mademoiselle," he whispered in cultured French. "The others won't come until tonight." Catching my eyes with his, he nodded almost imperceptibly, then rose and, taking the soiled bucket with him, turned and walked to the door.

I listened to the latch close and lock. Logic told me not to trust him, but my instincts and my stomach begged me to believe what he'd said. My muscles ached from dehydration. I picked up the bottle and gulped half the water, then fell greedily on the food. Another day without sustenance, I reasoned, and I'd be too weak to fight the drugs anyway.

In the end, the man proved honest in his kindness.

Salim and Hassan didn't come to my room until late that evening. They weren't alone this time. Werner came in with them and stood in the corner while the doctor did his business. Then my two tormenters left, and my host remained behind.

"How long are you going to keep me here?" I asked. It was a vain question, the answer most likely a lie or meaningless truth. It had long ago dawned on me that he had no intention of letting me leave alive.

Werner didn't answer. He stepped forward, put his hand on my scalp, and tilted my head back so my face was turned up to his. Then he brought his other hand up and ran his fingers along my neck and across the side of my cheek. He seemed at the same time to be looking for something and to have found it.

I spit at him as I had at Salim, and he dropped his hands and moved away. Something flared inside him, anger, disgust.

"I told you in Marrakech," he said coldly. "We will keep you here until you remember." He took a handkerchief from his pocket and wiped his face.

I looked up at Werner, and his stone gray eyes looked back at me. Something had happened to that young man at Les Trois Singes, I thought, something terrible and dark, to turn him into this person.

"Who am I?" I asked.

Werner cocked his head, considering the question. "A traitor, my dear," he said, "and a murderer." Then he turned and walked out the door, leaving me to my nightmares.

I lay back on the cot and said a silent prayer, this time for something to keep me from remembering. I was afraid, afraid to die in that awful little room, afraid I might not have the strength to lie if I did remember. I half believed what Werner had told me, that it was someone else who had had the sisters killed. But still, I couldn't imagine any good would come from whatever information he was looking to find. Werner was a dangerous man, that much was clear, and I didn't want anyone else hurt because of my cowardice.

The images that came to me that night were gruesome and violent, a horror-show loop of my own worst conjurings. I was back on the roof with Pat, while he slowly bled to death in my arms. I put my hands on his stomach, and the blood covered them. My clothes were sticky with it. It was in my hair. The smell was deep in my lungs.

I was in a hotel room, somewhere cheap and bland, with a dead man in the corner. He had been shot in the head, and his eyes were flung wide open, as if he'd seen the bullet coming. I was in that horrible warehouse again, heart pounding like a piston as I flew down the stairs.

I was at the abbey, inside the chapel, where the sisters had been slaughtered like sheep. There was blood on the altar and on the communion rail, blood pooling in the burnished wood curves of the pews, blood spattered on the old stone floor. Someone was singing the Magnificat. *My soul magnifies the Lord, my spirit rejoices in God my Savior.*

I was in my room at the Continental. On the bed was a Koran, the book open, the five letters from my ferry ticket forming the first line of the page. *Kaf. Ha. Ya. A'in. Sad.* Then the memory was ripped from me, and I opened my eyes to the low ceiling and narrow walls of my cell.

The man in the brown burnoose didn't bring breakfast the next morning. Salim and Hassan came instead, and in place of food they brought more desmopressin, a full syringe, and another bottle of water. This was the way it would be from now on, I realized, no respite, no time to recover, just a steady assault until they wore me down. When they were gone, I lay on the bed and wept. Then, my thirst overwhelming my judgment, I took a long drink of water and settled in to wait for the drowning to come.

They came again that evening, with more of the same. What I saw hadn't changed for some time, just sharpened in detail, the same dark reel running over and over again. My sickness gave me something to focus on besides the memories, and I drank more water, grateful now for the vomiting and the shuddering in my muscles, grateful for something, anything, even pain, to distract me.

Sometime in the middle of the night there was a quiet, almost inaudible knock on my door. I sat up and strained my ears, certain I'd imagined it, but the sound came again, just one short rap, then a key scratching tentatively at the lock. Standing, I moved toward the far wall and braced myself, rallying what strength I could. I had come to expect the morning and evening visits, and my foreknowledge was all that kept the desperation of my fear at bay. Now I could feel the angry jaws of panic snapping at my throat.

Was it Salim, I wondered as the latch clicked open, come to seek revenge for whatever it was that burned like a pyre in the depths of his eyes? The door swung forward, and I raised my fists. Had Werner decided to try more persuasive means of memory stimulation? If this was my last chance to fight, I would take it.

But it was not Salim. It was the man who had brought me breakfast the morning before. He had on the same brown burnoose. He opened it as he came toward me and unfurled a second hooded robe from the folds of his own. "Put it on," he said.

I nodded, slipping my arms into the arms of the cloak, pulling the hood over my head.

The man put his hands to his lips and stepped through the doorway. Motioning for me to follow, he slipped his babouches off and started, barefoot, down the long dark corridor, the white skin of his heels winking like two dim beacons. I obeyed, creeping behind, ducking around corners, up one short flight of stairs and down another, weaving through the labyrinth of hallways and rooms, the cerebral folds and cambers of the Casbah, the two of us silent and stealthy as the whip crack of a synapse sparking.

We came out from the depth, out from the heart of the great mud palace, and I could smell the desert air. Somewhere far off an aging car engine sputtered along. There was an archway up ahead, my guide's pointed hood silhouetted against the blue-black sky, and beyond, the wildly improbable shapes of the date palms, the strength of their slim bodies defying all reason and gravity. The only tree, I thought, that could bend flat to the ground during a hurricane and spring back unscathed. I had seen this, yes, I could remember it, the wind strong as a god, the sea heaving itself up onto the shore.

Just a few more feet, I told myself, but as I stumbled forward toward the opening I heard a man's voice, a gruff command in Arabic. I froze, shrinking back into the darkness. My guide turned his head and spoke back to the voice. An easy response, laughter, and the answer was easy as well. A second silhouette appeared, then a match sputtered and flared, and I could smell tobacco.

I pressed myself against the wall to keep from shaking, then reached up and steadied my lower jaw with my hand to still the clacking of my teeth. They smoked for what seemed like an hour, two hours, an entire lifetime of smoking, until, by some blessed intervention, a new voice called out. The interloper grumbled, an underling cursing authority, then tossed his cigarette to the ground and turned away.

My guide watched the man leave, then flicked his own cigarette into the dirt, turned back, and waved for me. "Quickly," he whispered. "Hurry."

I pushed off from the wall, willing myself forward. The old man grabbed my arm and pulled me along, scurrying across the gravel-and-sand drive that surrounded the Casbah. Then we pitched forward into the desert forest of the *palmeraie*.

"How far?" I panted. I could run, but I needed to know just how much of my flagging strength to give each breath.

My rescuer stopped short and raised his arm. "There," he said, pointing through the palms to a tiny speck of light that seemed to me to sit on the far horizon.

I nodded. "Let's go."

We ran in silence, moving through the trees toward the lone beacon. It took the very last of my energy to keep myself upright and mobile. The old man ran ahead, every so often stopping to wait for me to catch up. And then, suddenly, we were there, bursting out of the *palmeraie* and onto the hard-packed dirt of a road. I could see now that the light was a lantern, a goatskin lamp held aloft by a second hooded figure. Beyond the figure was a large truck.

My guide whistled, and the light was quickly extinguished. The figure moved, the coarse fabric of his burnoose rustling as he did; then the truck's door clicked softly open, and the engine started.

"*Montez!*" the old man said.

I climbed into the cab, the door was closed behind me, and the truck lurched forward. "Wait!" I yelled, panicking as the old man slipped away behind us.

Unheeding, the driver barreled ahead. He switched the headlights on, and the road ahead of us sprang into view, two washed-out ruts. "It's okay," he said. "He'll be okay." Then, peeling his hood back, he turned to me. His face was haggard, hollowed out by the green lights of the dash. It was Brian.

SEVENTEEN

I slept for a day and a half, freed from the assault of memory, swimming in the clean, dark waters of oblivion. I was aware of a woman who came and went, her hands tattooed with vines and stars, who brought me water and hummed while she arranged my sheets.

The room I was in was stark, the walls whitewashed plaster, the furnishings simple and clean, just as I wanted my mind to be, scrubbed and rinsed like the abbey kitchen when Heloise and I came down to start the bread. Out the open window I could hear the sounds of civilization, the distant buzz of mopeds, the intermittent rush of automobile traffic, the occasional human shout.

On the evening of my second day there, I woke to find Brian watching me from the far side of the room. I blinked my eyes and looked at him, still uncertain of what he'd delivered me to, still angry at his betrayal.

"How are you feeling?" he asked.

"Where am I?"

"Somewhere safe," he said, coming forward, taking a seat on the edge of my bed.

"Where?"

"A friend's house, in Ourzazate."

I sat up and faced him. "Who are you?" I demanded, the same question I'd asked that night in Marrakech.

He shook his head. "Later," he said. "You still need to rest."

I reached out and slapped him. "Now," I yelled, and I hit him again, my fists pummeling his chest, all the fear and exhaustion of the last few days finally finding a target. I hit him until my anger and frustration ground me down; then I leaned my head against him and sobbed.

He didn't say anything, just let me lie there, even after I'd stopped crying, till the only sound in the room was the ticking of the ceiling fan, and from far off, the muted thump thump of feet on leather, the sounds of a soccer game.

"Tell me who I am," I said, finally. I lifted my head and wiped my face with the heels of my palms.

"I'll tell you what I know."

There was a knock on the door, and the woman appeared with a tray. I was so hungry that the smell of the food made me nauseous. Gagging, I waved her away.

Brian spoke to the woman in Arabic, and she lifted a bowl of *harira,* a chunk of dry flat bread, and a bottle of water from the tray and put them on my bedside table. Then she left us, taking the rest of the food with her.

"Did you learn Arabic at Brown, too?" I asked when she was gone.

Ignoring my question, Brian picked up the soup and handed it to me. "You have to eat something," he urged, settling into the room's one chair.

I took a sip of the broth. It was hot and thick, rich with

cumin and chilies. "How did you know where Werner had taken me?"

"Fakhir," he said. "He works for us."

"The old man?"

Brian nodded but offered no further explanation.

"Is he in danger?"

"No. He'll be fine."

"And the 'us'?"

He was silent for a moment, as if contemplating a badly snarled thread, as if trying to decide which knot to loosen first. "It's not important," he said.

I set the soup aside and rolled out from under the covers. "Fuck you," I told him. I was tired of his game, tired of twenty questions and no answers in return. "Where are my clothes?" I asked, scanning the room.

"In the wardrobe," he said calmly.

I opened the cabinet and took out my clothes. They were clean and neatly folded. It had taken all my strength to stand, and now I could feel the room spinning around me.

"Sit down," Brian said, "and hear me out. If you still want to leave, I'll drive you to Marrakech myself."

"From the beginning." I sat back on the bed and eyed him skeptically. "You'll tell me everything, starting with who you work for."

He pressed the tips of his fingers together and looked down at them, as if expecting to find the answer to my question there. "I work for the Americans," he said.

"CIA?"

He raised his eyes toward mine. "Unofficially, yes. I do contract work, freelance, all strictly under the radar."

"You're a spook?"

He smiled grimly. "Just like in the movies. You know, the agency will disown any knowledge of you if things go wrong."

I let what he'd said sink in for a moment.

"Don't look too shocked," he said. "After all, we're in the same line of work, you and I."

"What's that supposed to mean?"

"You really don't know, do you?" There was a note of hostility in his voice.

I shook my head. "I told you. I don't remember."

"You were an independent contractor, like me. An arms specialist, by all accounts. Acquisition, mostly: foreign matériels, cargo divertment, engineering phony end-user certificates, stuff like that."

"That's how Werner knew me, knew Leila, I mean."

Brian nodded. "Bruns Werner's an old-school arms dealer. He started out contracting for the Pentagon during the Vietnam War."

Vietnam, I thought, rickshaws and women in white shifts, and *Easy Rider* at the Saigon cinema. Les Trois Singes. "Something tells me Werner no longer has a working relationship with the American government."

"We made him rich in Afghanistan," Brian said, "but he saw the end of the cold war coming before we did and moved to greener pastures. He's a bottom-feeder now. That's where all the money is, the real shitholes of the world: the former Soviet republics, the South American drug states, Africa, the Balkans, the Middle East. You were involved in a couple of transactions with him back when he was still getting us Chinese matériels."

"Not fond memories from what I could tell."

Brian's face lightened slightly. "Not many fond memories in this business."

"He claims I stole something from him. Information, he said. That's why they had me at the Casbah; they wanted me to remember."

Brian nodded. "A little over a year ago we picked up some intelligence indicating Werner and a man named

Hakim Al-Marwan were ironing out a deal. Only it wasn't a run-of-the-mill transaction."

"Why not?"

"Well, for one thing, there were no weapons involved. It was information Al-Marwan was getting."

"What kind of information?"

Brian paused.

"I'll walk," I warned him. "I swear to God I'll walk out of here, and you'll never see me again."

He cleared his throat and sat forward in the chair. "Al-Marwan's more than just a class-A asshole. He's an old friend of the CIA's from Peshawar, one of the Afghan alumni. He fought with the mujahideen; then, after the Soviet pullout, he came home to Algeria and helped start the GIA."

"What's the GIA?"

"Just your friendly neighborhood Armed Islamic Group. They specialize in village massacres, with the odd highjacking or car bombing thrown in for kicks."

"You still haven't told me what Werner was selling."

"A few years ago Werner contributed to the KGB retirement plan and got a bundle of documents for his good will. As far as we know, it was mostly outdated schlock. A sort of wholesale collection of things that wouldn't be missed. Municipal plans, satellite photos of power plants and major ports."

"You said 'mostly outdated schlock.'"

"There was one gem in the mix, and Werner knew it. Like finding a Monet at a garage sale."

"And the gem?"

"Detailed intel on every nuclear power plant in the northeastern United States."

"And this is what Werner was selling to Al-Marwan?"

"That's what we were hearing."

"So the Americans sent me down to Werner's Casbah

to steal the Monet back. Only something happened to me before I could deliver the goods, and now no one, not even me, knows what I've done with them?"

Brian got up from the chair and walked to the room's only window. "You've got it half right," he said quietly. His back was to me, his arm resting on the plaster sill. Down below us, in the street, a woman laughed, the sound fading with the dopplered rattle of a scooter.

"What do you mean, half right?"

"It wasn't the Americans," he said. "It wasn't the Americans who sent you."

"But I worked for them," I protested. "You said I worked for them."

Brian shook his head. "Not this time."

I caught my breath and held it. I had known this, I thought, that night in Joshi's apartment, and before that, in the piracetam nightmares. This thing I didn't want to believe.

"Who, then?" I asked.

"We don't know," Brian said. "At least I don't know. There are more than a few people who would want that information, and none of them are our friends."

"But why . . . why would I?"

Brian shrugged. "There are so many reasons, aren't there? Money, power." He turned to face me. "What do you think?"

"And last year?" I asked, ignoring his question. "In Burgundy? What happened?"

"We were trying to stop you," he said. "It shouldn't have happened the way it did."

"You mean I shouldn't have lived, or you should have made sure I had what you were looking for before you shot me?"

Brian shook his head. "No," he stammered, but it was a futile denial.

"And Pat? Not your brother, I assume."

"Pat worked for All Join Hands just like he told you. His work for us was purely incidental, mostly a matter of keeping his eyes and ears open."

"And what did he get in return?"

"As you already guessed, our boy had a gambling problem. We helped him out with his debts."

"And Hannah? Was that just a matter of keeping his eyes and ears open, too?" I thought about the picture Pat had taken of me on the train, the dreamy pleasure of it. "Is that what you've been doing?"

Brian didn't answer.

"You came for me at the Casbah," I asked, after a long silence. "Why?"

"We need you to remember," he said. "We need you to remember what you did with the plans you stole from Werner. We need to find them before anyone else does."

"It's not that easy," I said.

Brian thought for a moment. "When they found you in Burgundy, did you have anything with you? It could be something small, even, a piece of jewelry, a pen."

I shook my head. "The only thing I had in my pockets besides lint was that old ferry ticket."

"Do you still have it?"

I thought about my pack at the Hotel Ali. "Maybe," I said. "I left it in my backpack, in the hotel lockers in Marrakech."

"You need to rest for a while longer," Brian said. "Then we'll go together."

He got up and came toward me. For a second I thought he was going to move to kiss me, but he stopped at the end of the bed and stood there stiffly, as if unsure of himself, unsure of me.

"You've known all along that Pat was dead, haven't you?" I asked.

"We know what everyone else does, that he disappeared on that trip to Ourzazate. Beyond that, all we can do is guess."

"And your best guess?"

"Someone killed him."

"Who?"

He didn't answer, but when he looked down at me I could tell exactly what he was thinking, that it was Hannah who'd gone to Ourzazate with Pat, that only Hannah had come back.

"Who am I?" I asked. "Who was I before Hannah Boyle? Before Leila Brightman and the others?"

Brian shook his head. "I don't know."

"But someone does."

"Yes," he said. "Now get some sleep." Then he turned, walked to the door, and was gone.

I finished the *harira* and sipped at the water, then sank back into the pillows, trying to sift through the grains of Brian's story. If what he'd said was true, Werner had been right. I was a traitor and worse. Pat Haverman was dead because of me, dead on a Casbah rooftop, and I was the one who'd killed him. But why? There are so many reasons, Brian had said. Still, something didn't quite add up. I could have sworn it. Somewhere there was a flaw, a crack in Brian's story, invisible as the tiniest hair of a break in an uncut gem. This wasn't the person I had been; it couldn't be.

I closed my eyes and willed myself to dream. Something small, I told myself, a neat little package for carrying information. But what I dreamed of was not the thing I hoped to remember. Instead, I was back at Werner's Casbah, back in the *palmeraie*. It was nighttime again, the sky black above me. I was alone, wrapped in a burnoose and running, only this time I ran toward the Casbah instead of away from it, my boots snapping dry palm fronds as I barreled along.

Then, suddenly, I was inside, deep in the Casbah's heart. I was in an office, Werner's, I thought, breathing in the stench of expensive leather and cigars. I stopped for a moment, straining to hear over the silence, listening for the slightest movement above or below, a sleepwalker, someone wakened from a nightmare, but there was nothing. I crossed to Werner's computer and turned it on. The screen was blindingly bright.

I slipped something into my burnoose, then left the office and headed down the stairs, into the first-floor passageway, toward the door I knew led out into the *palmeraie*. This is it, I thought, hesitating a moment in the open doorway before stepping outside. This short dash across the drive the most vulnerable part of my journey. The wind had kicked up, and the palms rustled violently against each other. I looked out from beneath the hood of my burnoose, scanning the dark landscape, making sure I was alone; then I stepped outside.

But I had not looked carefully enough. As I emerged from the portal, I saw a figure slip from the shadows along the Casbah's outer wall. A man's voice called out, not unfriendly at first, a comrade out for a smoke. I stopped and watched the figure step toward me, the lit coal of a cigarette glowing at his side. Then the man spoke again, only a few meters away now, his voice moving toward irritation. I nodded, trying to think of a way out, coming up with only one. He took another step forward and tossed his cigarette aside. Run, I told myself, scrabbling across the drive, plunging into the *palmeraie*.

"*Sheffar!*" the man cried behind me, and I could hear other voices now. *Thief.*

I picked up the hem of the burnoose and ran as fast as

I could, weaving my way through the graceful forest, the palms lithe and supple as the legs of ballerinas. Someone was shooting. A palm trunk splintered. The ground in front of me erupted, spitting dirt and small stones. Then suddenly, I was on the road. A Jeep came careening down the two dry ruts.

"Get in!" Pat Haverman yelled, slowing just enough for me to hurl myself head first into the passenger seat.

I righted myself and peered back into the woods. The moon was a perfect half circle, a bright wedge climbing up through the clear sky. It cast just enough light for me to make out the half dozen figures sprinting toward us through the date palms. Another shot sounded, and the Jeep swerved, then corrected itself. I looked over and saw Pat holding his hand to his abdomen.

"I'm okay," he said, but I could tell he wasn't.

We drove with the lights off, bouncing along the dirt track until we reached a better-maintained dirt road and, finally, a paved two-lane strip.

"You're hurt," I said, as we turned our headlights on and started north on the paved highway.

Pat nodded. "There's a place not far from here, a safe place. I can call for help."

"Yes," I said, and then we were there, at the ruined Casbah.

Morning was coming, the day slowly unfurling itself across the valley, across the palm oases and the red cliffs, the great white prayer script that graced the opposite hillside. The roof we were on was ringed by tall ramparts, the wall notched out for defense or decoration or both. In the corner was the old stork's nest, its twig-and-branch construction dense and solid.

"You have to go," Pat said. "They're coming."

"Yes," I agreed, but I didn't move. I'd taken the burnoose off and torn it to put on the wound, but the makeshift bandage wasn't working. Pat's stomach was covered with blood.

"It's okay," he said. "I'll be okay. Now stand up."

For the first time I thought he might be right. I thought he was going to make it. I leaned down and kissed him, then forced myself to stand.

I woke in a sweat and threw my covers back. So I hadn't killed him, I thought, staring up into the darkness, feeling the heat rise off my body. I hadn't killed him, but he had died because of me, had died helping me. *Murderer,* I heard Werner say over and over as the dream receded and I drifted back to sleep. And then Charlie Phillips: *That boy had it bad.*

EIGHTEEN

"How does it happen?" I asked. Brian and I had left Ourzazate and were rattling up into the Atlas's desert foothills in an ancient Land Rover.

"How does what happen?"

"This," I said. "All of this. How did you become what you are? How did I?"

Brian downshifted and slowed, dodging two tourist vans that were stopped by the side of the road. "I've told you everything I know," he said as we picked up speed again.

"Or everything you can."

Out my window the road fell precipitously away, the crumbling hillside sweeping downward to a series of terraced dwellings, a village made of sticks and mud. Even here, on the bleak fringe of the Sahara, a handful of satellite dishes, like pale morning glories, perched among the settlement's flat roofs. Makeshift power lines tapped the electric cable that ran along the highway.

"What do you think they watch?" I asked, pointing toward the receding village.

"*Baywatch. Friends.* MTV," Brian hazarded.

"God, I hope not."

"American culture at its best. The new imperialism."

"You think it's better than the old?"

Brian shrugged. "Who am I to judge? But whatever else is true, they love our blue jeans and our music. A couple of years ago I saw a kid wearing Nikes and a Michael Jordan jersey burning an American flag."

"Where was that?" I asked, expecting no answer and getting none.

We drove on in silence for a few miles, dodging battered trucks and more tourist vans, the dinosaur traffic of the Moroccan road.

"Listen," Brian said, finally. "I'm not lying. I've told you everything I know."

"You mean everything they told you." I watched his jaw flex once. "Did they tell you I have a kid?"

He shifted his hands on the wheel. His eyes didn't move from the road ahead.

"I've got a kid somewhere," I told him. "A little boy or a little girl. I don't even know which. The doctor had to show me. She had to show me the scar. They didn't tell you that, did they?"

Brian shook his head. "No," he said. "They didn't tell me."

"Do you have a name?" I asked. "A last name?"

"Yes," Brian said, but the acknowledgment was as far as he would go.

The engine whined into a lower gear, and we slowed to a crawl. The road was climbing hard now, and ahead of us an ancient public bus led a small caravan of slowed vehicles.

"I grew up in Pittsburgh," Brian said, relaxing into his seat, giving in to the snail-like pace. "My dad's an electrician, and my mom sells real estate. I've got an older sister who lives in Cleveland. Her husband's a CPA. She's a soccer mom."

"And you wanted a life less ordinary?"

"I guess. I wanted to see the world at least. I joined the navy out of high school."

"Is that how it works?"

"That's how it worked for me. The agency came to me when I retired from the Special Forces."

"And for others?"

"I don't know exactly. Some come from the military. Some are just—" He paused, searching for the right words. "Some are just good at what they do."

"I assume you're not talking about cooking and sewing."

Brian shook his head.

"I killed people, didn't I? Was that one of my special talents?"

Again, Brian didn't answer. I took his silence for a yes.

"You know about the sisters?" I asked. "About what happened at the abbey?"

"Yes."

"Do you think it was Werner?"

"Who else?" He shrugged. "I'm sure he still has the connections to have tapped into the consular grapevine."

Of course, I thought, watching Brian shift his hands on the wheel. He ducked out into the opposite lane and craned his head, looking for an opportunity to pass. Whoever had found me had done so through the consulate, through whatever efforts had been made to get me to the States. I was reminded of the pictures in Werner's office, the grim record of slaughter, but still, something told me it wasn't Werner who had killed the sisters. He didn't seem like the kind of man to lie about such a thing, especially not to me, when his intentions had so obviously been not to release me, at least not alive.

No, I thought, someone else had murdered the sisters. Someone besides Werner had paved my way at customs. I was certain of it. Someone had put two and two together, the woman who'd been left for dead in that Burgundy field and an American trying to get home. The question, as Werner himself had pointed out, was who.

Brian found a clear moment, and we sped forward, overtaking the bus just before a blind curve.

"You don't have any idea who I was working for?" I asked, as we slipped back onto the right side of the road.

Brian shook his head and punched the accelerator. "No."

"But you believe it?" I asked. "You believe I'm a traitor?"

"Were," he corrected me. "I believe you were." The words were meant for me, a show of conviction, but it seemed to me it was himself he was trying to assure.

We came into Marrakech from the north, skirting the red walls of the medina and the stone-pocked cemetery outside the Bab el-Khemis, plunging down the Route Principale toward the Bab Larissa and the Avenue Mohammed V. We passed the Koutoubia Mosque, then turned onto the Rue Moulay Ismail, pulling to the curb in front of the Hotel Ali.

"Wait here," I told Brian. Praying Ilham had kept my storage locker, I climbed out of the Land Rover and headed into the hotel's lobby.

The proprietor was at the front desk, her hair neat as

always, the blue eye shadow that colored her lids a perfect match to her djellaba, the robe a light azure shot through with gold threads. She smiled graciously when she saw me enter. *"Mademoiselle!"* she said, her smile fading to a scowl as I approached. "You have been ill?"

I nodded. I must have looked terrible. "I went to Ourzazate. I was too sick to travel back."

"La pauvre!" she exclaimed, reaching out and taking my hand in hers. "I was so worried for you. Gone off without your things. I didn't know what to tell your friend."

"My friend?" I asked.

"Yes. She was here this morning. A friend from the States. She said you had gone on across the mountains, that you had sent her to get your things."

My stomach dropped. "She took my pack?"

"But of course not." Ilham fished in her djellaba and withdrew her key ring. "I'm sorry, Mademoiselle, but you said nothing to me about this. I told her you would have to come yourself."

"What did she look like?"

"A woman." The proprietor shrugged, coming out from behind the desk, opening the door to the storage room. "Rather tall, with blond hair. You do understand, don't you? I can't just let anyone in here. If you had told me yourself . . ."

"Yes," I said, catching a glimpse of my pack in its wire locker. "You did the right thing." I flashed her a weak smile, my gratitude as real as it gets.

"I'm afraid I'll have to charge you. It's five dirhams a day for luggage storage." She undid the lock and stepped aside.

"Of course." I reached up, undid the pack's top flap, and fished deep in the inside pocket. "Here," I told Ilham, pulling out a one-hundred-euro bill, then handing it to her.

She shook her head vehemently. "But, Mademoiselle, I couldn't possibly have change for this."

"Please." I pushed the bill into her hands. "Take it and keep it."

"Got it?" Brian asked as I slid into the passenger seat of the Land Rover.

I nodded, hauling the pack in after me. "Someone was here asking about me. A woman."

"When?"

"This morning," I said. "She wanted my pack."

"It doesn't look like she got it."

Shaking my head, I opened the pack's top flap. "Thank God for inscrutable hotel managers."

"Thank God," Brian echoed.

"Here." I withdrew the tattered ferry ticket and handed it to him. "My sole worldly possession."

He took the scrap of paper and examined it carefully.

"There's something on the back," I told him. "I always thought it was a code of some sort."

I watched him flip the ticket over and mouth the characters silently to himself.

"Or maybe a combination," I hazarded.

"It's not a combination," he said. He handed the paper back to me, started the Rover's engine, and pulled out onto the street.

"Where are we going?" I asked.

Brian turned onto the Avenue Mohammed V, heading in the direction of the Ville Nouvelle. "We need to find a Koran."

We parked on a side street behind the post office and walked the few short blocks to the All Join Hands offices.

It was early afternoon and the building was still open, but the offices were nearly empty. Charlie Phillips and a pretty but overly thin young black woman with an upper-class British accent were playing darts in the common area while a scrawny American kid with bad acne played a video game at one of the many computers.

It was a strange threesome, each of them a misfit, each so obviously wounded in his or her own way, at large in the world, trying to find some comfort in exile. For why else would you leave? What else but belonging would you be looking to find in a place so far from home?

Charlie glanced back when he heard us come in. For a split second he looked less than happy to see us; then he tipped his mouth up into a wide grin.

"Bri," he said jovially.

Brian stepped forward, and I followed. "Hey, man," he said. "You mind if we make use of your library?"

Charlie smiled uncomfortably. Something was wrong, I thought, though it could have been just that we'd busted in on his hustle. "Sure," he said.

Brian started for some bookshelves on the far side of the room. "Don't let us keep you from your game."

Charlie looked over at the woman. "She's beating me anyway." He chuckled nervously. "You know Fiona, don't you?"

"Hey, Fiona." Brian acknowledged the woman, then turned to the stacks, his finger running across the rows of worn spines. He pulled a leather-bound volume from the shelf and took a seat at one of the desks, motioning for me to join him.

Brian opened the Koran to the back cover and began paging backward. "The ticket," he said, stopping about a third of the way through the text, setting the book flat on the desk.

I pulled the ferry ticket from my pocket and handed it to him.

He laid the paper on the page.

"What is it?" I asked.

"Mary," he said. "The letters are from the first line of the sura called Mary. Only here you have them written backward."

"What do they mean?"

Brian shrugged. "No one's quite sure. Some people think they're the initials of the original scribe. Another camp believes they have some mystical significance."

He ran his finger down the page. "Verse twenty-one," he said, reading the text out in Arabic.

"What does it say?" I asked.

"It's the angel, talking to Mary about the Immaculate Conception. She wants to know how she can have a child when she's a virgin. The angel tells her these kinds of things are easy for God. *The Lord saith: It is easy for Me.*"

Easy, I thought, it is easy for me. Where had I heard that before? "Abdesselom," I said, remembering the Koran I'd found in my room there.

"What?"

"At the Hotel Continental. It was the first thing he said to me when I went to check in. *It is easy for me*. I thought he knew me. I could have sworn he knew me."

NINETEEN

We left the city and headed north, retracing the route I'd taken down from Tangier, through the green heart of the country, the emerald patchwork of barley and new hay. After the austere Atlas, the landscape seemed extravagant, overrun with row upon opulent row of crops. Women in bright robes, colorful as songbirds, dotted the fields and dirt roads. Discarded Tide laundry soap packages littered the riverbanks where the day's linens had been scrubbed, the familiar fluorescent orange-and-blue packaging scattered like petals from some strange fruiting tree.

The sun was beginning to set when we crossed the blue curve of the Oued Oum er-Rbia. Shadows stretched themselves across the stubbled plateau. Women and men headed in from the fields for a bowl of *harira* and a cigarette, that first glass of water to break the fast. As we drove toward the sea, the sky slowly darkened, the few high clouds stained pink to violet, the blue vault above us sliding from deep indigo toward star-speckled black.

We drove in shifts through the darkness, hugging the coast through Casablanca, Rabat, and the fortified towns along the Atlantic. It was close to two in the morning when we reached Tangier, and except for a few straggling tourists and a Senegalese whore or two, the city was a dark ghost town. Brian drove us in through the Ville Nouvelle to the southeast ramparts of the medina.

The Rover was too big to squeeze in through the old plaster gate on the Avenue d'Espagne, so we parked it on the Rue du Portugal and climbed the last three hundred meters up the steep cobbled street toward the Continental. I took my pack with me, hooking the Beretta in the back waistband of my pants. The gun sat snug against my skin, a spare clip bulging from my back pocket.

We will make of him a revelation for mankind and a mercy from Us. I repeated the second half of the twenty-first verse of the sura Mary as I followed Brian up past the Great Mosque, past Joshi's apartment building, toward the hulk of the old hotel. *And it is a thing ordained.*

Mercy, I thought, and then I heard the sisters, all dead without mercy. *Kyrie eleison,* Lord, have mercy on us. And the Gloria: *Domine Deus, Agnus Dei, Filus Patris: qui tollis peccata mundi, miserere nobis.* I took a deep breath and let the rich stink of the bay fill my nostrils. Didn't we all die without mercy?

A pair of rats scrambled across the alleyway in front of us and slipped into a storm drain. *They're coming,* Pat had said, his lids closing, his eyes scanning some unknowable dream, some paradise of his own making. An Eden of memory, I had thought, the synapses firing back toward childhood, a slow dance in a grade-school gym, paper streamers and a girl's cheap perfume, or a boat ride across a green lake, an island capped with pine trees, his skis skimming the water, dipping back and forth across the wake.

Isn't this what we all wanted, the succor of our memories, the wave upon which we could ride and ride? Not heaven, but a return, a backyard full of fireflies, the cool prickle of mowed grass on the soles of our feet, that time-softened place with which we all long to be reconciled.

And yet, I realized for the first time, this was not what Pat had meant. There had been someone coming. *There's a place,* he'd said in my dream. *I can call for help.* He had called, and they had come, but they had not saved him. Someone with wings, I thought, not wings but the sound of wings, rotors thrashing the air. Pat had called for help, and it meant something, only I couldn't say what.

Brian turned in to the Continental's rambling courtyard, and I hesitated a moment beneath the gate, trying to discern dream from memory, wishful fiction from fact. It's not about guarantees, Heloise had said once when I'd questioned the idea of omnipotence; it's about surrender. But to what? I wondered, watching Brian's dark form. Was I a traitor? A killer? Someone's mother? Someone's daughter? The girl of someone's dreams? Or was I all these things, like Heloise's cruel God, the baby in the crèche, the man on the cross?

Brian turned back to me, and I willed myself to follow. There was a light fog coming off the bay, softening the patio lights, and the old hotel glowed like a dew-brushed rose. We climbed the wide stone steps to the veranda, pushed open the double doors, and stepped inside.

As late as it was, the lobby was deserted, the front desk unmanned. A handwritten sign on the counter indicated an electric doorbell and advised us to "please ring for service." Brian pressed the button, and we heard the muted chime somewhere far off, in the depths of the old building.

It seemed like a good ten minutes passed before our call was answered. We stood there, our silence accompanied by the tick of the old grandfather clock, by the shuffling of our own feet on the lobby's tiles. Then, miraculously, the door behind the desk rattled and shook, and Abdesselom appeared. His eyes behind his wire spectacles were half asleep, his shoulders slightly hunched in his gray wool cardigan. He came forward and stopped just on the other side of the counter from us.

"We will make of him a revelation for mankind and a mercy from Us," I said.

Abdesselom blinked at me. For a second I thought I was wrong, that we'd made the trip for nothing; then the old man nodded, slowly, carefully. *"It is a thing ordained,"* he answered.

"You have something of mine," I told him, more question than statement.

"Yes," he said, glancing from me to Brian and back again. "Who is he?"

I moved toward Brian. "A friend."

He seemed less than reassured by my statement. "Wait for me in the alcove," he said, craning his neck to indicate the short hallway that ran back from the lobby stairs. Then he turned and slipped through the same door he'd emerged from, closing it silently behind him.

Brian and I made our way down the corridor toward the little sitting alcove. The room was gaudily Moroccan, ringed with richly upholstered banquettes and dotted here and there with handworked leather ottomans. The walls were orange, inset with faux windows latticed with bright blue five-pointed stars. The archway that served as a door was plaster, intricately carved, and above the plaster the wall had been carefully pieced with a blue-and-white zillij mosaic. Wool kilims in bright patterns covered the floor.

I took a seat on one of the banquettes. "Do you trust him?" I asked.

Brian stood near the door. "We don't have much choice, do we?"

The lobby door opened and Brian tensed visibly, but it was only some late partiers. There was drunken laughter, male and female, then the sound of feet starting up the stairs.

I leaned back into the silk pillows that lined the banquette. I felt like a bride before a wedding, or like Judas in those last seconds before the kiss, trapped in that long bewildered moment before the great shift toward one's promised self, that moment when there's still time to act, but when action seems impossible.

He would know, I thought, that old man in the gray cardigan, a package, a person, even a child. There was so much I wanted to ask him, about Hannah Boyle, about why I'd come to Morocco.

The revelers dispersed to their rooms, and the hotel fell silent once again. Down the hall, I heard Abdesselom emerge from his doorway and the sound of his slippers on the terra-cotta floor. He appeared in the archway, his face more relaxed than it had been.

"My dear," he said. He smiled and came toward me. "I had heard you were dead."

I shook my head. "No," I told him, "not dead."

"I thought it was you before. Only it had been so long. You've changed. Of course I should have known. After the last time you disappeared."

"The last time?"

"Yes, my dear. Five years and not a word. We thought you were dead then as well. But I thought we had agreed you were going to send someone else this time."

"Who?"

The old man shook his head. "I don't know. You only

said you would send someone, someone who would know our signal."

Reaching into the pocket of his sweater, Abdesselom pulled out an object about the same size and shape as a fat fountain pen. "Here," he said.

I put my hand out and took the offering. I could see now that it was some kind of portable memory. Where the tip of the pen would have been was a circle of metal and a cluster of tiny pins for fitting into a computer's USB port.

"What is it?" I asked. "What's on here?"

Abdesselom shook his head. "I don't know," he said. "It was my place only to keep it."

"Thank you," I said, trying to decide where to begin, what to ask first. There were so many questions.

Abdesselom opened his mouth to say something, but he never got the chance. Over the hotel manager's shoulder I saw Brian raise his arm. In his hand was a gun, a dark and solid piece of metal. He lifted it, bringing the full force of his fist and the stock down across the back of the old man's neck. For just an instant a look of surprise crossed Abdesselom's face; then he slumped forward onto his knees like a man begging for something. I watched him fall, his glasses knocked off by the blow, his rag-doll head careening forward with the rest of his body. He hit the floor with a thud and lay there, motionless.

I spun backward, reaching for my Beretta, but I was too late. When I turned my head, the first thing I saw was Brian's gun, the barrel of the Browning staring down at me like a vacant eye.

"Give me the pen drive," he said.

It took me a moment to understand what he meant, that he was going to kill me, that he had known for some time that this was how things would end. I thought back to Ourzazate, how he'd stepped toward me, then drawn back, how I'd expected him to kiss me and he hadn't.

He'd known then, I was sure of it. He was going to kill me, and in the end I didn't believe in mercy or grace.

"Give me the pen drive," he repeated.

I turned my face up to his and opened my eyes wide. "Patrick Haverman was alive when I left him," I said, the truth of what had happened snapping into place as I spoke. "He was the one who called for help. Think about it; who would he have called?"

Brian's knuckles were white on the grip of his pistol, his forearms tensed and taut. "I'm sorry," he said.

"Think about it," I pleaded. "I didn't kill him. Don't you want to know what happened? You have to want to know."

Brian shook his head, but I could see him wavering, fighting to push back the part of himself that knew I was right. "Just give me the pen drive, Eve. Don't make me do this."

The grandfather clock in the lobby rang out, three long chimes, and Brian turned slightly, his head moving over his shoulder, not to the sound of the clock but to something else, something moving in the dark hallway. A figure slipped past the archway, a swath of golden hair catching the light.

I ducked, watching the gun swing away, and Brian's arm with it. Now, I told myself, everything in me leaping toward this moment of distraction. I thrust the heel of my right palm against Brian's throat and brought my left hand down on his right wrist. He doubled over, struggling for breath, his grip faltering.

"Get the gun," a voice said behind me as the pistol clattered to the ground. I bent down and lunged for the Browning, glancing back to see a woman in the doorway, her feet planted firmly in place, a pistol in her right hand.

"Down on the ground," she said to Brian, motioning

with her gun. "Face down." She took a step forward into the light, and her mercurial features resolved themselves.

The American, I thought, the solo traveler with the fanny pack and the sensible boots, the woman I'd seen in the bathroom at the El Minzah that night. I'd seen her somewhere else as well. I blinked and tried to remember. Was she the one who'd come looking for me at the Hotel Ali? A blonde, Ilham had said.

Still gulping for air, Brian lowered himself onto the carpeted floor.

"Hands on the back of your head," the woman commanded.

Brian stretched himself out and interlaced his fingers behind his neck, wincing as he did so.

The woman turned to me. "C'mon!" she said. There were voices in the hallway, someone ringing the bell at the front desk, getting no answer.

"Who are you?" I asked.

"A friend," she said. "Now come on!"

TWENTY

We took the back way from the hotel, out a service entrance and into the pitch-dark hive of the medina, groping our way up one long flight of stairs and into a wider alleyway. There was a light rain falling, a fine mist that sifted down over the rambling stage set of the Old City, the crooked streets and houses like some child's nightmare backdrop. A breeze blew in from the strait, carrying with it the stench of low tide, seaweed and sewage and exposed dock timbers.

A friend, I thought. It was the same thing I'd told Abdesselom. We ricocheted around a corner, and I slipped the Beretta from my waistband, then grabbed the woman's arm and shoved her against the damp wall.

"Who are you?" I asked, jamming the gun up into the soft space below her chin.

She reached for her pocketed gun, and I nudged her harder with the Beretta. "Leave it," I told her.

Her face was wet, her breath hot on my face.

"Who do you work for?" I asked.

"The Americans."

"Fuck you," I said. "That's what Brian told me."

She turned her face upward and blinked against the rain. "Same team, different players. Brawn versus brain. We're the quiet ones."

"You'll have to do better than that."

The woman swallowed hard, the muscles in her neck tensing against the barrel of the Beretta. "NSA," she said.

The National Security Agency, I thought, remembering Sister Claire's videos, the various incarnations of American might. "Bullshit," I told her. "The NSA's a bunch of computer geeks. They don't have people in the field."

"You're right," she said calmly. "Ask anyone, and they'll tell you I'm not here."

I shook my head. "Who am I?"

"You don't remember. You call yourself Eve, but your passport says you're Marie Lenoir. You entered the country just over a week ago on the Algeciras ferry, a feat that would seem virtually impossible considering Marie's corpse lies six feet under in a churchyard in Burgundy. You spent the last year in a Benedictine convent."

"And before that?"

"Before that you were Hannah Boyle."

"And before Hannah?"

"That's where things get tricky. We know a woman named Leila Brightman did contract work for American intelligence. European work mostly, Amsterdam, Vienna, the arms pipeline. But you were here in North Africa as well. That was a few years ago. We have some other names: Michelle Harding, Sylvie Allain."

"And Hannah, did she work for the Americans, too?"

"No."

"How can you be sure?"

"Hannah herself, for starters. It's a civilian alias, something you most likely got on your own. Hannah Boyle died over a decade ago in a car wreck outside of Bratislava. The agency doesn't use dead girls. They don't have to."

I eased my safety back on and lowered the Beretta just an inch. "Why should I believe you?"

"You shouldn't, not any more than we should believe you've lost track of three decades of your life. Come on," she said. "There's a safe house not far from here."

I lowered the gun to my side.

"I saved your life," she reminded me. "That's got to count for something."

"What's your name?" I asked, taking a step back.

She peeled herself off the wall. "Helen," she said. "You can call me Helen."

Helen hit a switch on the wall, and a single bulb flickered on, illuminating a narrow corridor and, beyond it, a larger, windowless room. "It's one of our old listening posts," she explained. She stepped forward into the main space, and I followed behind.

The room was sparsely furnished. Dusty boxes were stacked in the corner. A wooden crate turned into a makeshift table held a grimy coffeemaker and an electric hot plate. In the middle of the room was an old wooden desk and chair, and behind them, an army cot and sleeping bag. A curtain half covered a door in the far wall, through which I could see the partial outline of a toilet.

Helen got down on her knees, slipped a penknife from her pocket, pried one of the old plank floorboards free, and pulled a laptop from the space in the subfloor. There was something mercurial about her, shape shifting. Here, in the room's tired light, she seemed older than she had at the hotel, her face and body a blank canvas.

"At the Mamounia," I said, remembering the tall blonde with the overdone breasts. "That was you in the casino?"

"Yes," she said. She stood and carried the computer to the little desk.

"And at customs in Algeciras? You had them let me through, didn't you?"

"We needed you to get on that ferry," she explained, drawing the pen drive from her pocket, sliding it into the laptop's USB port.

"Why?"

"What did Brian tell you?" she asked.

I hesitated a moment, unable to let myself trust her.

"He didn't know, Eve," she said. It was strange to hear that name in her mouth. "He didn't know he was lying to you. He didn't even know who he was working for."

"I told you, he said he was working for the CIA."

"Well, he wasn't, not this time. Someone in the CIA, yes, but not the agency itself. Same story with your old friend Patrick Haverman."

"I don't understand."

"What did he say was on the drive?"

"Documents from old Soviet files," I told her, finally deciding I had nothing to lose.

"What kind of files?"

"Municipal plans for U.S. cities, full specs on American nuclear power plants. Bruns Werner was selling it all to someone named Al-Marwan."

Helen shook her head. "He said Al-Marwan was the buyer?"

"Yes."

"And how do you fit into all of this?"

"I stole the files off Werner's computer," I explained.

"Brian said I was working for someone, someone who wanted the information for himself."

"Did he tell you who?"

"No."

"And you believed him?"

I thought about the question for a moment. "I don't know," I told her finally.

Helen crossed to the overturned crate that held the coffeemaker and hot plate. She blew dust off a rust-speckled coffee can, opened the lid, and sniffed the contents. "You willing to chance it?"

"Sure." I shrugged, watching her spoon the dry grounds into a filter. "What did you mean when you said Brian didn't know?"

Taking the glass decanter with her, Helen crossed to the tiny bathroom. She turned the tap on and let it run for some time. I sat down in the desk chair and perused the utilitarian contents of the room. It was a place stripped down to its essentials, sleep and waking, and the work that filled the hours in between. A listening post, Helen had said, but for listening to what? In Claire's movies these places were always futuristic, filled with shelves of complicated electronics. There was always a woman, too young and pretty for the job, or a man with long hair and strange taste in music. The rooms were nothing like this one, which was worn and tired and, even after years of disuse, still conjured up the creeping pace of boredom.

"I mean he didn't know," Helen said, emerging from behind the curtain. "I'm sure he believed everything he told you. I'm sure he thought he was working for the good guys, just like always."

"And who was he working for?"

Helen started the coffee machine, then pulled a folding chair from behind a pile of boxes. "Let me start at the beginning," she began. "Last September we intercepted a satellite call coming out of southern Algeria." She set the chair down next to mine and took a seat.

"The deal between Werner and Al-Marwan," I said.

"That's what Brian told you."

I nodded.

"According to our information, Werner wasn't the one selling."

"I don't understand."

"Werner was the buyer," Helen explained.

"But that doesn't make sense," I protested, trying to get a handle on what she was saying. "Why would a terrorist be selling something like that to an arms dealer?"

"You're right," she agreed. "It doesn't make sense."

I looked at the monitor in front of us, the screen patiently awaiting a command to read the pen drive. "What's really on there?"

"The call Al-Marwan made to Bruns Werner wasn't the only call we intercepted," Helen said. "Al-Marwan was definitely shopping his wares around, looking for the highest bidder. One of the other communications we intercepted was between him and someone in the States, another prospective buyer."

"My mystery employer?" I guessed.

"Not yours, Brian's. These communications were with someone in the CIA."

"Do you know who?"

Helen shook her head. "For about a year before all this happened we were tracking a leak coming from somewhere in the agency."

"What do you mean, a leak?"

"Someone on the inside, someone the agency didn't even know about, was passing information to Al-Marwan."

"What kind of information?"

"One of Al-Marwan's buddies is a guy named Naser Jibril."

"I know that name."

"Jibril's the founder of a group that calls itself the Islamic Revolutionary Army."

"They're the ones who shot up that synagogue in Turkey last year," I said, remembering the news footage of the carnage.

"Among other things. Two years before that they bombed the El Al ticket counter in Rome. The year before that they hijacked a passenger flight out of Karachi."

"They're based in Egypt, right?"

Helen nodded. "They were our friends during the Soviet invasion of Afghanistan, part of the waves of Arabs who joined up to fight with the mujahideen. But Jibril's been on the run for almost a decade now, since he was sentenced to death for his part in the assassination of a Jordanian diplomat. He was holed up in the Sudan for a while, then spent some time in Libya and Afghanistan and Iraq. He's got about a half dozen countries on his tail, including us, but he's always managed to stay one step ahead of everyone."

"And you think your CIA mystery man was helping him out?"

"There's no doubt someone on the inside was tipping him off."

"Why?" I asked. I was thinking about what Brian had said in Ourzazate. *There are so many reasons.*

Helen got up and walked to the coffeemaker. Taking two Styrofoam cups from a dusty sheath, she poured us each a cup of the hot, brown liquid, then crossed back toward the desk and sat down.

"I'm hoping we're about to find out," she said, leaning toward the laptop, typing in a command.

The screen went black, then flashed on again, the colorful display replaced by a grainy black-and-white image. The shot had been taken from a rooftop, the camera perched near the edge. In the front of the frame was a slice of a gutter, and below, a patchwork of rooftops, a semi-urban landscape, but a non-Western one, closer to the aimless, industrial suburbs of Rabat or Casablanca than Paris or Lyon. Off in the distance a mosque poked up from the grimy skyline, a domed roof capped by a sickle moon. The sky was a bright, monochrome gray above it all, cloudless or fully overcast, it was impossible to tell. In the distance, a flock of birds, black and stark as punctuation marks on a white page, rose skyward, then winged from view.

"It looks like a video that's been transferred to digital," Helen remarked. "The quality's pretty poor."

"Any idea where it was taken?" I asked.

Helen squinted, taking in the view as the lens panned to the left. "It's hard to say. I'm pretty sure it's Peshawar. It's definitely Pakistan, though."

The camera tilted upward, jostling, then came to rest, as if the operator had lifted it to his or her shoulder. We could see the rooftop in its entirety now, a flat tarred surface, and several yards away, a hutlike protrusion that I assumed held the building's stairwell.

In the foreground, just a few feet from the camera, was a woman. She was a Westerner, her face obviously European, her hair, or at least what was visible of it, was dark. Her head and torso were draped and wrapped in long folds of fabric, and in her hand was a microphone. She was talking easily with the cameraperson, smiling, the microphone down by her side. With the woman's clothes so carefully covered, it was hard to date the scene, but there was something about the microphone, the size of it, or even its presence, that told me the film we were watching had been made some years earlier. And then there were the woman's boots, a style some fifteen or twenty years past their prime.

"Is there sound?" I asked.

Helen shook her head. "I don't think so."

Suddenly, the woman's demeanor changed. She snapped to attention, motioning to something behind the camera operator. The lens panned violently around and swept downward, catching the blurred sky, the fractured cityscape, coming finally to rest at the edge of the roof again. We were looking downward now, at the alleyway below, and a battered box truck.

The truck's back door opened, and a pair of men jumped out, each with an automatic rifle on his shoulder. They were in civilian dress, loose-fitting pants and shifts. Several other similarly clad figures emerged from a nearby doorway, and the whole crew set to work unloading a cargo of long, coffinlike wooden crates. They made short work of what was in the truck, and when they had emptied it, they began filling it again with the same type of crates they'd just unloaded.

Helen paused the video as the second crate was carried from the building.

"Here," she said, touching her finger to the screen.

The side of the box had tilted briefly upward toward the camera, revealing black letters.

"SA-7s," Helen said.

"What does it mean?" I asked, squinting to read the grainy, Cyrillic text.

"They're Soviet shoulder-fired missiles," she explained, starting the video again.

As the crate continued on its journey to the truck, two newcomers stepped out of the building and stood watching. The camera angle and the film quality made it impossible to see their faces, but the first man, the shorter of the two, stood out in Western garb, tan fatigues, light pants and a short-sleeved collared shirt. The second man was dressed as the men unloading the trucks were, though even in his baggy pants and long shirt, he was unquestionably an authority figure.

"Any idea who they are?" I asked.

"No," she said, pointing to the first man, "but I'd give you a hundred–to–one odds this guy's CIA."

"Our mystery man?"

"Maybe."

"What do you think was in those boxes they took off the truck?"

"Heroin, most likely."

"All transported courtesy of the Central Intelligence Agency," I remarked.

"No use letting those trucks come back to Pakistan empty," she said, a slight hint of sarcasm in her voice.

"You think what we were doing was wrong?" I asked.

"It's not my place to think," she countered.

"Is that the kind of secret someone would want to keep?"

"At the time, maybe, but this is all pretty much common knowledge now."

"The drugs?"

Helen shrugged. "Everyone knows that's how the mujahideen financed their war."

"But why the Soviet weapons?"

"Most of the weapons we fed into Afghanistan were either replicas of the Soviet stuff or real foreign matériel bought on the black market. Stuff the mujahideen could have picked up on the battlefield. A lot easier to explain than a truckload of American Stingers."

Two more crates had emerged from the building while we spoke. As the second was being hoisted into the truck's bed, one of the men holding it fumbled momentarily and lost his grip. The wooden box tilted sideways, its base striking the ground, its top sliding ajar. There was a moment of harried activity as the two men scrambled to

right their load. The lid was put back on, and the crate slid
into the truck and out of our view.

"Did you see that?" Helen asked, running the video
backward.

"See what?" I asked, watching the crate fall again.

"There's nothing in there," she said, pausing the film as
the top opened and slid away. "There's nothing in the box."

"I don't understand," I said, looking into the bare
crate. She was right, there seemed to be nothing inside,
but I didn't see why that mattered.

"No SA-7s," she said. She ran the video backward
again, back to the moment when the men had stepped out
of the building with the first crate. "Look at how they're
carrying them," she noted, moving her face closer to the
monitor.

I shrugged. Whatever she saw was lost on me.

"A shoulder-fired missile is a pretty weighty thing, but
look at these guys."

I followed her gaze to the screen. What I had missed
the first time seemed obvious now. The men carrying the
crates moved easily, too easily for men with even moder-
ate burdens. "There's nothing in any of them!" I
exclaimed.

"But why the empty crates?" The question was meant
for herself, not me, but I answered anyway.

"Maybe someone wanted it to look like there were
SA-7s in there," I offered.

Helen didn't say anything. Her eyes were glued to the
monitor. We watched the tape roll on past what we'd already seen. Several more crates were loaded into the
truck. Then, suddenly, something rattled the men on the
ground. One of the pair with the automatic rifles pointed
upward, in the camera's direction, and all the other heads
followed, faces moving in unison toward our rooftop van-
tage point.

"C'mon," Helen murmured, talking to the two observers, the Westerner and the other man. "This way. Look this way."

And then, as if by a miracle, the two men turned to look up.

"Jibril," Helen said, touching her finger to the image of the taller man.

"And the other one?" I asked. "The American?"

Helen paused, scanning the face. "I don't know," she said.

Jibril gestured frantically, and the gunmen sprinted across the alley. The camera followed as they barged through a door directly below and disappeared.

"They're coming up," I said, my heart beating as if I were on the roof with them.

What followed was a flurry of confusion, two sets of feet, one male, one female, the legs and blurred torsos of the cameraman and the woman with the microphone. The camera sped across the roof, bumping dizzyingly against the man's hip, then plunged into a dim stairwell. The lens caught a nauseating jumble: a pile of filthy rags, a line of metal railing flaring light, a rat fleeing the commotion, a broken window.

"Oh my God," I whispered, leaning in closer to the monitor, transfixed by the familiar setting, this panicked descent I'd made so many times in my dreams.

"What?" Helen asked. "What is it?"

"I've seen this before," I told her.

The couple reached a landing and hesitated. The cameraman pivoted, searching for something, another way out, perhaps. Then he leaned forward, and we saw what he saw: figures moving in the semidarkness below, a man with a gun climbing the stairs, and behind him a second man.

The cameraman ducked through a doorway off the

stairs and the woman followed. Here was the same room I knew so well, the cathedral-like ceiling and grimy windows. In the paltry light I caught my first full glimpse of the woman since I'd seen her earlier on the roof. The wrap had slipped from her head, and her hair was wild and disheveled, slick with sweat where it fell around her face.

"This woman," Helen said, as the camera swung down again, catching dusty floorboards and feet.

"What?"

"I know her. I think I know her."

As if in response the lens pitched upward suddenly and caught her face again, the angles of it exaggerated by the room's shadows, by the grainy tape. She was terrified, that much was certain, afraid of what she knew was to come. I could, I thought, feel the moment as she felt it, the cold slant of the light, the abandoned smell of the place, the sound of the man next to me struggling to get his breath back.

"What do you mean?" I asked.

"I was in Islamabad from 'eighty-seven to 'eighty-nine," Helen explained. "It was my first foreign gig, the tail end of the war. God, I can't remember her name."

"But you knew her?"

"I knew who she was. She was with CNN, I think. It's been so long. I used to see her around, you know, the local watering holes."

We both watched as a hand reached into the frame and grabbed the woman's hair.

"They're going to kill her," I said, my knowledge of what was about to happen as certain as if I had been there. And hadn't I? Hadn't I felt the knife against my own throat?

Something winked in the dim light, a flash of metal. The scythe of a blade crossed the woman's neck, carving a single dark line across her throat. Not me, I thought, but her, and yet the realization brought little relief.

"It was my second summer there," Helen said as we watched the monitor in silence, waiting for something else, anything that would tell us we were wrong. But there was nothing more to see. "It would have been 'eighty-eight. July, I think. None of us knew what had happened. They dumped her body onto Aga Khan Road, right outside the Marriott."

As the tape went black, I thought of Heloise, and of the other sisters, and Inspector Lelu, the way the word *massacre* had spilled from his mouth.

"Jibril was blackmailing him," Helen said, pointing to the unknown figure. She had run the tape back to the moment when the two men lifted their faces to the camera.

"With the murder of the journalist?" I asked.

Helen shook her head. "It's more than that. If this had been a CIA operation, our friend wouldn't have had anything to hide, at least not from the agency. They wouldn't have been happy, but they would have covered for him. No, this was a private deal, a one-on-one arrangement between Jibril and our man. That's why there were no missiles in the crates."

I puzzled through what she was saying. "These guys were moving heroin out of Afghanistan under the guise of American intelligence and pocketing the cash themselves."

"I doubt a single penny was going to the war effort. The boys at Langley would not have been pleased."

"But why would Jibril sell the tape if it had bought him an ally inside the agency for all these years?"

"Jibril didn't sell it," Helen said. "We had several uncomfirmed reports that he died the summer before last in Algeria. I'll take this as confirmation. With Jibril dead, Al-Marwan must have decided the tape was worth more to him on the open market."

"Where do you think Werner fits into all of this?" I asked.

"Honestly, I don't know. A little personal dirt can go a long way in the arms business. Werner could have had a deal working with our friend from the street. Maybe he needed a little leverage. Or maybe he was just looking to buy himself some insurance. You know, for a rainy day."

"Maybe," I said, but I wasn't satisfied. "Brian said it was Werner who came for me at the abbey. Do you think he was right?"

Helen took a sip of her now-cold coffee and made a face. "It wasn't Werner," she said.

"Al-Marwan."

"We don't think so."

Neither of us said what we were both thinking, that this left only one possibility.

Helen rubbed her eyes, glanced at the room's single cot. "Maybe things will make more sense in the morning," she said.

"What about the pen drive?" I asked.

"Normally, I'd upload everything on there and send it home to the geeks in Maryland, but this is too sensitive to put out into the ether. I'll have to hand-deliver it."

"I'm coming with you," I told her.

She looked over at me, her face open, almost expectant. "You don't even know where I'm going."

"I don't care," I said. "I'm going. I need to know who I am."

She nodded. "I've got a friend in the Petit Socco we can see tomorrow about getting out of here. It's not safe to take you through immigration right now. In the meantime you should try to get some rest."

I looked at the cot. As tired as I was, I doubted I'd manage any sleep that night. "Why don't you take it?" I said. "I know I should be tired, but I'm not."

She hesitated a moment, then got up. "There should be some spare blankets in one of these boxes if you change your mind."

"Thanks," I told her, watching her slide in under the sleeping bag without taking her boots off.

I sat there for a few minutes and listened to the silence of the room, the distant hiss of water in a pipe somewhere, the sound of Helen's body shifting. What about me? I wondered, my gaze drawn to the two men on the monitor, Jibril's hollow features and the somehow boyish face of the other man. What was my place in all of this?

Brian had been wrong about what was on the pen drive, but as far as I could tell he'd been right about who I was, at least who I had been. Helen had said it herself. *We know a woman named Leila Brightman did contract work for American intelligence.* Couldn't my employer and Brian's have been one and the same? Couldn't he have been the one who'd sent me to Werner's Casbah?

I started the video again, as I'd watched Helen do, and reran the last horrible moments of the tape. The final panicked seconds of the woman's life. Something in me said I knew her, though perhaps it was just the intimacy of the tape, the intensity of her fear. Yes, that was it, for how could I know her, a woman most likely dead all these years, dead when I would have been little more than a child? But still, I couldn't let her go.

I ran the footage back once more, this time pausing it on her frightened face. Yes, I thought, I knew her, only a younger her, and smiling. She was the woman from Les

Trois Singes, the blurred face in Werner's photograph. My memory at the Casbah had not been faulty. There was another print, a picture captured just before Werner's, before the girl in the white shift had stepped into the frame, before the woman in the center had moved her head to speak or laugh.

I had seen that photograph, not just once but many times. I was certain of it. I had known this woman, just as Werner had known her, just as the man on the video had. For it was him in the picture as well, the handsome one, the swimmer, so at ease in his white cotton shirt, the same man who stood with Naser Jibril while her throat was slit. No, I told myself. I hadn't been working for anyone. I'd known all along what was on the video, and it was to solve her murder that I'd come to Morocco.

I put my hand to the computer's screen and touched her face, the tear forming in her right eye. My mother, I thought, the knowledge as certain as my own presence in the world.

TWENTY-ONE

I had fallen asleep, arms crossed on the desk, head cradled in them. When the knock came, it slapped me awake and I sat up, eyes wide open, heart frantic. Helen was up, too, her feet rolling from the cot to the floor in one swift motion. Her gun was drawn, her finger to her lips in a warning for silence.

The knock came again, a heavy fist rattling the thick wood.

"You expecting anyone?" I whispered.

Helen shook her head, then paused for a moment, her knuckles white on the stock of the gun, her feet deciding which way to move.

"Police," a man's voice called from the other side of the door. "Open the door."

Stepping in my direction, Helen reached into her pants pocket and pulled out a rumpled business card.

"Anything happens to me," she whispered, "you go to

the Café Becerra in the Petit Socco. Ask for Ishaq. Give him this." She handed me the card. "He'll get you to Spain. From there you'll need to get yourself and the pen drive to Paris. Can you do that?"

I nodded.

"Good. When you get to Paris, go to the American church. Post a note on the bulletin board, the one outside. It should read: *Uncle Bill, In town for the weekend. Ring me at the George V. Katy.* Tell me what the note says."

I swallowed hard. "Uncle Bill," I repeated, "In town for the weekend. Ring me at the George V. Katy."

"Okay. There's a tearoom across from St.-Julien-le-Pauvre. Go there the next day at four in the afternoon. Take a table alone and order a pot of Darjeeling. Can you remember this?"

"Yes."

"St.-Julien-le-Pauvre," she said.

"A pot of Darjeeling," I repeated.

She pointed to the card in my hand. "Café Becerra. Ishaq," she said. Then she started for the door, motioning toward the bathroom as she went.

I nodded and slid off my chair, pulling the pen drive from the laptop, slipping it and the business card into my pocket as I made my way to the bathroom.

I drew the curtain closed and made a careful survey of my surroundings. The room was the size of a small closet, the only fixtures an old pull-chain toilet and a tiny sink. On the opposite wall, next to the sink, was a small window. Barred, I noted, though the metal grate was fastened directly into the plaster outer wall. The screws that held it in place were corroded and rusty.

I heard Helen undo the latch on the front door's iron porthole. The tiny hinges creaked open; then a pop sounded, the muffled thump of a silenced gunshot. Helen let out a strangled cry, her body thudding against the wall, her gun clattering to the floor.

I leaped upward, grabbing for the old pipe that ran across the bathroom ceiling. Gripping the metal, I swung forward and hit the grate feet first. The plaster loosened, and I felt the screws wrench partway free. I swung back and kicked again. I could hear commotion in the room now, a man's voice speaking Arabic. Salim, I thought, the old vasopressin memories coming back to me.

I kicked at the grate again, and this time it popped loose. Dropping to the floor, I scrambled up onto the sink and pulled myself through the narrow opening. It was a thankfully short drop to the roof below, but I landed on my side, jarring the shoulder I'd hurt in my tussle with Salim that night outside the Mamounia.

Wincing at the pain, I rolled up and drew the Beretta. I could hear Salim above me, his voice through the open window, and then the distinct crack of an unsilenced gunshot. The bullet erupted at my feet, sending up a spray of gravel and tar.

I sprang forward and sprinted, dropping down onto the neighboring dwelling. A second shot sounded, this one just missing my heels. I crouched in the shelter of the roof's edge and fired back, the action coming easily. Steady, aim, shoot, I told myself. The plaster wall shattered, and the head in the window dropped from view.

Taking a deep breath, I steadied myself and waited for Salim to reappear, but the window went dark instead. Yes, I thought, I knew how to do this kind of thing. I had been this person, and she lived inside me still, this woman I'd denied, this woman I'd feared. Now my very survival rested with her. I glanced behind me and saw the path I would take, the roofs of the medina forming an unbroken pathway. A way out, I told myself, as I scrambled forward and leaped down onto the next house. Everything would be fine.

It was early daylight when I finally made my way down the Rue Dar el-Baroud. The morning was gray, the bay dark as oil, the chop etched in froth. The Continental glowed against the ashen sky and filth-streaked medina like a rose at dusk. I passed the old hotel without stopping and headed east through the medina. Stopping at a shop on the Rue as-Siaghin, I bought a plain brown burnoose and a cheap leather shoulder bag, then wandered down the Rue des Almohades till I found a grimy and nondescript pension.

Twenty dirhams got me an unplumbed room on the second floor. Another outrageous fifty, and the manager reluctantly produced a bowl of greasy broth, a wedge of stale bread, a handful of dates, and a hard-boiled egg. Hardly a feast, but it was enough to take the edge off my hunger. I ate in my room, then slipped the burnoose on, put the Beretta, my money, and my passports in the leather bag, and headed out again.

It was just midmorning, but already the Ramadan hush had settled over the Petit Socco. A few old diehards played chess over ghosts of mint tea or sat alone in the cafés with imagined cigarettes and coffee. But save for them and the occasional tourist trying to recapture the Tangier of William Burroughs or Paul Bowles, the square was nearly empty.

I found the Café Becerra easily. The tiny establishment sat on the northeast corner of the plaza, its handful of outdoor tables clustered beneath a grime-streaked awning, its only clientele three scrawny stray cats asleep on the patio. Stopping several yards from the café, I pulled the burnoose down low over my face and slid Helen's card from my pocket. There was neither name nor address on the plain white rectangle, just a simple representation of the Hand of Fatima, the Moroccan good-luck talisman, a woman's palm facing outward.

Keep us safe, Lord, I whispered, the old compline prayer. Reaching into my bag for reassurance, I touched the barrel of the Beretta, then crossed the last few yards to the café's open front door.

It was dark inside the restaurant, the air rich with the smell of the evening's *harira* already on the stove. A shriveled old man in a brown burnoose had either died or fallen asleep at one of the inside tables. His hood was pulled down over his eyes, his mouth open slightly, his hands clasped on his chest. A cane rested against the table. A dark young man who looked as if he was fresh from the king's prisons sat behind the bar thumbing through a dog-eared girlie magazine. It was a cheap publication, the women all fat and amateurish, with greasy hair and bad makeup.

His eyes shifted slightly, taking in the burnoose, and he grunted something in Arabic. When I didn't move, he looked up at me. "Closed," he said in French, sneering at the Western face behind the hood.

"I'm not here for tea," I told him.

He shrugged, then slowly turned the page. "We are closed," he tried again in English.

"I'm looking for Ishaq," I explained.

The man scanned the page in front of him, the glossy picture of a fleshy woman in black leather underpants and a merry widow. "Sorry," he spat. "No one here by that name."

"A friend sent me," I said, setting the card on the woman's crotch.

He looked down at the Hand of Fatima for a moment, then pushed the card off the magazine and across the bar toward me. "Where's Helen?" he asked.

"Dead," I told him, returning the card to my pocket.

He considered me for a moment, his eyes hard and black as coal. Part of a tattoo was visible above the collar of his shirt, the top of some intricate decoration. "There," he said finally, nodding toward the motionless old man.

He called out in Arabic, and the wizened figure opened his eyes and stared out at me from beneath his burnoose. The two had a brief exchange of words; then the old man beckoned me to his table.

"You must excuse Kahlil," he said, motioning to the barman as I took a seat opposite him. "He is a little rough around the edges." He spoke perfect French, cultured and easy, each word delicately formed.

"Of course."

"And you," Ishaq said, resting his knotted hands on the table. "You have come for transportation, no?"

I nodded. "Yes. Can you get me to Spain."

"Anything is possible," he conceded, with fake modesty. His eyes were bright beneath the shadow of the burnoose.

"How much?" I asked.

"May I assume time is of the essence?"

"You may."

He drummed his fingers on the table. "I could arrange for something tonight, but for a white woman, on such short notice, I would need at least four thousand, American."

"Two thousand," I said. "I'll give you the cash right now."

"You are trying to insult me?" he protested. "I couldn't possibly do this for less than thirty-five hundred."

"Three thousand," I told him.

The old man shook his head and flashed me a look of reluctant disgust. "Three thousand," he conceded.

I opened my bag and counted out half the money, then

slid the bills onto the table in front of him. "Half now, half on delivery," I told him.

He shook his head. "I'm afraid that's not how we do business, Mademoiselle. This is a dirty affair, I know, but you'll just have to trust me. It's three thousand now, or the deal's off."

Reluctantly, I counted out the remaining fifteen hundred and passed it to him.

He smiled at the sight of the currency. "Take the number fifteen bus tonight from the Grand Socco toward Cap Malabata," he said, secreting the money into the folds of his burnoose. "The last one leaves at around eight. Get off at Ghandouri and walk toward the cliffs at the eastern end of the beach. There will be a boat sometime after midnight."

He looked right at me. "Don't worry, my dear. There will be a boat. Now, if you will excuse me, it seems I have other business to attend to."

I stood and turned. Three men had come in while I was with Ishaq, West Africans, Senegalese or Ivory Coasters from the looks of them, no doubt shopping for the same thing I'd come for.

"It has been a pleasure, Mademoiselle," I heard the old man say as I headed for the door.

TWENTY-TWO

I slept like a corpse in my narrow bed at the pension and awoke to darkness outside my window. It was close to seven by my watch. Down in the street voices clamored and hummed, crowds driven by newly full stomachs and nicotine. I got up, went down the hall and relieved myself, then came back to the room and washed my face and hands in the cold-water sink.

We all live with a variety of illusions, the crooked nose, the lazy eye, the faint scar no one else can see. Or the promise of courage under fire, the belief in some kind of undeniable inner virtue. For so long I'd had nothing but the face in the mirror, nothing but what I'd come with, the careful tracery of the bullet, this delicate boundary between the self I'd been and the one I wished myself to be. Now, in the room's paltry light, in the cheap warped glass, I barely recognized myself.

I dried my face, pushed my hair back, and checked the

old scar. And then, without warning, I thought of the child. I could smell it as if it were there in the room. Soap and powder and the faint odor of sour milk.

Turning to the bed, I slipped the black box from the leather shoulder bag and spread the seven passports out on the worn coverlet. Five years, I told myself, paging through the blurred immigration stamps, confirming what I'd seen that night in the bathroom at the El Minzah. Not one of the passports had been used in the past five years. Hadn't Abdesselom said as much at the Continental? *Five years and not a word*.

And yet here I am, I heard Heloise say that summer morning in the kitchen. I could see her still, tan forearms shining with steam and sweat, eyes closed as she gave herself to the pleasure of her cigarette, to that single moment of unfettered quiet.

Yes, I thought, that's how it works, not five times a day, not ten, but hundreds, each fragile instant of faith a surrender to the unknown, to the story we all must choose for ourselves. For in the end, the only thing certain is what we can never really know. Memory or not, we are all dumb and blind, fooled, like Brian, by some hollow reflection of ourselves. In the end, all we are is what we believe.

Yes, I had been these women in the passports, but I had also chosen to leave them behind. I'd had a child somewhere in those five years, and another life, one in which Leila and the others didn't exist. When I had come back, it had not been as a traitor, but to find out what had happened all those years ago in Pakistan, to learn who had killed my mother.

And Patrick Haverman? He had loved me. He had believed me when I'd told him why I'd come, had loved me enough to help me. And the truth, not just hope or hazard, was that I'd loved him back. That's why the people who were supposed to help him had silenced him instead.

This, then, was my story, my faith, the one I chose. Someone's mother, someone's child, the girl of his dreams. Of this I could be certain, but there was much more I didn't know.

There was still the man, the American, the face at Les Trois Singes, and outside that Peshawar warehouse. It was he who'd had the sisters killed, who'd left me to die in that field. I was sure of it now. But what had I been doing in France in the first place? *You only said you would send someone,* Abdesselom had told me, *someone who would know our signal*. Had I gone to find that person?

It wasn't far from the pension to the main gate of the medina and the Grand Socco, a fifteen-minute walk at most. I slipped back into the anonymity of the burnoose and set out with just the leather bag, the passports, the Beretta, the pen drive, and what little money I hadn't yet spent, a meager haul, but far more than what I'd brought to that damp field. Hannah's clothes and pack I left behind.

The narrow streets of the Old City were jam-packed, the Petit Socco teeming with humanity, the patio at the Café Central overflowing. Monklike figures in burnooses scurried along, faces hidden under pointed hoods. Southern African whores called out from doorways. Voices whispered from dark corners, *Something special, my friend*. It had rained while I slept, but the shower had served only to heighten the smells of the Old City. There was a pervasive dampness and stink: the stench of wet donkey shit and cheap perfume, urine and bile, and the jumbled odor of spices, cumin, cayenne, black pepper, ginger.

I turned away from the Petit Socco and started down the rue as-Siaghin, letting the crowds carry me past the long-neglected Church of the Immaculate Conception, its gray face smeared with some twelve decades of black filth. Just past the church, the crowd knotted and slowed as the deluge of bodies fought its way out through the old arched gateway. Then suddenly we were free, streaming loose from the bottleneck into the Grand Socco.

It was closer to nine than to eight when the last number fifteen bus finally lurched into the square. The Grand Socco is where the Old City meets the new, where the wide colonial streets collide head-on with the medina's narrow alleyways, and as a result, it's a perpetual traffic jam, a tight clog of taxis and private cars fighting to get in through the old gate.

The bus crawled toward us, and the crowd that had been waiting picked up their bags and cases in anticipation of its arrival. A few passengers disembarked, but at this hour the flow of traffic was definitely away from the city. The bus filled quickly, and by the time I got on there were just a handful of free seats. I found a place near the back, next to a stylish young woman in a black turtleneck and jeans.

We rumbled out of the city, past the long dark stretches of beachfront, the Club Med and the white high-rise apartment buildings that lined the eastern shore. Gradually, the surroundings turned more and more rural, until stretches of dark scrub marked the distance between homes, and the road dropped sharply toward the sea on our left-hand side.

Ghandouri was not much of a place. The lights of a half dozen homes and a small café shone in the darkness. I asked the only other passenger to disembark with me for directions to the beach. He pointed hastily to a dark space in the cliffside, then disappeared quickly, the hard soles of his shoes tap-tapping on the road.

I could smell the beach, and I could hear it, the easy cadence of the Mediterranean, the brackish odors of fish and flotsam. I stood at the edge of the road for a moment,

letting my eyes adjust to the darkness, then started toward
the path. The little trail was overgrown with sea holly and
evergreen shrubs, and I had to pick my way down to the
water. But once I was there, the beach opened outward in
a long expanse of sand and surf.

To the west lay Tangier, a crescent of light against the
utter blackness of the sea. To the east, its silhouette just
barely visible in the moon's dim light, was the lighthouse
at Cap Malabata. A few lone ships winked from the Strait
of Gibraltar, tankers fighting the powerful fist of the current. It was no place for a small boat, and yet in a few
hours I'd be out on those black waves in a craft I could
only hope would prove as large as a fishing boat.

The temperature had dropped substantially, and the
sky was clear, the stars bright and plentiful as at the abbey. For an instant I was back in Burgundy, back in the
yard, heading to the kitchen to ready the bread for its second rise. Down the hill the Tanes' dogs were barking,
their call and response filtering up through the woods.
Muffled by the stone walls of the chapel, the sisters read
that night's psalm in unison, their voices catching the
rhythm of the verse.

> *My God, my God, why hast Thou forsaken me?*
> *Why art Thou so far from helping me, from the words*
>   *of my groaning?*
> *O my God, I cry by day, but Thou dost not answer:*
>   *and by night, but find no rest. . . .*
> *. . . But I am a worm, and no man: scorned by men,*
>   *and despised by the people.*

Shivering, I turned east and headed for the cliffs, for
the bright beacon that burned at the base of the rocks. As
I neared the fire, a cluster of dark and silent faces came
into view, teeth and eyes catching the light, skin reflecting

the flames. A figure beckoned me forward, and I stepped closer, pulling back the burnoose to reveal my distinctly European face to the all-male group.

Whether they had been told to expect an outsider, or whether they recognized me for what I was, someone, like themselves, simply looking for a way out, I don't know. But they shifted without hesitation, making a space for me in the soft sand near the fire's warm glow. Someone touched my arm, and I looked over to see a steaming cup of tea. I nodded my thanks and lifted the drink to my lips. The liquid was miraculously hot and sweet.

There were some two dozen men in all, all like the trio I'd seen earlier at the Café Becerra. And on other beaches? Doubtless there were more fires like this. What had Brian said that first night in Joshi's apartment? *You know how many Africans disappear into the Strait of Gibraltar each year?*

I finished the tea and handed the cup back to the man beside me. I would make it, I told myself, looking out past the fire to the dark water. We would all make it. And then what? I would go to Paris. I would do what Helen had asked. This man would help me. Someone had to know me. And if not? The threads I had to follow seemed even thinner than the ones that had brought me to Morocco. My mother's face on a video, a man I didn't know. And there was Hannah Boyle as well, dead some ten years earlier. I had chosen her. Perhaps I had known her.

Someone started singing, and a handful of other voices joined in, the tune melancholy as a hymn or a lullaby. I closed my eyes, and I could feel the child, the shape of its body in my arms, the unsteady weight of its head.

It was very early in the morning when the boat came. At first it was just a single light, a spot blinking in and out of the chop. Then, slowly, the outline of the craft appeared, the boxy cabin, the prow and stern. The boat pulled up in the surf and weighed anchor.

I scrambled to my feet with the rest of the group, shaking the cold from my legs, stumbling across the sand and into the water.

"Quickly!" a voice called, and I felt a hand on each shoulder, two men lifting me onto the deck. I lay there for a moment, heart pounding, chest heaving, like a fish fighting the air. By the time I gathered myself enough to stand, we had hauled anchor and were moving. I looked back to the shore, but there was nothing to see. The moon had long since set, and the cliffs of Ghandouri beach were invisible in the darkness, the lighthouse at Cap Malabata only a memory.

When I turned to face northward again, the deck was clear, the open hatch my fellow passengers had disappeared through gaping like a dark maw. The captain stood silhouetted in the dim lights of the cabin's instrument panel, his hands on the wheel, his gaze firm on the invisible Spanish shore.

Beside the captain was a second man, his body tall and graceful, his hands crossed over his chest. He was turned in my direction, his face in shadow, but still I knew him without question. He started forward, surefooted on the pitching deck.

"Nebesky," he called out, raising his voice to make himself heard above the noise of the engine.

I shook my head and took a step back, contemplating the dark waves, the distance to the shore, the beach receding farther from swimming distance each second.

"Nebesky," he said again, coming closer. "You wanted to know my name. It's Brian Nebesky. My grandparents were Czech immigrants."

The top buttons of his shirt were undone, and in the

boat's pale running lights I could see the dark shape of a bruise on his throat.

"You were right," he said. "I want to know."

"They'll kill us both," I told him.

Brian grinned, showing a row of perfect white teeth. "I'll take my chances."

TWENTY-THREE

"How did you find me?" I asked.

It was too cold to stay on deck, and our presence seemed to be making the Spanish captain nervous, so we'd climbed down into the hold with the rest of the passengers. The cramped space reeked, of seawater and sweat born of fear, but it was warm and dry. A small propane lamp hung in one corner, shining on the tired faces of our shipmates.

"I figured you'd be trying to get out of the country, so I did some asking around. The Café Becerra was my second stop. Believe it or not, there aren't too many European women looking for illegal rides across the strait. I hadn't counted on you being alone, though."

I swallowed hard, thinking of Helen.

"Who was she?" Brian asked.

"NSA," I said, lowering my voice. We were the only

ones speaking, and even at a whisper we seemed pro-
fanely loud.

"What happened?"

"Werner's men," I told him.

"She's dead?"

"Yes."

"Did you get a chance to look at the pen drive?"

I nodded. "Whoever hired you lied to you, Brian. It's
not what you think."

I told him everything, about Helen, the old videotape,
the warehouse in Peshawar, and the empty crates. I told
him about the woman, my mother, and the photograph in
Werner's office, about the five missing years and why I'd
come back, why I thought Pat had helped me at the Casbah, how I was taking the pen drive to Paris.

"Do you know who he is?" I asked when I had finished. "Whoever it is you're working for?"

Brian shook his head.

"There must be someone who contacts you," I insisted.

"Everything is arranged on-line," he said. "There's a
chat room I go to. The times are agreed on in advance."

"How do they pay you?"

"I've got an account, through a bank in Geneva; the
money goes there."

"When are you supposed to make your next contact?"

"Last night," Brian said. "They'll know by now something's gone wrong."

I wrapped my arms around my damp shins and set my
head on my knees.

"Eve?" Brian asked.

"Yes."

"You said Helen thought there was a leak in the
agency, someone passing information."

I nodded. "Why?"

"I'm not sure," he said, "but if I had to guess, I'd say this was more than one person."

"How many?"

Brian shrugged. "I don't know, but there's money here." He hesitated a moment, letting his words gather weight. "Lots of it."

The little boat took a wave across the port side and pitched uncomfortably. A collective shudder ran through the hold; then the craft found its equilibrium once more, bobbing upright like a cork.

I was suddenly exhausted, too tired to reason through the implications of what Brian had just said. "Helen's contact in Paris," I told him. "He'll know what to do."

Brian leaned back against the hold and closed his eyes. "I hope so," he said.

Once, on a cold spring morning, I happened upon a freshly hatched swarm of baby spiders in the back of the abbey's henhouse. At first all I could see was a single dark stain and the ruptured puff of white gauze at its core. When I looked closer, each tiny creature resolved itself, legs scrambling purposefully across the rough wood boards, black arachnid body glistening in the coop's filtered light.

I stood there for some time, shivering in my thin sweater, and watched the swarm disintegrate, till each hatchling was gone and only the wispy shell of their abandoned home remained. Their disappearance seemed the greatest of miracles to me, the purpose with which they entered the world, their determination toward some unknown point. What a boon, I'd thought, watching the last body scuttle through a crack in the wall. What a thing to know, without thinking, the direction of your life.

When our boat weighed anchor off the wind-scarred

Spanish coast and my fellow passengers leaped into the surf, I was immediately reminded of that spring morning in the henhouse. It was early, the dark sky broken only by a bloody smear of daylight on the eastern horizon. Brian and I stood together on the deck and watched the men start across the black gulf between us and the shore.

It was hard to imagine toward what they were headed, bad jobs and poor pay, a season of lettuce picking in southern France, a roach-infested apartment, a bed shared with two other men, each missing his wife. And yet each of these possibilities offered something better than what they had left behind.

"Let's go," Brian said, as the last of the men slipped into the water.

He put his hand on my arm, and I nodded, raising the leather bag above my head. Brian did the same with the pack he carried. We'd both taken our boots off and hung them over our shoulders.

The water was frigid, the bottom rockier than I'd imagined, and I had to struggle to keep my balance. It wasn't far to the shore, twenty meters at most. Already some of our shipmates had reached land and were scrambling across the beach, disappearing into the dark scrub and up the rocky bluffs on the other side of the sand.

"You okay?" Brian asked, looking over at me.

"Fine." I shivered, my chest half-submerged.

"Don't think about the cold," he said. "You're almost there."

I nodded and closed my eyes briefly, my bare toes fumbling blindly ahead. But in truth I wasn't thinking about the cold. For the first time that I could remember, I was thinking about my past, about my mother, her face in the darkness above my bed at night, her pale, aqueous body suspended in the blue of an ocean, her arms and legs treading water. I was thinking about Paris as well, about the distance between us and the tearoom near St.-Julien-le-Pauvre, about what we would find when we got there. For the first time that I could remember, my own purpose seemed certain as the day to come.

When we finally staggered up onto the beach, Brian set his pack down and pulled what looked like a cell phone from the front pocket.

"GPS," he explained. He hit a button, and the small screen phosphoresced. "The captain said there'd be a village not far from here, but I want to make sure."

The last of the men from the boat crossed the sand in front of us and disappeared, fading into the darkness and scrub as if he had never existed. I brushed the sand from my feet and started to put on my boots.

"It looks like about five kilometers to Bolonia," he said. "We can get a room and get cleaned up."

I nodded, clamping my jaw shut to keep my teeth from chattering.

We climbed the bluff, then bushwacked for a kilometer or so. When we finally emerged onto the washed-out dirt road Brian's GPS map had promised, dawn was spreading upward fast, a stain of cool blue, seeping into the dark sky like bright ink into water. By the time we'd crested the last hill and started down into Bolonia, wan daylight illuminated the tiny village, revealing a cluster of whitewashed houses huddled around an alabaster beach. Beyond the town sat the wind-worn remnants of an ancient Roman seaport, crumbling columns and stone archways stark against the blue bay.

The little beach town was mostly closed for the winter, the first two hotels we came across shuttered against December's punishing wind. Finally, a bleary-eyed old man in slippers and a bathrobe opened the door to us at the Hostel Bellavista, his eyes narrowing as he surveyed our damp clothes, dirty faces, and scant luggage. It took a wad of euros, and Brian's confident Spanish, to salve his suspicions. Just two crazy Americans, Brian had said, laughing, shaking the man's hand, pulling bills from his pack. And two rooms, please, you know how the ladies can be. The man had glanced over at me, smiling at Brian as if to say, yes, I know. Then he tucked the money into the pocket of his bathrobe and led us upstairs.

My room was drafty, the radiator cold to the touch, but the shower was mercifully hot. I stripped myself of my clammy clothes and stood under the steaming water for a good half an hour, letting the feeling come back into my feet. I had just gotten out of the shower and climbed into bed when there was a tentative knock at the door.

"Eve?" It was Brian. "You up?" he whispered.

Swinging my feet to the floor, I wrapped the bedcover around myself and padded across the room.

"I hope you weren't asleep," he said apologetically when I'd opened the door. He glanced down at the bed-cover, and I thought I detected a hint of color rising to his cheeks.

"No," I told him. "Not yet."

"Sorry," he offered sheepishly, nodding to indicate the breakfast tray he held in his hands. "I thought you might be hungry."

"Starving," I conceded, surveying the food. The tray held a plate of chocolate-dipped churros, two large pieces of bread with butter and marmalade, several slices of ham, and a pot of coffee and two cups.

"How did you manage that?" I asked, stepping aside to let him into the room.

He set the tray on the bedside table. "Our host can be quite accommodating when provided with enough incentive." He smiled, producing a stack of folded clothes he'd tucked under his right arm. "His daughter's. I don't know how well they'll fit, but they're clean and dry."

"You don't like this look?" I asked, pulling the bed-cover tight around me.

"Cute, but I'm not sure it's practical."

"Thank you," I said. I took the clothes and set them aside.

Brian smiled. "Do you mind if I take a look at what's on that pen drive? Just to see if I recognize anyone. I've got my laptop."

"Sure," I told him, starting for my bag.

Brian went out into the hall, and I heard the door to his room open, then close. He reappeared with his laptop.

I handed him the pen drive and sat down on the bed. "If it's all right with you, I'd rather not watch it again."

"Of course," Brian said, moving to the far side of the room.

I drank my coffee and ate while Brian watched the video in silence. When he was finished, he closed the laptop and came over and poured himself a cup of coffee.

"Anyone look familiar?" I asked.

"I'm sorry," he said, shaking his head. "I'm so sorry." He flexed his hands awkwardly at his sides and rocked almost imperceptibly on the balls of his feet, as if waiting for something, as if trying to decide how to navigate some great impediment between us.

"At the Continental," he said, then hesitated. "You know I couldn't have . . . I didn't know."

"You knew what you wanted to know," I told him.

He turned away slightly, as if from a blow.

I shook my head, regretting what I'd said. He was here now, and that was all that should have mattered. "I shouldn't have said that," I told him. "I know you wouldn't have hurt me." But the truth was that neither of us knew.

I lifted my hand to his and pulled him toward me, letting the bedcover slip away. I felt almost giddy, drunk on exhaustion, and I didn't want to think about the Continental.

Brian got down on his knees and rested his head against my bare stomach. He'd showered, too, and his hair was still wet, cool and damp on my skin.

"It's okay," I said again.

I lifted his face to mine and bent down and kissed him. No, I thought, we would never know. He might have killed me that night in Tangier, but for now I would choose to believe otherwise.

Moving carefully, I eased my hand under his sweater and lifted it over his head. His skin was hot, like a fire kindled from within. Outside, the wind kicked up, needling the windowpanes with fine sand, singing through the cracks in the old stone building. Brian put his hand on the side of my breast, and I shivered. Yes, I told myself, for now I would choose to believe him.

TWENTY-FOUR

We slept through the day and left early the next evening, heading toward Seville in an old Seat Brian had managed to talk the hotel owner into selling us. We'd paid almost twice what the car was worth, but it hadn't fazed Brian. When the old man had named a price, Brian had produced a roll of euros from his pack without flinching. *There's money here,* I remembered him saying on the boat. *Lots of it.* Evidently, he'd taken his share.

It took us a night of hard driving to cross Spain, with nothing but the vast Iberian landscape and the occasional looming silhouette of one of the massive Osborne bulls for company. We took turns at the wheel, pushing north through Cordova and Madrid, then up across the Cordillera Central to Burgos and San Sebastián. Some twelve hours after we'd left Bolonia and the coast, we crossed France's southern border.

Road-addled and red-eyed, we pulled into a truck stop

outside Biarritz for breakfast and coffee, then headed out again, straight into Bordeaux's morning rush hour and on toward Paris. I was grateful to be taking the western route across the country, thankful not to have to see Burgundy again. But in the hazy winter daylight the bare vineyards of Bordeaux and the Loire Valley seemed too much like home.

It was midafternoon when we reached the southern suburbs of Paris. Brian was asleep in the passenger seat, and I shook him awake.

"Can you get us to the American church?" I asked.

He nodded reluctantly, rubbing the sleep from his eyes. "I think so."

"Good."

I followed his directions into the heart of the city, then followed the skeletal beacon of the Eiffel Tower toward the Seine.

I'd made one trip to Paris during my year at the convent, a brief visit during which I'd spent most of my time filling out paperwork at the U.S. Consulate. I'd only stayed two nights in the city, in one of the abbey's sister convents, in a hard-up neighborhood near the Bois de Vincennes, but in my spare few hours I'd crossed the Pont de l'Alma from the consulate and walked through the Champ de Mars.

It had been only a month or so after the sisters had taken me in, I remembered now as we headed along the Quai Branly, the Trocadero gardens on our left, the Eiffel Tower on our right. I had been slightly afraid as I wandered among the tourists on the park's elegant pea-graveled pathways, fearful that one of the doughy Americans in their running shoes and sun visors would recognize me. Afraid, and yet half hoping someone would.

We squeezed the Seat into a parking spot a few blocks

off the Quai d'Orsay, then walked back toward the American church. It was a beautiful day, sunshine slanting through the bare trees, a nearly empty *bateau-mouche* gliding along the Seine. An old woman, a solitary birdlike silhouette led by a tiny black dog, shuffled along the quai, her feathered hat ruffling in the wind, her pumps picking their way across the graveled path. It was full-on winter here, colder even than when I'd left Burgundy, the mournful, diesel chill of a European city. I shivered in the canvas jacket the old Spaniard had thrown in with the car.

The church sat not far from the Pont de l'Alma, an immaculate gray stone structure tucked in among its high-rent neighbors, across from the hazy sprawl of the Triangle d'Or. A small, scattered crowd lingered on the sidewalk and steps out front, American backpackers fresh off the train, middle-aged Asian women in the neat attire of the would-be domestic worker, exchange students in loafers and pea coats.

"Excuse me," I said, approaching two American girls on the steps. "Can you tell us where the bulletin board is?"

"Which one?" one of them asked.

"The one outside," I told her, remembering what Helen had said.

"There." She pointed with authority to the church's covered entryway.

"I'd like to post something. Do you know if there's a fee?"

She took a drag off her cigarette, looking far too young to be smoking. "You have to go inside to the office. It's a couple of euros, I think."

"Thanks."

We passed by the glass-fronted bulletin board on the way inside, and I stopped to take a look. It was neatly maintained, the notices written on index cards, arranged by category, a sort of clearinghouse for the expatriate community in Paris. You could, it seemed, find anything here, child care, domestic services, tutors, apartments, experienced dog walkers.

On the far side of the board was a space for miscellaneous messages. The communications were between travelers mostly, people looking to meet up with friends they'd lost along the way.

Julia on the train from Madrid to Seville. We talked about Capri. You said you'd be spending December in Paris. Am here until New Year's. Please leave a message saying where I can reach you. Michael.

Phillip from New Haven. Remember tacos at Jo's Bar in Prague? Do you still think Kafka is overrated? Please call. Jennifer.

"Do you think he'll call?" Brian asked as we headed inside.

"I hope not," I said. "He sounds like a jerk to me."

The office was on the first floor, at the end of a bright hallway plastered with church notices, invitations to the Bloom Where You're Planted women's coffee group, a schedule of yoga and aerobics classes offered in the church basement, a list of twelve-step meetings in English. It would be possible, I realized, reading the multicolored notices, to live for years in Paris without ever really leaving the United States.

"I bet someone here can tell you where to find cranberry sauce at Thanksgiving," Brian remarked, as we neared the reception desk.

I smiled, conjuring up a scene from some movie, a well-dressed family, the sound of a football game in the background, and a long table groaning with food, turkey and mashed potatoes and some quivering red mass in a bowl.

A cheerful woman in a tastefully dull beige sweater set took my message, carefully transcribing it onto an index card, nodding approvingly at the mention of the Hotel George V.

"It'll go up today?" I asked.

She nodded, adding the card to a small pile of similar messages. "I post the new cards by five."

"What now?" Brian asked as we walked back to the SEAT.

"I guess we should find somewhere to stay," I said. "I don't meet Uncle Bill until tomorrow at four."

"I know a place in Montparnasse," Brian offered. "It's not the George Cinq, but I don't think anyone will look for us there."

Brian was right: the sex shop–lined rue de la Gaîté was no Champs-Elysées, the fraying Hotel de l'Espérance about as far from the gilded Hotel George V as one could get. But there was no doubt this would be the last place in Paris anyone would think to find us. Thirty-five euros got us a room with a double bed and a private bath. The dead cockroach in the sink was complimentary.

We both showered, then went out for an early dinner at the grease-scented brasserie on the corner. By nine we were in bed, bathed in risqué red neon, dreaming the road behind us.

TWENTY-FIVE

It was just after three the next afternoon when Brian and I ascended from the metro under the gaze of St. Michael, his stone feet trampling the writhing form of evil. *And the great dragon was thrown down,* I thought, conjuring up the passage from Revelation, *that ancient serpent who is called the Devil and Satan, the deceiver of the whole earth.*

John's psychedelic vision of the apocalypse had always been one of my favorite parts of the New Testament. I'd liked the utter unambiguousness of it, the way the crazy hermit had seen the end of the world in good and evil, a clear delineation, each of us marked with the sign of the beast or the name of the Father. But as I looked up now at St. Michael, at his upstretched wings splattered with pigeon shit and his feet littered with cigarette butts, I was unconvinced. For wouldn't evil, when it did appear, know better than to come as the serpent? Wouldn't it hide itself? In the folds and feathers of an angel's wings. In the face in the mirror.

As cold as it was, the Place St.-Michel was still jammed with bodies, a Latin Quarter mixture of Parisian students meeting friends and earnest tourists looking to soak up the fifth arrondissement's exiled-artist mystique.

"This way," Brian said, pulling me after him as he started down the narrow rue de la Huchette.

We'd be early. A good thing, Brian had said. Time to get the lay of the land. We'd been over our plan a dozen times at the hotel, but as we neared the rue St.-Jacques, Brian put his hand on my arm and pulled me to the side of the street.

"One last time," he said.

"We split up here," I told him. "I cross the Petit Pont, then come back through Notre Dame. Before I go into the tearoom, I stop at St.-Julien-le-Pauvre and say a quick prayer, left side of the aisle, second row back."

"And after?"

"You'll be watching from the church. When I leave the tearoom, I walk straight back to the St.-Michel metro stop. You'll meet me on the platform."

"Good. And if anything goes wrong?"

"We meet back at the hotel. If one of us isn't there by seven, the other one goes."

Brian nodded. "Don't wait for me," he said. "I won't wait for you."

He put his hand on my back, touching the butt of my Beretta through the canvas jacket. "You're okay," he said, as if reassuring himself of this fact.

"I'll see you at the church," I told him, my eyes steady on his, my hand on the pen drive in my pocket. Then I turned away and started down the rue St.-Jacques toward the Ile de la Cité and Notre Dame.

• • •

City of Tourists. That's what Sister Theresa called Paris, her distaste for the crassness of the visitors apparent. She'd grown up rich here, a daughter of privilege, Heloise had told me one night over a mound of brioche dough, obviously not meaning to flatter. I'd been taken aback by the revelation, surprised by the deep-rooted sense of class in a place I'd naively assumed to be above such distinctions.

Theresa had been the last of the sisters to warm to me. Even after I'd gained her trust, she'd had a particular way of correcting me, of pointing out the flaws in my French, the imperfections in my cooking. You see, she'd say, biting into one of Heloise's éclairs, this is the real *pâte à choux*. As if the fate of the republic rested on my inability to make the perfect pastry.

As I made my way toward the imposing spires of Notre Dame, I was reminded of Theresa's prejudice. The island was clogged with sightseers, many of them obvious Americans, harried families running from one great European monument to another, guidebooks and digital cameras in hand. I could understand the nun's snobbery. Yes, there was a coarseness to these people, an arrogance borne of unchallenged comfort. What I still couldn't see was my place among them.

And yet, Theresa had seen it. So had Mohammed, my little friend from the train tracks. American, he'd insisted, when I'd tried to say otherwise. And so I was, though surely in no way these compatriots on the Ile de la Cité would recognize. There was something besides the clothes, the T-shirts and athletic shoes, besides the blank and bewildered faces staring up toward Notre Dame's exquisite facade. There was something other than loyalty even. *The real pâte à choux,* I heard Theresa say, her tongue clicking accusatorily. Later, after everyone had gone to bed, I'd sneak down into the kitchen and taste mine against Heloise's, trying in vain to tell the difference.

I made the loop Brian and I had discussed so many times, crossing the Pont au Double, then walking west along the river before heading down the rue Viviani toward St.-Julien-le-Pauvre. I got my first glimpse of the tearoom, a tiny establishment tucked into the first floor of a medieval town house, before turning through the iron gate into St.-Julien's churchyard.

The church's door was closed, but it swung open easily, ancient hinges groaning in protest. I stepped inside and stood for a moment in the warm foyer, letting my eyes adjust to the absence of sunlight, taking in the little stone chapel. Not Catholic, I thought, noticing the ornate icons on the altar. No, whatever its origins, St.-Julien-le-Pauvre now belonged to the Greek Orthodox order.

Unlike its flashy cousin across the river, the unassuming St.-Julien drew few visitors. There were just a handful of us today, a young Italian couple studiously surveying the twelfth-century architecture, a stooped old woman in widow's black saying her rosary. And in the second row back, on the left side of the aisle, a solitary man with his head bowed in prayer. Brian.

I checked my watch, making sure we were on schedule, then slid into the row in front of him. He leaned forward onto his kneeler and put his hands on the back of my pew.

"It's hard to tell," he said, "but I don't think there's anyone else waiting for your meeting. It should just be you and your mystery date."

I looked up at the lurid crucifix, the gilt images of the saints.

"There's a back way out, but it's a tight alley, with just one exit. I wouldn't use it unless I had to."

Nodding almost imperceptibly, I leaned forward and crossed myself once, fingers moving from head to gut to shoulders as they'd done so many times at the abbey. Then I slipped from the pew and started for the back of the church.

There was something unnervingly quaint about the little low-ceilinged tearoom, something ominous about the white-aproned serving girls, the tiny sandwiches, and the thick slices of gingerbread with delicate dollops of cream. Close as we were to Notre Dame, I'd expected a mob of tourists and the bad food that inevitably accompanied them, but it was obvious at first glance that the establishment catered to locals.

Most of the customers were old Parisian ladies, archaic creatures in hats and smart wool suits, but there were three male patrons as well. The first, a grandfatherly type with salt-and-pepper hair and a neat mustache, sat alone near the back of the room, deeply engrossed in a copy of *Le Figaro* and a slice of fruit tart. The second, a rumpled bureaucrat in his late fifties, sat closer to the door, an untidily folded copy of *Le Monde* on the table in front of him, his brown wool overcoat occupying the opposite seat. The third man was even younger, a university student, I figured, sharing a weekly tea with his grandmother. Either that or he was a gigolo, catering to the over-eighty set.

None of the three seemed a likely match for my enigmatic contact. Certainly not one of them had taken even the slightest note of my arrival. I scanned the room one last time, searching for something I might have missed, then took the last free table. It was exactly four o'clock by my watch. One of the waitresses came over, and I ordered a pot of Darjeeling, just as Helen had told me to do.

The tea came, hot and smoky, and I poured myself a cup, dousing it liberally with cream, checking my watch again. It was a quarter after now, and still no sign of whoever it was I was supposed to meet. Of course the message had gone up late, I told myself. I could always try again tomorrow.

Then, out of the corner of my eye I saw the *Le Monde* reader get up from his chair and shrug into his coat. Reaching into his pocket, he fished out a euro note and some change and laid the money on the table. He was just a few feet from me, and when he moved I thought at first that he was heading for the door, but he stepped toward me instead, his heavy coat brushing clumsily against the narrowly spaced tables.

"Katy?" he asked, stopping just in front of me.

I set my tea down and looked up into his face. "Uncle Bill. You got my message."

He nodded, his eyes nervously taking me in, his hands gripping the old newspaper.

I motioned to the chair opposite mine. "Sit down."

He shook his head, then smiled unconvincingly. "We should go," he said. Fumbling in his pocket with his inky fingers, he pulled out money for my tea.

Something was wrong, I thought, glancing out the tearoom's front window toward St.-Julien's gray facade. My gut told me so, and so did the man's hands, the way they shook when he laid the coins on the table.

"We should go," he said again.

I nodded and started to get up.

Beyond the man's elbow I saw the young student rise as well. He reached into his jacket as he came up, his body pivoting toward us, the nickel nose of an automatic sliding out from beneath his coat.

"Get down!" I yelled, diving for the floor, but my voice was drowned out by the crack of the first bullet.

The man in the brown overcoat spun around, his paper dropping to the floor, his head suddenly knocked backward as if by an unseen hand, a dark rose of blood staining the skin behind his ear. He fell sideways, taking one of the tea tables with him, hitting the floor in front of me in a hail of bullets and broken china.

The granny was up, too, her prim suit open to reveal a shoulder holster and, beneath her shirt, two firm young breasts that put her age closer to twenty than eighty.

I crawled backward, reaching for my Beretta as I went, taking advantage of the few seconds of chaos that followed the opening round of fire to find shelter beneath one of the tables. The rest of the patrons were on the floor, too, a jumbled mass of floss-white hair, lavender water, and fear. Toward the back of the room someone was crying, but everyone else was dead silent.

I took a breath and surveyed my options. My back was to the wall, literally. The first shooter, the man, stood directly between me and the front door. My best bet was the alley exit, but it was ten meters at least, across a minefield of upturned tables and huddled figures. I wouldn't make it without help. I turned and glanced toward the front window again, praying Brian had heard the shots, hoping my choice to trust him this time hadn't been a fatal one.

The fake granny took a step forward, her pumps crushing broken glass. One of the old ladies beneath the table next to mine lifted her head and blinked up at me. There was a smear of blood on her powdered cheek, a piece of clear glass, part of a bud vase, lodged in her skin. She put her index finger to her eye, then motioned to something behind me.

I followed her direction, my eyes moving once more to the front window. A shadow ducked beneath the frame, a head slipping from view. Brian, I thought, though I couldn't be sure. When I looked back, the old woman nodded at me, and I nodded back. Yes, I'd seen it too. I smiled reassuringly, then mouthed the word *Down* in French. The woman lowered her head, laying her uninjured cheek against the floor.

Moving carefully, I dodged out from my cover, sighting for the woman with the gun, squeezing two rounds off. The first bullet went wide, but the second found her left shoulder. She flinched and spun sideways, her gun hand flying to her wound. Her partner fired in my direction, his rounds splintering the flimsy tabletop. Then both he and the woman hit the ground.

Someone else was firing now. I looked over to see the front window shatter and Brian's face appear above the frame.

"Go!" he shouted, clearing what was left of the tattered pane with the barrel of his Browning.

I moved in a tight crouch, navigating my way from table to table, heading toward the back of the establishment while Brian occupied the two shooters in the front.

I wouldn't use it unless I had to, I heard Brian say as I neared the alley door. Suddenly, *had to* had become an unfortunate reality. I glanced back one last time, and Brian waved me on with his gun. "Now!" he yelled, firing once more, then slipping from my view.

I rose up and hit the door with my shoulder, stumbling blindly out into the alley, slamming into the stone wall of the opposite building. The little passageway was barely the width of a footpath, not even a meter across, too narrow for me to outstretch my arms. It smelled of centuries of waste, both human and animal, and a perpetual lack of daylight. White scum streaked the walls.

Keeping a tight grip on the Beretta, I edged forward. Out the alley's mouth I could see one of the quarter's cramped side streets and a steady stream of foot traffic passing by. Somewhere in the distance a police siren let out its frantic wail, the noise growing louder and closer with each passing second.

I reached the street and slid the gun back into my jeans, hesitating a moment to get my bearings. There was no going back for Brian. He wouldn't have done it for me, I told myself, merging into the crowd, heading west toward the Place St.-Michel. Besides, if anyone could take care of himself, Brian could. He'd be waiting for me in the metro. If not there, then back at the Hotel de l'Espérance. He'd be fine.

There was no sign of Brian on the crowded platform at the St.-Michel metro stop. I took the Porte d'Orléans line south to Montparnasse, then walked the rest of the way to the hotel. It was five-thirty when I got back to our room, and still Brian was nowhere to be found. We'd asked the maid not to come in, and it looked as if she'd heeded our request. The bed was unmade, the dirt streaks from her last visit untouched. Still, I made a quick check of my leather bag, reassuring myself the passports were still there. Satisfied, I sat down by the window to watch the street below.

The half dozen sex shops on the rue de la Gaîté did a booming afternoon business. The clientele was mostly male, white-collar commuters and manual laborers making a quick post-work stop, but there was the occasional single woman as well, the ubiquitous gaunt-faced urbanite in torturously high heels and a grim gray suit. The shop directly across from the hotel, a tiny storefront through whose open door blared the disco whine of Rai music, seemed the most popular of the establishments. A steady stream of customers filtered in and out, no doubt lured by the neat row of leather restraints that hung in the front window, the flaccid forms like roasted ducks in a Chinese butcher shop.

I watched the parade of neon-lit faces for a good hour. By six-thirty I was starting to worry. *If one of us isn't there by seven, the other one goes.* We'd agreed to it a dozen times, and yet it hadn't occurred to me that it might happen. I glanced at the SEAT keys on the bedside table, our meager possessions, my bag and Brian's pack. *I won't wait for you,* Brian had told me, and yet, if I left now, there was nowhere for me to go.

I went into the bathroom and splashed cold water on my face, then lay down on the bed's dusty coverlet, tracing the cracks in the plaster ceiling. My watch clicked past six-forty-five, then six-fifty. I should get ready, I told myself, but I couldn't bring myself to move. Six-fifty-five, and like a miracle, a key rattled in the lock.

TWENTY-SIX

"I took the train out to Bobigny," Brian explained. "I wanted to make sure no one followed me back here." He sat down on the bed and shrugged off his jacket. The right shoulder of his shirt was stiff with dried blood, the fabric plastered to his skin. "It's just a scratch," he said, fumbling with his shirt.

"It looks like more than a scratch to me," I told him, pushing his hands aside, pulling his head and unhurt arm free of the shirt. The fabric around the wound was glued to his arm. "Don't move," I said. "I'm going to have to soak that off."

There were no washcloths in the bathroom, but I found a clean hand towel and ran it under the hot tap.

"Was it a bullet or glass?" I asked, laying the warm towel on his shoulder.

"A bullet," he said, wincing at the pressure of the cloth. "But it's just a flesh wound."

"Still," I told him, "you should have it looked at."

He shook his head. "There are some antibiotics in my pack. I'll be fine."

"Do you have a pocketknife?"

He nodded. "In the pack, front pocket."

I retrieved the knife and the antibiotics, then peeled the towel back and cut the arm of his shirt away. He was right; it was just a flesh wound, but a bad one, deep enough that it should have gotten a couple of stitches. The skin around it was pink and puckered, flushed with the first hints of infection.

"You need antiseptic and bandages," I said, folding the towel, laying the still-clean side of it back on his shoulder. "I'm going to find a pharmacy."

There was a night-duty pharmacy not far from the hotel, and I found it easily, following the desk clerk's directions. On the way back to the room I stopped at an *épicerie* and bought some rudimentary dinner supplies: cheese, ham, a loaf of bread, a bag of oranges, some bottled water, and a couple of bottles of Kronenbourg.

Brian had showered and changed into a clean T-shirt by the time I got back. I doctored his cut as best as I could, swabbing it with iodine and antibacterial ointment, then covering it with clean gauze. He'd have a nasty scar, that much was certain, but other than that he'd be fine.

When I was done, I cracked the two beers and spread the preparations for our cold meal on the room's battered little table.

"Thanks," Brian said, tearing off a chunk of bread, then cutting a thick wedge from the small round of Camembert I'd selected.

I took a pull off my Kronenbourg. "It was my job at the abbey," I said, "making sure everyone ate."

"You cooked for the nuns?" Brian asked, washing the bread down with a swig of beer.

I nodded. "There were two of us who did all the kitchen work."

"Do you miss it?"

"Yes." I thought about the question for a moment, the inadequacy of language. To say merely that I missed the sisters and the abbey was such a gross understatement that it verged on sin. It was not just the only home I had ever known but the grounding on which my entire being was built.

"And your life before?"

I took an orange from the bag and pierced the skin with my thumb. "You mean, do I miss it?"

Brian nodded.

"There's nothing there to miss," I said, stripping the peel away, separating the sections.

"But you said there's a child. You must think about the child."

"Sometimes."

"There's nothing you remember? Nothing at all?"

I shook my head, but it was a lie. In truth there were pictures, flashes so brief and fragmentary I had never let myself trust them. And there were things I was sure of, too, sensations of touch and smell that were too visceral to be anything but real.

"What about you?" I asked, putting a section of the orange in my mouth. "You must miss your family."

Brian shrugged. "I go back every few years. There's less and less to miss. My parents were older when they had me. My dad's got Alzheimer's, and my mom's so worn down from taking care of him she's crazy in her own way."

"I'm sorry."

"Don't be. This is the life I signed on for."

"Do you ever regret it?"

He took a sip of his beer. "All the time. But I've never been able to see myself doing anything else, either."

"I guess I've sort of screwed things up for you."

"I've got some money put away."

"What will you do?"

"I don't know. Disappear. There's a little island off Tortola with a wreck of a bar I've always wanted to buy. But first we need to straighten this mess out, don't we?"

I nodded. "Who do you think they were, the couple at the tearoom?"

"Associates of my former employer, I suppose. Contract hires, like me."

"Do you know anyone at the NSA, anyone we might go to with the pen drive?"

Brian shook his head. "I've got a few contacts in Central Intelligence here, but I wouldn't trust any of them right now. Like I said, I think this runs deeper than just one person."

I cut myself a piece of bread and took some of the ham. I was hungrier than I'd thought, and the Kronenbourg was starting to go to my head. "What about Werner?" I asked. "Can you get in touch with him?"

Brian looked at me incredulously.

"He's the only person I'm sure knows who our mystery man on the tape is. And he knew my mother. There was a photograph in his office, a picture of the three of them together."

"In Pakistan?"

"Vietnam. I'd seen it before, only I couldn't remember where, another copy. My mother must have had one."

"He would have killed you, Eve," Brian reminded me.

"He wants what's on the pen drive. Maybe we can make a deal. A copy of the tape for whatever he knows."

"This is crazy," Brian said.

"If you have a better idea, I'm all ears."

We ate in silence for a while, each of us mulling our own thoughts. I knew my plan was sketchy, but it seemed like the best option. I wanted my life back, and from what I could tell, Werner had a big chunk of it to give.

Finally, Brian drained the last of his beer and set the empty bottle on the table. "I've got a friend," he said, the reluctance audible in his voice. "In Bratislava. A pilot. He flies for Werner sometimes. He owes me a favor or two."

"Thank you," I told him.

Brian shook his head. "Don't thank me yet."

We left early the next morning and drove east, through Strasbourg and Munich and on toward Salzburg and Vienna. It was close to midnight when we crossed the border into Slovakia, heading past the dark remnants of the iron curtain toward the Danube and Bratislava. We hadn't bothered with papers when we'd taken the old SEAT, and it took some slick talking on Brian's part and a one-hundred-euro note to convince the border guard that the car wasn't stolen. It was snowing when he finally waved us through, fat wet flakes settling like dander on the guard's dark wool coat.

We could see the space-age turret of the Novy Most long before we reached the city, the Soviet-era bridge hovering over the Danube, shadowing the old city's quaint buildings like an invading spacecraft. On the hilltop beyond, its dour stone facade washed in light, its towers looking imperiously down on the town, sat the old Bratislava castle.

"What time is it?" Brian asked as we motored through a vast stretch of socialist suburbs on the southern side of the Danube.

"Almost one," I said, watching the endless high-rises

glide by. It was a grim utopia, the monolithic buildings no one's idea of inviting. Here was a place built to contain, designed for easy eavesdropping and the systematic dampening of resistance. And here, once more, was a place I knew.

"I've been here," I said.

Brian glanced over at me. "Do you remember something?"

"No. It's just a feeling. A long time ago, I think. Before the end of the cold war." I'd felt it at the border, too, a visceral reaction, a dark memory of barbed wire and Kalashnikovs, of serious young men in Soviet uniforms who'd slid mirrors under the car.

Hannah Boyle had been here as well. According to Helen, she'd died here, too. And for some reason I'd chosen her name to use as my own.

We started onto the bridge and over the river. It was snowing hard now, veiling the black water of the Danube in a lacy curtain, obscuring the waterfront and the old city beyond.

"Should we find a place to spend the night?" I asked.

"I thought we could try and hook up with Ivan," Brian said. "It's about time for him to be up and about."

Our first stop was a jazz bar in the Old City, a cramped, smoky little place around the corner from the Primatial Palace. The crowd was young and hip, pale thin boys in black jeans and leather jackets and tough-looking college girls cultivating the physical style of longtime heroin addicts.

When Brian asked at the bar for Ivan, the bartender's face turned sour. "That cocksucking Russian hasn't shown his face here for a couple of weeks," he spat in contemptuous English. "But if you see him, tell him I'd like the twenty-five hundred koruna he owes me."

"Any suggestions on where we might find him?" Brian asked. "Just in case we wanted to pass your message along."

The bartender poured out the two martinis he'd been mixing, then barked something in Slovak to a hostile-looking cocktail waitress in a black minidress and knee-high boots.

She set her tray on the bar and lit a cigarette, giving Brian the once-over, her eyes flicking briefly and dismissively in my direction. "Lately he's been hanging out at Charlie's Pub," she said. "Over on Spitalska. You know it?"

Brian nodded.

The waitress took a long drag off her cigarette, then let the smoke filter slowly out through her nostrils. "Will you give him a message from me, too?" she asked. "Tell him Yana says to go fuck himself."

"Your friend Ivan's a popular guy," I said as we made our way back to the SEAT.

"I never promised Mr. Congeniality," Brian countered. "Besides, he's not all that bad. People don't like Russians here."

"He does seem to have a way with the ladies."

"You picked up on that, huh?"

"Speaking of ladies, I think that waitress had the hots for you."

Brian smiled. "She's not really my type. I'm more a marked-for-death amnesiac kind of guy."

"Thanks," I said. "But seriously, how do you know this Ivan character?"

"I hitched a ride out of Khartoum with him a few years ago. We had to lay over for twelve hours at Lake Victoria waiting for a load of frozen tilapia. He and I just kind of hit it off."

"And what were you doing in Khartoum?" I asked as we reached the Seat and stopped walking.

Brian put his hand on the car's roof, suddenly serious. "You really want to know?"

"Yes," I told him.

"I was escorting a shipment of small arms to the SPLA," he said grimly. Then he unlocked the SEAT's door and slid into the driver's seat.

I slipped in beside him and tugged my door closed. Brian started the engine, pulling away from the curb.

"Did you really believe it?" I asked, as we rattled down the narrow, cobbled streets. "I mean God and country and all that. Weren't there times when you didn't know?"

A cluster of snow-dusted bar hoppers stumbled into the street in front of us, and Brian braked to a stop. We watched in silence as they crossed our headlights, arms linked for warmth and balance, breath rising in one great cloud, like steam from some giant engine.

"Are you asking about me?" Brian said finally. "Because I can't tell you how you felt, whether you knew or not." The last of the group raised a mittened hand and waved his thanks to us, then stepped up onto the sidewalk and out of our lights.

"That wasn't fair," I said.

Brian sighed. "I've never pretended our system is perfect, but it's the best I've ever seen." He shifted the Seat into gear and eased forward on the slick cobbles, then gestured to the world beyond the car windows, the snowy streets and dark Hapsburg buildings. "The alternative didn't work out too well here."

"No," I agreed, though I wasn't sure the failure of the Soviet system was a justification for greed. Such logic seemed cynical at best. "Were you here?" I asked. "During the cold war."

Brian shook his head. "That was before my time. I watched the Berlin Wall come down on a TV in the base canteen."

I'd seen news footage of the fall of the Berlin Wall, the crowds at the Brandenburg gate. Several of the sisters at the convent had been old enough to remember when the city had been divided, and had talked of brothers and sisters separated from each other.

"My family in the Czech Republic lost everything after the war," Brian said as we pulled to a stop across from a brightly lit building fronted by four movie marquees. "That's when my grandparents came to the U.S., after the Communist coup in nineteen forty-eight. My father was still a boy." He cut the engine and looked over at me. "Here we are."

I could see why the notorious Ivan had chosen Charlie's as his home base. The clientele here was far less sophisticated than at the little jazz bar, and conveniently more transient. A good portion of the women were obvious non-locals, Americans and Brits searching for something off the well-beaten Prague and Budapest path. Ivan could piss people off here to his heart's delight, secure in the knowledge they'd be gone in a week or two, and that someone just as willing would take their place.

The large club was a model for sensory overload, crammed with big-screen televisions, pulsating with loud pop music. There was no dance floor, so people gyrated among the tables, lit cigarettes waving dangerously about. I followed Brian to the bar and waited while he flagged down one of the bartenders, a suspiciously tan woman in a halter top and hip-hugger jeans.

It was too loud for me to hear their exchange, but the woman said something to Brian, the now-familiar look of disgust on her face telling me we'd most likely found our man. Sneering, she pointed toward a table in the far corner of the bar where a wiry man with slicked-back hair and a long leather coat was drinking with two blondes.

"There's our man," Brian said, starting toward the threesome.

Whatever favors Ivan owed Brian must have been far less odious than his debt to the bartender at the jazz bar. The Russian spotted us well before we'd reached the table, and stood up with his arms out in a ready embrace, seeming genuinely pleased by the interruption. After clamping Brian in a bear hug, he turned to the two blondes and dismissed them, then motioned for us to sit.

"Son of a bitch." Ivan grinned, punching Brian jovially on the shoulder. His accent was pure Russian, almost a caricature of itself, the *i* in *bitch* long and hard so that the word came out sounding more like *beach*. "What the fuck are you doing in this shithole?"

"We just drove in," Brian said, then motioned to me. "This is my friend Eve. Eve, meet Ivan."

Ivan looked me over, then flashed Brian a look of collusion. "This cocksucker saved my life," the Russian bellowed, hooking his arm across Brian's shoulders, leaning close enough to me that I could smell the liquor on his breath. "Did he tell you that?"

I shook my head and glanced at Brian.

"It's a long story," he said.

Ivan downed the remaining contents of his glass. "You

here on business or pleasure?" he asked, scanning the crowd.

"We need a favor," Brian told him, shouting to be heard above the music.

Ivan caught sight of a cocktail waitress and waved to her, holding up three fingers, making a circular motion around the table. The woman nodded and started for the bar.

"A favor?" Ivan said, raising his eyebrows, pulling a pack of Marlboros from his coat.

"You still flying for Bruns Werner?" Brian asked.

"Sometimes, yeah."

"We need you to arrange a meeting with him."

Ivan laughed. "Go fuck yourself, man."

"I'm serious," Brian told him.

The waitress appeared and set three shotglasses on the table. Ivan paid her, then waved her off. "Drink!" he exhorted us, picking up his glass and draining it with a quick tilt of the head.

"What is it?" I asked Brian, sniffing at the clear liquid.

"Slivovitz," he said. "Plum brandy. Nasty stuff."

I took another sniff and drank most of the shot. It was rough and potent, like the brandy the Tanes made from what was left of the wine pressings each fall.

"Look," Ivan said. "Werner's a good client. I can't afford to screw things up with him."

"He'll want to see us," Brian assured him.

Ivan was skeptical. "The two of you?"

"Yeah."

The Russian lit a cigarette and leaned forward in his chair. "You're not going to tell me what this is about, are you?"

Brian shook his head.

"Motherfucker," Ivan said, looking far too serious before his mouth split into a wide smile. He leaned over and put his meaty hand on Brian's shoulder. "I just can't say no to this man," he said to me. Then he looked up and waved to the waitress, signaling for another round.

It was almost four when we left Charlie's and stumbled the few blocks to Ivan's apartment, stopping at the SEAT to pick up our bags. Ivan's place was an old Soviet-era flat, boxy and plain, the two rooms and small kitchen no doubt built to house a family of four. But it was roomy enough for Ivan and his collections of bad pornographic art and electric guitars.

Ivan insisted on a nightcap before leaving us to the fold-out couch in the living room. It was after five before we could coax him into calling it a night. He seemed deeply disappointed by our lack of stamina, saddened by our frailty. After we'd settled into bed, we heard him slip out the front door. He returned sometime near dawn, but not alone. Half asleep, I heard the front door click open and the sound of hushed female laughter.

Whoever she was, she was gone when Brian and I woke late the next morning to the sound of singing, the smell of frying eggs, and the unsightly spectacle of Ivan's hairy body and scrawny legs clothed only in some old blue slippers and a pair of leopard-print bikini underwear.

The Russian finished the last chorus of "Material Girl," then turned to us, spatula in one hand, cigarette in the other, like the fry cook in some bad pornographic movie.

"Good morning, my sleepyheads," he said jovially.

TWENTY-SEVEN

I've said that some new memories are to be savored, and it's true that certain sensations, felt again for the first time, are like unexpected gifts. It's also true that there are some experiences we all wish we could forget. The feeling of waking up in Ivan's living room, my throat dry, my gut churning, my head reeling from my first hangover, was one of those experiences.

"Why do people do this to themselves?" I asked Brian as we stumbled toward the kitchen table, drawn forward by the smell of strong coffee.

He laughed weakly. "It's a kind of amnesia, I guess. You tend to forget just how bad it was."

"You guys look like shit." Ivan grinned, setting two mugs of coffee on the table, pouring a water glass of vodka for himself. "You want?" he asked, offering the bottle to us.

I shook my head, stomach reeling at the smell.

Ivan laughed, then turned back to the stove. Anchoring his cigarette in the corner of his mouth, he opened one of the kitchen cabinets, pulled out three large plates, and piled a generous helping of eggs, potatoes, and sausage onto each one.

"Good news," he said as he set the plates on the table in front of us, then slid into a free chair. "I called Werner this morning. Whatever this is about, it must be important because I thought he was going to piss himself when I told him you two wanted to meet." He stubbed his cigarette out, then laid a napkin across his bare legs. He had a tattoo on the right side of his chest, a faded dragon and a woman in chains. Just beneath the woman's feet was a large, starburst-shaped scar.

"He agreed?" Brian asked.

I lifted a forkful of potatoes to my mouth. It felt good to get something in my stomach.

"He's flying up to Vienna this afternoon," Ivan said. "I wasn't sure how you wanted to work this, so I told him I'd call him back to arrange the details."

"Thanks," Brian said. "When you talk to him, tell him he can meet us at nine tomorrow morning at the war memorial on Slavin Hill. Tell him we've got what he wants and we're willing to bargain."

Ivan nodded, then touched his scar, the movement unconscious, automatic.

"And tell him to leave his goons at home," Brian added.

"How long have you been in Bratislava?" I asked Ivan when we'd finished eating and Brian had gone to take a shower.

The food, combined with three cups of coffee, a liter of water, and some aspirin had given me half my brain back, and I was starting to think about Hannah Boyle, wondering if she'd been like those expatriate girls at Charlie's Pub or the woman I'd heard whispering at Ivan's the night before.

"Since 'ninety," he said.

"I had a friend," I told him, "an American girl. I was wondering if you knew her. Her name was Hannah. Hannah Boyle."

Ivan thought for a minute, then shrugged. "There have been one or two Hannahs, but your friend, I don't know."

"She died. In a car accident. It was a long time ago. Ten years at least."

"Sorry," Ivan offered.

"Brian says you know a lot of people here," I said, choosing my words carefully.

Ivan's pectoral muscle flexed, and the dragon moved its tail. "It's my business to know people," he said.

"She was a good friend of mine, you see, and I've never been able to find out what exactly happened. Surely there's a record of the accident. With the police, maybe."

"Maybe."

"We have the afternoon," I said. "Is there somewhere I could go, someone you think I should ask?"

Ivan narrowed his eyes at me, his look saying he knew I was bullshitting, and that he wanted me to know it, but he would do this for me anyway.

"There are some people," he said. "I will make a few calls."

After Brian got out of the shower, he and I left Ivan and walked over to the Tesco department store. The clothes Brian had bought off the Spaniard for me were well past road-weary, reeking now of sweat, cigarettes, and plum brandy, and I was desperate for some clean essentials.

"I asked Ivan to do some snooping around for me," I said as we crossed the tramway and headed for the giant store.

"Snooping about what?" Brian asked.

"Hannah Boyle," I told him. "I've been here. I can feel it. And according to Helen, this is where Hannah died. If I can find someone who knew her..." I shook my head at the absurdity of it. "I don't know, but there's a reason why I chose that name in Tangier."

"If there's anything to know," Brian said as we merged with the crowds and pushed our way through one of Tesco's front doors, "I'm sure Ivan will find it."

Needless to say, living at the convent had taught me little about fashion. What clothes I'd always had, mostly hand-me-downs, were picked for practicality, for warmth in the winter, function, and ease of care. Not so with the racks upon racks of leather miniskirts and spangled blouses in the Tesco ladies' department. If I'd been alone, I might have given up and gone back to Ivan's empty-handed.

I stood there for a moment, paralyzed by the selection, before Brian took over, navigating me toward a rack of blue jeans. An hour later we emerged victorious onto Spitalska Street, our bags stuffed with two pairs of jeans, some plain knit shirts, a sweater, several changes of underwear, socks, black boots, and a dark wool pea coat.

Ivan was waiting anxiously for us when we got back to the apartment. He'd changed from his bikini and slippers into black jeans, a black sweater, and a pair of shiny black cowboy boots.

"I found your friend," he said when we walked through the door.

"Already?" I asked dumbly, setting my Tesco bag down.

"Well, not her exactly, but the police report. I've got a friend who works in the municipal archives." Ivan beamed at his success. "She wants us to meet her in an hour," he said, glancing at his watch. He looked from me to Brian and back again, then cleared his throat. "I should bring her a gift, perhaps. For her troubles."

Taking the hint, I crossed to where I'd set my leather bag and pulled out a fifty-euro note. There was, I was starting to think, nothing one couldn't buy.

Ivan glanced at the note, then shook his head. "Inflation," he explained sadly, while I produced a second bill.

I'd thought the one hundred euros would be more than sufficient, but on the way to the archives Ivan insisted we stop at a perfume store in Kamenne Square for a bottle of knockoff Chanel.

"So as not to be tacky," he explained, slipping the euros inside the black-and-white box. "She's a classy lady, my friend."

At first glance, the Bratislava municipal archives seemed a model of modern record keeping, a civic office like any other, sustained by all the comforts of technology, computers and fax machines and multi-line telephones. It was only after we'd met Ivan's friend, Michala, and descended into the building's bowels that the true nature of the archives was revealed. Down underground stretched the vast vaults of the pre-computerized era, room after room of metal shelves buckling under the weight of boxes and files, a dusty monument to the beast of Soviet bureaucracy and the sheer amounts of paper required to feed it.

Ivan may have been a cad with bartenders and waitresses, but he obviously knew when a relationship was too valuable not to coddle. Whether it was flattery or sincerity, I couldn't be sure, but he treated our hostess with a charm and tact I'd yet to see him exhibit.

I wasn't sure *classy lady* was a term I would have used

to describe Michala. Like many aging civil servants, eager to proclaim their individuality, she dressed with a gusto that veered toward bad taste. Her cantilevered breasts were squeezed into a bright pink sweater, her thighs sheathed in black leather. Here was a woman who was no stranger to the racks at Tesco.

Brian and I followed behind as Michala and Ivan led the way through the dimly lit passageways, Michala's heavy key ring jangling like a tambourine as it knocked against her wide hips, her singsong Slovak echoing through the empty halls. Finally, she stopped in front of a blank door and began sorting through her keys.

"The files do not leave," she announced in English as she slipped the correct key into the lock and put her hand on the doorknob. "Understood?"

"Of course." I nodded.

She looked at Brian as if for emphasis, then pushed the door open and pressed the light switch, illuminating several rows of shelves.

"Police reports," she explained as we entered the room. "From post-revolution until the divorce." Then, noticing my confusion, she added, as if to a small child, "From the fall of the Communist system until our split from the Czech Republic."

She started forward, her heels tap-tapping at the concrete. "This way, please."

We followed her about halfway down a row of shelves, then watched while she reached deftly up and pulled out a thin file folder. "Hannah Boyle," she said, the name strangely Slavic in her mouth.

"Thank you," I said, opening the folder and scanning the report's unintelligible writing. In several places sections of text had been blacked out with a dark ink pen.

There was a photograph paper-clipped to the first page, a picture of a crumpled white Peugeot. The car had been hit in such a way that the driver's side was completely obliterated, the engine thrust back against the steering wheel, the dash shoved back into the seat. The passenger's side, however, had been spared the full force of the trauma. The door was open slightly, as if someone had gotten out and neglected to close it. On the back windshield was an oval sticker identifying the car's home country as Austria.

The picture had been taken at night, and the background, outside the glare of the flash, was pitch-black, as if the world consisted entirely of the car and the thin border of glass-spangled asphalt, and nothing else, but I was aware of each object in that dark beyond as clearly and fully as if I were standing there. To the right, outside the frame, was the truck that had hit us, its bumper dented only slightly, its headlight smashed and broken, a tiny figure of St. Christopher on the dash. To the left was the ambulance, the emergency workers smoking cigarettes while Hannah's body lay lifeless inside.

It was a cold night, the air crisp with the smell of coming snow. Cars whipped by on the roadway behind us, some slowing to rubberneck, some too preoccupied with the upcoming border crossing to care. The broken glass crunched under the soles of my shoes. I shuddered at the crispness of the memory.

"Ouch!" Ivan said, glancing at the photo over my shoulder, his voice wrenching me back to the dusty basement room.

"Can you tell me what it says?" I asked Michala, offering her the file.

She opened the pair of gold reading glasses that hung from a chain around her neck and slipped them on, then took the folder.

"December twenty-one, nineteen eighty-nine," she read, her finger sweeping across the text as she went. "Head-on collision on the Bratislava-to-Vienna road. It says here the driver of the lorry was drinking. The driver of the Peugeot, Hannah Boyle, an American, was killed at the scene."

She hit one of the blacked-out passages and stopped, knitting her eyebrows together as if puzzling through a complex problem.

"What is it?" I asked.

"I don't know." She shrugged. "A mistake, perhaps." She skipped over the black ink and flipped forward, reading silently. "The rest is technical," she explained. "Speed, force of impact..."

"And the parts that have been crossed out?" I wondered. The neat obliteration of the words seemed far too deliberate for the correction of an error, unless the error had been putting the information in the report in the first place. I suddenly wished I could read Slovak.

Michala shook her head. "I can't tell. I'm sorry, I really don't know." She seemed genuine in her apology, aware that the information she was providing was less than complete, and I believed her. "Now, this is funny."

"What?"

She motioned toward the signature on the last page, the name typed neatly underneath it. "Stanislav Divin," she said, "the detective who signed off on this. You see these letters by his last name?"

I nodded.

"It's not appropriate," Michala said, with the confused indignation of someone used to extreme order. "It's not normal for him to investigate an accident like this."

"Why is that?" I asked.

She put a laquered fingernail to the man's name. "This is simply not his department. He's a narcotics detective."

Stanislav Divin. I read the name to myself, then read it

and reread it again, committing the spelling to memory. If I couldn't take the file, I told myself, I'd at least take this.

"Divin." Ivan mulled the name as we made our way out the front door of the archives building.

"Do you know him?" I asked, reaching up to shade my eyes. Even thinned as it was by winter's smog, the sunlight seemed unbearably bright after our time underground.

Ivan shook his head. "He must be retired."

"Can you ask around?" Brian said.

Ivan took a long pull off his cigarette, exhaling loudly. "Sometimes, man," he growled, glancing at his friend, "I wish you hadn't saved my life." Then he reached into the pocket of his leather coat and pulled out his cell phone.

Whoever Ivan was trying to reach had evidently gone home for the day, but the Russian assured us he'd left a message and that we'd hear something the next morning. It was late when we got back to the apartment. I got cleaned up and changed into my new clothes; then we went out for an early dinner at a place called Montana's Grizzly Bar, an American burger-and-steak house bizarrely situated in the medieval tangle of streets that lay in the eastern shadow of the castle.

"Montana!" Ivan remarked as the waitress delivered our food. He waved his fork at the campy decor, the mangy stuffed animal heads and American beer signs, then looked at me. "What part of America are you from?"

"I don't know," I said.

Ivan stopped for a moment, his fork plunged into his bloody T-bone, his knife in midair. "What the fuck?" he started to say, but then he looked at Brian and whatever glance they exchanged said to leave it at that.

We left Ivan at the bar after dinner, our early departure softened by the arrival of three British flight attendants, and walked back to the apartment.

"We meet Werner in the morning," Brian reminded me as we crossed Hlavne Square, our feet marking the dusting of fresh snow that had fallen while we were in the restaurant. The burghers' houses that ringed the square were tucked in for the night, eaves edged in icicles, windows aglow. "Do you know what you're going to say?"

I shook my head and took a breath of the cold, dry air.

Brian turned his face toward me. "We need a plan," he said. "We'll make a plan."

"Yes," I told him, but in truth I wasn't thinking about Werner or the meeting. Instead, I was thinking about Hannah Boyle's white Peugeot, about the way the car's passenger door had been slightly ajar, and the long black ink stains on the police report. I was close to something, I could feel it, close to the place where all this had begun.

TWENTY-EIGHT

It had snowed heavily overnight, and from the top of Slavin Hill the Old City looked quaint as a miniature Christmas village, its baroque spires and Gothic rooftops cloaked in cottony white. The sun was shining, the sky crisp and blue, the golden crown atop the steeple of St. Martin's cathedral glistening in the morning light. A tram ran along the river, then turned inland, stopping to unload a cargo of tiny figures before continuing on. Above it all, the castle sat gray and silent, watching the Danube and the plains beyond for the next invading force, as it had for some six hundred years. Only the hypermodern bridge, shuddering with rush-hour traffic, and the ugly high-rise suburbs across the river broke the illusion of perfection.

As early as it was, the war memorial was almost deserted, the only visitors besides us two old men sweeping snow from the wide steps, their stooped frames dwarfed by the monument's immense pillar. A bronze plaque in several languages informed the ignorant of the six thousand Soviet war dead the memorial commemorated, boys who'd perished pushing the Nazis out of western Slovakia.

"Nine o'clock," Brian said, glancing at his watch, stamping his feet to ward off the cold.

I pushed my hands deeper into the pockets of my new coat, my right fingers brushing the stock of the Beretta, my left fingers finding the memory card that Brian had copied the contents of the pen drive onto the night before. We'd left the original at Ivan's apartment.

Two figures appeared from behind the memorial and started across the wide plaza in our direction. As they drew closer, I recognized them both. One was Werner. Beside him was my old friend Salim.

"You ready?" Brian asked.

"He's brought his thug," I whispered, curling my palm around the Beretta, resting my thumb next to the safety.

"I thought we asked you to leave your goons at home," Brian said as Werner and Salim neared.

Werner stopped walking. "Mr. Aziz is my personal assistant."

I shook my head.

"Come on," Brian announced, grabbing my arm. "Let's go."

Werner let us walk toward the edge of the plaza. "Let's be reasonable," he called out finally, dismissing Salim with a wave of his hand. The younger man started back toward the memorial.

"We're willing to trade," Brian said as we retraced our steps. "But we do this on our terms."

"Fair enough," Werner agreed. "You have the film?"

I pulled the memory card from my pocket and held my hand out for Werner to see, then slid it back into my coat. "Here's the deal," I said. "First, you tell me who they are, the man and the woman on the tape. Second, I want a meeting with him. I don't care how you arrange it; just make it happen."

Werner looked at me with a mixture of pity and contempt. "My dear," he said. "What makes you think I know the man on the tape?"

"You do," I assured him.

"Sadly, I was robbed of the film before I got a chance to watch it. That said, I must admit I lack your conviction."

"You mean you don't know what's on here?" I asked.

"To the contrary," Werner corrected me. "I know exactly what is on the film. That's why I agreed to buy it. There's a murder, is there not?"

"Yes," I said. "A woman, a journalist. A friend of yours. The man was a friend of yours, too."

Werner rubbed his gloved hands together. His nose and cheeks were red from the cold, his lips pale and dry. "For a woman who remembers nothing," he observed, "you know quite a lot."

"The picture in your office in Marrakech," I told him, "of you at Les Trois Singes. The man and the woman on the film are the same."

Werner pulled the collar of his coat up around his neck. It was a distraction, a gesture meant to conceal, but for the briefest of moments he looked like a man who'd just taken a hard punch to the gut.

"You were in love with her, weren't you?" I asked, remembering the photograph of the three of them, the way both men's heads were turned in the woman's direction, the looks on their faces.

"You're certain this is the man?" he asked stonily, ignoring my question.

"Yes."

Werner hesitated for a moment, looking past us toward some point on the far bank of the Danube, as if expecting the Hussites to come riding in at any moment. "Robert Stringer," he announced. "That's his name."

"And the woman?" I asked.

"Catherine," he said, his eyes hard on my face, his expression answering my earlier question. "Catherine Reed."

There it was, I thought, a name. If I had nothing else, I had that. "Who were they?" I asked.

"Catherine was a journalist, like you said. An American."

"And Stringer?"

"When we first met in Saigon, he was working for USAID."

"And in Pakistan?"

"Officially, he was with the Asia Foundation."

"And unofficially?"

"Everyone knew he was CIA."

"Even Catherine Reed."

"Catherine knew."

"And Stringer's side business with Naser Jibril?" I asked. "Did everyone know about that?"

Werner shook his head.

"But Catherine knew?"

"Because I told her," Werner said, fumbling with his coat again.

"But you said you didn't know it was Stringer on the film," I reminded him.

"I didn't," he agreed, stopping for a moment before continuing on. "In my business, one hears things, a lot of it rumor, some of it fact. A friend of mine in the Pakistani border guard told me there was an American moving empty arms crates into Afghanistan. The guards were all thrilled because they were getting twice the regular payoff. It didn't sound right to my friend, and it didn't sound right to me, so I told Catherine, as a favor. I thought there might be a story there."

"But you didn't have anything to do with Stringer's little pipeline?"

Werner shook his head. "I told you, I didn't even know it was him."

"And it never occurred to you that your favor might get Catherine killed?"

Werner shivered visibly. "I've told you enough," he said. "I'll arrange your meeting with Stringer. It will be my pleasure, but we're done here. You'll give me the film now."

I took the memory card from my pocket. There was little use in holding on to it, now that Werner knew it was Stringer on the tape. "One more thing," I said. "Leila Brightman worked for Stringer, didn't she?"

"You really don't know, do you?"

"No," I told him.

"You worked for Stringer then, just like you were working for him when you stole this film."

"You're wrong about that," I said. I held my hand out and offered him the memory card. "I went to your Casbah on my own."

He took the card and stashed it in the inside pocket of his coat. "And why would you do that?" he asked.

I hesitated for a moment, part of me wanting to tell him the reason, that this woman he had loved I had loved as well. But something got the better of me. "I had my reasons," I said.

"Don't we all," he agreed. Then he looked at Brian. "I will call Ivan in the next day or two."

"We'll be waiting," Brian said.

Werner nodded and turned from us. It took him a while to cross the plaza, his heels kicking snow as he went. Alone, against the stark white plaza, with the monument and its monolithic pillar looming in front of him, he looked tired and defeated, just an old man on a winter morning. When he reached the memorial, he stopped and looked back at us, lingering briefly before disappearing from our view.

"Do you trust him to make this meeting with Stringer happen?" I asked Brian, as we started back toward where we'd parked the SEAT.

"Do you?" Brian asked.

"Yes," I told him.

He nodded. "So do I."

Ivan was already up and gone when we got back to the apartment, but he appeared almost immediately with breakfast supplies: fresh eggs, pastries, a loaf of bread, and a brand-new bottle of Russian vodka.

I'd been hard asleep and hadn't heard him come in the night before, but from Ivan's wan face and shaky hands I could tell he'd had another late night. There was a dark red bruise on the side of his neck, an oval the size and shape of a woman's lips. I could see why some people found Ivan annoying, but there was also something fundamentally endearing about the Russian. There was an honesty to him, an unapologetic glee to his self-destruction that just made me like him.

"How did your meeting with the big guy go?" he asked, setting the food down, taking his coat off. "Everybody get what they wanted?"

"I hope so," I said.

One of Ivan's best qualities was his discretion. He hadn't asked either of us why we'd wanted to meet Werner, just as he hadn't pushed me on Hannah Boyle, and I was grateful to him for it.

"You got any plans for the next couple of days?" Brian asked.

Ivan shook his head. "I don't have a flight until next week."

"Good," Brian told him. "We have some more business with Werner. He's going to call you in the next day or two."

"No problem, boss." Ivan smiled, but I could tell he wasn't at his cheery best. He set the pastries on a plate, put a pot of water on the stove to boil, and slumped down at the kitchen table with a cigarette. "I think I'm getting too old for this crap," he admitted.

Brian laughed. "I think that happened a long time ago."

Ivan's cell phone rang, and he reached into the pocket of his coat to answer it, flashing Brian the middle finger of his free hand.

"Ivan," he grunted into the receiver. A garbled voice crackled back at him.

Ivan mumbled something in Slovak, then got up and opened one of the kitchen drawers, pulled out a pencil and a piece of scrap paper, and scribbled a hasty note. A brief conversation ensued, with much laughter on Ivan's side; then Ivan snapped the phone shut and turned to us.

"Got it," he said triumphantly.

"Got what?" I asked.

"Stanislav Divin," he said. "I talked to my friend at the police department while you guys were out. That was him calling back with Divin's address. Apparently, he's retired to the countryside, bought himself a little farm." He handed me the piece of paper. "Some shithole outside of Kosice."

I looked down at the paper, at Ivan's barely legible scrawl. "Where's Kosice?"

"Eastern Slovakia," Brian offered. "Near the Hungarian border."

"Can we get there by tonight?" I asked.

Brian looked at his watch. "There and back, if we leave soon."

TWENTY-NINE

Catherine Reed. I said the words to myself as I peered out the SEAT's back window at the fallow fields rushing by. The snow was thick and downy, the land beneath sculpted into shallow ripples by the last pass of the plow. Off in the distance the ghostly peaks of the Carpathians rose up through the ever-present Slovak industrial haze.

If all else failed, at least I had the name. That, coupled with what little else I knew, that Catherine had worked for CNN in Islamabad, that she'd died there in the summer of 1988, would surely be enough to find out more. Someone would know what had happened to her daughter, what had happened to me.

What did people do in situations like that? There would have been grandparents, aunts and uncles, a father. The same people who were taking care of the child I had left behind. Though I would have been old enough to take care of myself, I thought, calculating the best guess at my age against the timeline of history. I would have been somewhere around nineteen or twenty in the summer of 1988.

A truck passed us, barreling down the highway, spewing snow across the front windshield of the SEAT, and I felt my heart power up into my chest. The little car shuddered, pushed sideways by the truck's wake. For an instant I thought of the Peugeot, the body crumpled like an aluminum can. But there was more to my fear than the fear of dying.

I could find her, I thought; not the little girl at the Cluny abbey, not this shadow daughter of my imaginings, but a real child. A real person, out of whose life I had walked one day, into whose life I somehow expected to return. She was out there, some part of her no doubt having forgotten, some other part waiting for me.

"Maniac," Brian swore, struggling with the wheel as the truck disappeared down the highway.

Stanislav Divin's farm was some twenty kilometers outside of Kosice, a ragtag little homestead nestled in the foothills of the Low Tatras. The address Ivan had given us was vague at best, and it took some time to make our way through the villages north of Kosice, stopping occasionally so that Brian could ask directions in his imperfect Slovak.

It was nearing sunset when we turned through Divin's battered gate and started down the unplowed drive to the house. The property was worn but tidy, the outbuildings patched and repatched. It wasn't much in the way of a farm, just a chicken coop, a small barn, and a couple of broken-down Skodas, but it was exactly the kind of place a city cop would dream of retiring to. I could only imagine it in the summertime, with the mountains green in the distance and the smell of freshly mowed hay.

Not wanting to scare Divin off, we purposely hadn't called in advance, and I was relieved to see lights on in the house and a thin line of smoke snaking up from the chimney. As we pulled up to the house, the curtains in one of the front windows opened and a gray face peered out at us from behind the glass.

"I guess they know we're here," Brian said as he cut the engine and we climbed out of the SEAT.

The front door opened, and a woman in a wool shirt and pants appeared on the porch. She was close to Divin's age, or what I would have guessed his age to be, a robust seventy-something, stocky and self-reliant. His wife, most likely.

Brian started toward the house, calling out in Slovak as he went, his tone light and genial.

"Smile," he called out to me over his shoulder, as the woman peered in my direction.

I broke into an idiot grin while Brian laid out his most charming appeal.

I could see the woman hesitating, her mind contemplating the possibilities, these two obvious foreigners in a Spanish car asking to see her husband. It couldn't have seemed right. And yet she turned toward the door and beckoned us forward.

The house was luxuriously toasty inside, heated to a near sub-Saharan warmth by an immense woodstove. Dinner was cooking in the kitchen, and the air was perfumed with the smell of long-simmered meat and baked apples.

"Divin's in his shop," Brian explained as the woman disappeared into the back of the house. "She's going to get him."

"Did you tell her why we're here?" I asked.

"I said it's about one of his old cases. I told her you're an American, and that your sister was killed in a car accident. I said there's a lawsuit pending and that there could be money in it if he knows anything that can help us get a settlement."

"And she believed you?"

Brian shrugged. "As far as I could understand."

There were excited voices from somewhere in the back of the house. Finally, the woman reappeared with her husband in tow. She said something to Brian, then left us and headed into the kitchen.

Stanislav Divin was a slight man, his trim but vigorous body in stark contrast to his wife's wide hips and meaty hands. He was dressed simply, in worn jeans and a frayed work shirt, his forearms powdered with a fine film of sawdust. In his right hand was a wooden figurine, a beautiful and delicate rendering of a hummingbird in flight.

He smiled at me, and for a moment I was worried that he might recognize me, that if I had been in the car with Hannah he would surely remember, but his expression said nothing of the sort. He looked to Brian next, then motioned for us to sit. How many hundreds of cases, I told myself, and this one so long ago. Even I might not have recognized the girl I had been then.

"My wife says you've come about an old case of mine," Divin said in barely accented English. He settled himself into an armchair near the woodstove and set the bird in his lap.

"Yes," I said, slipping my coat off, taking a chair opposite him. It was hot near the hearth, unpleasantly so. "My sister," I told him, following Brian's lead. "She died in a car accident some years ago. I've been told you were the investigator."

"An accident?" Divin mused.

"Yes. In December of nineteen eighty-nine. She was driving a white Peugeot with Austrian tags. A truck hit her on the Bratislava-Vienna road."

"A white Peugeot," Divin said. He put his hand on the

bird's head and turned his face up toward the ceiling, as if looking for the memory in the roof's old wood beams.

"She was an American," I offered. "Her name was Hannah. Hannah Boyle."

The old man nodded. "Yes," he said. "I remember. It was a nasty collision. The girl..." He winced, then looked at me. "I'm sorry."

"It's been a long time," I said, showing him a thin smile, the dregs of grief. We were both silent for a moment while I tried to decide how to continue. A log shifted in the fire, the sound echoing in the stove's iron belly.

"I understand you were a narcotics detective," I said finally, taking a chance.

Divin shifted in his chair, glancing quickly from me to Brian. He said something to Brian in Slovak, and Brian answered back. Whatever Brian said must have been convincing. When they had finished their exchange, the old man turned back to me. "You understand correctly," he said.

I smiled encouragingly. "It's all right," I told him. "My family is well aware of my sister's problems." I took another chance. "She wasn't just a tourist, was she?"

Divin shook his head.

"Heroin?" I guessed.

"Hashish," he corrected me.

"How much did she have in the car with her?"

"Several kilos," Divin said. "I don't remember exactly."

"And the other girl, what happened to her?"

Divin looked down at the wooden bird. Gently, he lifted the figure from his lap and set it on the low table next to him. When his eyes met mine again, they were clear and steady. "I don't understand," he said. "What other girl?"

"My sister's friend," I tried. "She was traveling with another woman, an American."

"Surely you're mistaken," the old man insisted. "There was no one." He set his hands in his empty lap. "This lawsuit of yours? Who exactly is involved?"

I looked to Brian.

"Peugeot," he said quickly. "There was a problem with their seat belts."

Divin nodded. "Well, then," he said, rising from his chair. "Surely I've told you everything I know that could help. The Boyle woman's seat belt, as I recall, was still buckled when we got to her. Now, if that's all, I believe our dinner is almost ready."

"Seat belts?" I said as we climbed into the SEAT. "Was that the best you could come up with?"

Brian pulled the door closed behind him. "I'm not sure anything I could have said would have made much difference at that point."

He was right, of course. Divin was no dummy, and our story was full of holes, but still I couldn't help thinking there was a lot more to the car accident than the old detective had told us.

"You think it was you, don't you? In the car with Hannah." Brian asked as we started out the gate.

"Yes," I told him.

"You know they don't mess around with that kind of stuff here. The drugs, I mean. If that was you, you'd still be sitting in some Slovak prison."

I stared out the dark window, at my own ghostly reflection, and the wedge of moon in the distance. "But I'm not," I said, thinking about the Peugeot, the open passenger door, and the glass littering the asphalt around it, each shard shimmering like a diamond in the glare of the police flashbulb.

I pushed the image from my mind and tried to focus on

what I knew, the order in which things had happened. In the summer of 1988, Catherine Reed was murdered in Pakistan. Some eighteen months later, during the frenzied fall of communism, Hannah Boyle died in a car full of hashish, and Catherine's daughter, riding in the seat beside her, emerged unscathed. No, something didn't add up.

THIRTY

The call from Werner came the next evening. Brian, Ivan, and I were having dinner at a Thai place in the Old City when Ivan's cell phone rang. The conversation was short, the Russian all business.

"It was Werner," Ivan said when he'd hung up. "He'll meet you at the boat terminal at Devin Castle. Morning after tomorrow, ten o'clock. He said to tell you Stringer will be there."

I set my fork down and looked to Brian, panic flashing in my eyes. As much as I trusted Werner to deliver Stringer, I couldn't forget what had happened at the Casbah.

"It'll be okay," he said. "Don't worry."

Ivan shoveled a forkful of fried rice into his mouth. "Werner's a motherfucker," he said, chewing while he talked. "But he doesn't go back on his word. It's all he's got."

I believed Ivan, but still, it seemed strange to me that Werner had agreed so readily to my request. And why, I wondered, would Stringer be so willing to meet?

"Don't worry," Brian assured me. "I'll be there with you."

Even on the bleakest of winter mornings the drive out to Devin Castle along the Danube was a pleasant one, the dark river mottled with sheets of ice, the gentle foothills of the lower Carpathians rolling northward. Snowbound and denuded as they were, stripped of all foliage, there was miraculously little sign along the Danube's banks of the massive razor-wire fences that had scarred them for so long. Nor of the old guard towers, once spaced within sight of each other, the guards looking not outward to Austria, but in.

I had made this trip before, in different weather, at a far different time, and I had a brief but clear memory of it now, the fence crawling with summer vegetation, the river glinting in the sun. And every few hundred meters a rusty sign forbidding photographs.

The castle itself was nothing more than ruins, the remnants of what had once been a massive structure perched high atop a rocky fist, its one remaining tower balanced gracefully over the half-frozen river, like a diver about to leap. The parking lot was deserted when Brian and I pulled up in the SEAT. In fact, the whole complex was closed for the winter, the souvenir stands and little café shut up tight.

"You can take a boat out here from the city in the summer," Brian explained as we parked the SEAT in front of the shuttered ferry terminal.

"Why are you doing this?" I asked. I wanted more than just the answer he'd given me on the boat from Tangier, more than just some vague allusion to the choice between right and wrong and the knowledge necessary to make that distinction.

Brian rested his hand on the top of the steering wheel and looked down at his knuckles. "I meant what I said that night at the Mamounia," he told me quietly.

I thought about the desert garden, the orange trees and poinsettias, the smell of baked earth cooling in the darkness, and the stoic minaret of the Koutoubia Mosque. *If I'd met Hannah Boyle at the Ziryab,* Brian had said, *I would have fallen in love with her, too.*

And what about that night at the Continental? I wanted to ask but didn't. No matter what Brian said, it would always be there between us.

Brian pointed across the parking lot, and I looked up to see a black Mercedes coming toward us. "You ready?" he asked.

"Yes," I lied.

The Mercedes pulled to a stop near us, and the driver's door opened. Salim climbed out, walked over to the SEAT, and tapped on Brian's window. "Mr. Werner will see her alone," he said, as Brian rolled the glass down.

Brian shook his head. "I'm coming, or she's not."

Salim shrugged. "Then neither one of you will be meeting Mr. Stringer today."

I put my hand on Brian's arm and popped my door. Somehow I had always known this would be something I would have to do alone. "It's all right. I'll be fine. You said it yourself."

"Your gun," Salim said as I climbed out of the car. Without waiting for me to surrender it, he reached into my coat pocket and pulled out the Beretta. Then he walked over to the Mercedes and opened the back door. I could see Werner inside.

I looked back at Brian one last time. "It's okay," I reassured him.

"You can go back to the city," I heard Salim tell Brian as I climbed into the Mercedes's back seat. "We will deliver her wherever she wishes when we've finished." Then he closed the door behind me and walked to the driver's door.

The town car was spacious and warm, perfumed with the smells of expensive leather and Cuban cigars. As we pulled out of the parking lot, Werner touched a button and a dark glass panel slid noiselessly to the ceiling, separating the front seat from the back.

"He makes you nervous," Werner observed, motioning to the dark silhouette of Salim's head.

I laughed at the absurdity of the statement. "It's hard to imagine why."

Werner shook his head. "I'm sorry about what happened in Morocco. I hope you understand; that film was very important to me."

"Sure," I quipped. "No hard feelings."

Werner watched me for a moment, like a fighter sizing up an opponent. "You know, you look like her," he said finally. "I should have known all along. There was one night at the Casbah when I saw it, but it was so brief, and I never imagined."

"I don't know what you're talking about," I told him, unable to bear his satisfaction at knowing.

"It was the photograph," he continued, "that gave you away. At the war memorial you said she was the woman from the photograph in my office. Only, as you know, her face is blurred in that picture."

I looked away from Werner and out the window toward the snowy hills. We were heading farther away from the city, and the land here was striped with row upon row of vineyards, each plot perfect in its geometry, each plant clipped and gnarled, bound neatly to its makeshift cross.

"But there was another photograph, a better one,"

Werner went on. "Catherine kept that one. You've seen it, haven't you?"

I turned back to face him. "Where are you taking me?"

"To a friend's villa," he explained. "Where you can talk with Mr. Stringer."

"He's agreed to this?" I asked.

Werner smiled. "In a way, yes."

We drove on in silence for several kilometers, moving slowly north along the flanks of the hills. Then the Mercedes turned onto a dirt road and began a gradual upward ascent.

"You know I wouldn't have told her," Werner said as we pulled through an old gate and onto the grounds of a sprawling villa. "If I had known she would be in danger. If I had known what was really going on.

"Your mother was not someone who let that kind of thing stop her," he explained. "Fear, I mean. You are like her in that respect."

Suddenly, I wanted more than anything to remember my mother, to know her as Werner had, this woman who couldn't sit still for the time it took a camera's shutter to open and close, this woman who had made her living telling the story of war. I wanted to understand what she had seen in Werner, what she had come to love. There must have been something, a person in him that I could not see. Of course, it occurred to me, I might never have known her, at least not that intimate part of her.

"Did you love her?" I asked, repeating the question I'd put to Werner at the war memorial.

"We were lovers," he said. "In Vietnam and then again in Pakistan. But we were realists, too. I'm not sure our lives would have allowed us anything more."

The Mercedes looped around toward the back of the villa, stopping near one of the building's rear entrances.

Werner opened the door, then climbed out, motioning for me to follow. "This way," he said.

We entered the house through the kitchen, a large industrial space renovated to serve the modern banquet. I could see little of the villa, but the few glimpses I was offered, open doors that led to long corridors and high-ceilinged rooms, hinted at a level of opulence I had never before encountered. What staff there was, if any, was silent and invisible. Salim had left us at the car, and from what I could tell, Werner and I had the whole building to ourselves.

Beyond the kitchen was a short corridor that led to a large pantry and, finally, a locked doorway. Werner drew a key from his pocket and undid the lock, opening the door to reveal a flight of stone stairs that disappeared downward into cold, musty darkness. I shivered, reminded of the days at the Casbah, my subterranean cell.

"Don't worry," Werner said, flipping a light switch, illuminating the grotto below. "I have no intention of harming you. You have my word."

What had Ivan said? *It's all he's got.*

We started down together, Werner leading the way into the villa's ancient wine cellar. The cave was stocked to overflowing, the walls filled from floor to ceiling with bottles, each shelved neatly like a book in a library. We'd kept a cellar at the abbey, but this was nothing like the sisters' meager cave. Centuries of mold covered the racks and stone walls, dripping like wispy stalactites, cocooning everything in a soft gray web. The air was thick with a primordial stench, the odor of rich and unfettered decay, the smell of the grave.

"In Soviet times," Werner explained, motioning to the staggering collection, "this villa belonged to the party."

They'd had more than a proletariat's appreciation for wine, I thought, as we turned down a narrow passageway and stopped before another locked door. Werner once again drew a key from his pocket.

"You may ask Mr. Stringer what you like," he said, holding the key to the lock. "I believe he is ready to tell you whatever you might want to know."

There was something in his voice that I recognized instantly, a tone I'd heard that morning in his office in Marrakech. No, I thought, Stringer had not come here of his own accord, and he wouldn't be leaving of it either.

Werner opened the door to reveal a small square room, lit wanly by a single bulb. It was, in fact, much like my quarters at the Casbah, sparse and bare, furnished with a cot, a chair, and a bucket. Seated in the chair or, more accurately, slumped in it, his arms bound behind him, his feet bare, was a man in his late fifties with a thick mop of salt-and-pepper hair.

There had obviously been some attempt to tidy both the room and the man for my visit, but the reality of the situation was undisguisable. The smells of vomit and feces lingered in the small space, and there was blood on the man's face and filthy shirt. From the looks of him, Robert Stringer had been Werner's guest for some time. No doubt Werner's men had found him not long after our meeting on Slavin Hill.

"Hello, Cathy," Stringer said, looking up at me. His left eye was swollen nearly shut, his lower lip puffy and split. "I've been expecting you."

I must have blanched at the name, because Stringer's cracked mouth opened in a weak but contemptuous grimace.

"Yes," he sneered. "Catherine Reed, same as your mother."

"It was you who sent the men to the abbey," I said, looking for something, anything, that would justify

Werner's cruelty. I knew all too well what it meant to be on the receiving end of Bruns Werner's hospitality.

Stringer looked at Werner, then back at me. "Yes," he admitted.

"Had you thought I was dead?" I asked.

"It's what I was told, yes."

"By the men in the car, the ones who put me in the field that day. They worked for you, too?"

Stringer nodded.

"Where was I going?" I asked.

"You were coming to Geneva," Stringer said. "To meet me. You'd called from Morocco to say you'd seen the tape and me on it. You were upset. I told you I could explain."

"You didn't know then that I'd left the pen drive in Tangier?"

"No," Stringer said.

"But you knew I'd been to Werner's Casbah, that I had the tape. How?"

Stringer opened his mouth to answer, but I stopped him. "No," I said. "Let's start at the beginning." I thought for an instant, trying to understand where that might be, in the warehouse in Peshawar or years earlier. "You knew my mother in Vietnam," I said finally.

Stringer glanced at Werner again, and in the look that passed between them I understood that the two men had never been friends, that from the beginning she had come between them.

"We were friends," Stringer said, the last word hard and bitter in his mouth.

Of the two men in the photograph, he had seemed the more likely choice for Catherine, tall and lean, so much more elegant than the awkward Werner, and yet it was Werner my mother had picked.

"You would have liked to have been more, wouldn't

you?" I asked. "Is that why you had her killed in Peshawar? Because she loved someone else?"

Stringer cleared his throat and spit. A dark globule of phlegm and blood landed on the stone floor at Werner's feet. "Catherine died because someone sent her snooping where she didn't belong. She came to me beforehand, you know," he said, addressing Werner. "She said you'd given her a line on a story, some American using the CIA pipeline in an unusual way. I tried to tell her it was garbage, tried to get her to let it go, but she wouldn't. You know how Catherine was."

"So you stood by while Jibril's men killed her?" I asked.

Stringer raised his head and looked directly at Werner. There was a recklessness to him that came with being so badly broken. "She shouldn't have come."

Werner clenched and unclenched his fists, rage in his every pore, though whether at himself or at Stringer, I couldn't tell.

"Tell me about Hannah Boyle," I said. "I was with her that night, wasn't I?"

"Sharp as a tack," Stringer said, leaning forward, straining against his ropes. "You were always so smart."

"I talked to Stanislav Divin. He told me about the hashish."

"I was just keeping a promise. Catherine didn't tell you she had a daughter, did she?" he asked Werner, then turned back to me. "When she came to me in Peshawar, she told me she was afraid. She asked me to look out for you if anything happened to her."

"And you did, only not in the way she might have meant."

Stringer's eyes flared. "If it weren't for me, you'd still be sipping gruel in a Slovak prison."

"You got Divin to take my name off the report," I said.

"I saved you," Stringer told me. "You may have survived the accident, but by the time I found out what had happened you were sitting in a cell in Bratislava looking at twenty more years. I made a deal for you. It wasn't easy."

"Only your generosity didn't come without strings."

"I gave you a life with meaning. It was what you wanted, what you all wanted. There were so many idealists here then that this country stank of them, and you wanted in as much as anyone else. Just to be part of it, instead of some pathetic life trucking drugs across the border. And I gave it to you."

"You ran me as a contract agent, just like Patrick Haverman, just like Brian. You told me I was working for the CIA, but I wasn't always, was I?"

"You were always working in the best interests of the country," Stringer said.

"And who decided that? I should have known the truth," I told him.

"You knew what you wanted to know," he countered.

It was the same thing I'd said to Brian in Spain, and I couldn't help thinking Stringer was right, that in some way I must have chosen to believe him.

"You let me go because of the baby?" I asked.

"You were always free to go."

"But I came back," I said, "for the tape. How did you know?"

"You called me from Tangier," Stringer began. "You said some old friend from the business had gotten in touch with you, that he'd heard through the grapevine that Al-Marwan had an old tape on the market, something that sounded like it could have been your mother, and that he and Werner had worked out a deal for it. You needed my help."

"And you offered it?"

"You couldn't have done it alone."

"So you sent Patrick Haverman to me, to take the tape once we found it. Only you didn't count on him having a change of heart."

"He was a fool," Stringer snapped.

"And when your men didn't find the tape on me in France, you sent Brian to Tangier to find it."

Stringer grimaced. The reserves that had held him together so far were nearly tapped. "I said you were smart. You don't really need me to tell you any of this."

"My child," I asked. "Where is she?"

Stringer coughed, doubling over as far as he could. Something rattled in his chest, like a stone in a piece of hollow wood. "She's with her great-grandparents," he said. "Catherine's parents. Outside of Seattle."

"You told them I was dead?"

"Yes."

"Did they know why I left?"

Stringer shook his head.

"What's her name?"

He spit again, more blood this time, then forced himself upright. "Madeline."

I closed my eyes and repeated each syllable to myself. Madeline, the name I had chosen for my daughter. Now that I had this, there was nothing more I needed from Stringer, not even revenge. Suddenly, the tiny room seemed unbearably claustrophobic, the stench oppressive. I looked to Werner, wanting out, but he took a step past me, moving toward Stringer.

"She's mine, isn't she?" he demanded, stopping just inches from the other man, his fists still clenched, every muscle in his body shivering.

For a moment I thought he was talking about Catherine, but then his face turned back to mine and I understood what he had meant.

Stringer smiled. "She was afraid to tell you," he said, "afraid you'd want her to get rid of the baby. The last two months in Saigon she cried on my shoulder almost every night, and you never knew. I hated you for it. You didn't deserve her.

"She never thought you loved her," he went on. "All those years later in Peshawar, she still couldn't bring herself to tell you you had a daughter."

Werner stared down at the other man for a moment, then slowly turned away from him. He was wearing a dark suit and a long wool overcoat, but he seemed suddenly naked, as vulnerable as the bloodied figure in the chair. He turned to me and opened his mouth as if to speak, but nothing came out.

For a moment I could see the person he'd been before any of this had happened, before my mother's death had changed him. I could see the young man from the photograph, the man at Catherine Reed's side in that Saigon café. At the same time I could see the old man he'd been that morning on Slavin Hill, a defeated figure shuffling away from us through the snow.

He raised his hand slightly, like a priest about to offer a blessing; then he opened the door and stepped out into the passageway.

I stopped a moment before following him, taking one last look at Stringer. "You're not alone, are you?" I asked, thinking about what Brian had said on the boat, what I had suspected for so long. The men at the abbey, the couple at the tearoom, there was too much here for just one man.

He stared up me, grinning like a man who knows he's going to die. "We're all alone."

"No," I said. "I mean, in the agency, you're not the only one."

"I know what you meant," Stringer wheezed.

I could call Werner back in, I thought, and find out everything. I could make Stringer tell me. But the truth was there was nothing more I wanted to know, nothing more I could know.

Wasn't that the true nature of memory and knowledge, the thing I'd never quite understood? Wasn't that what Heloise had tried to tell me that night in the convent's library, looking up at the peeling walls? That the past is a puzzle for everyone, a tattered collection of memory and desire. That even those people we most long to understand remain no more than a sum of those static moments we've chosen to hold them in. A figure on a boat, a face in the darkness above one's bed at night, a woman in a Saigon café. All I wanted now was the life I'd left, and my daughter.

Stepping toward Stringer, I reached into my jeans and pulled out the pen drive. "You're wrong," I said, slipping the drive into the breast pocket of Stringer's shirt. It was Werner's now, as was Stringer, to do with whatever he wanted. "We're anything but alone."

Werner and I didn't speak on the way back to the city. It was afternoon when we reached Bratislava, snowing again, the white flakes immolating themselves in the black oblivion of the Danube. Whatever there was to be said between us would not be spoken that day, and we both knew it, both understood the importance of silence, the danger of the one word, *father,* that hung between us.

When we pulled up in front of Ivan's apartment building and I reached for the door handle, Werner leaned across me and put his hand on mine. "I did love her."

"I know." I nodded. I should not have wanted to give him such a gift, but I did it anyway.

"Please let me help you," he said. Reaching for his

wallet, he pulled out a handful of one-hundred-euro notes.

He pushed the money toward me, but I shook my head. "I'm fine," I told him. "I'll be fine."

"Whidbey Island," he stammered. "It's where Catherine's parents live. She used to tell me about it. They have a house on the water."

"Yes," I said, opening the door, setting one foot on the curb. "I know. And a sailboat."

Werner put the money back in his billfold, took out a business card, and forced it into my pocket. "Whatever you need," he said as I climbed out.

I stepped to the front entryway of the building and scanned the roster of names, my finger hovering over Ivan's bell while I listened to the Mercedes drive away. When the car was gone, I turned and started up the sidewalk, my feet following the creeping dawn of recognition toward SNP Square.

The weather had chased everyone inside, and the sprawling triangle of the square was oddly deserted for midafternoon. A tram pulled to a stop, and a handful of passengers climbed off, scurrying away, flakes sticking to their fur caps. The old bronze monument to the infamous *Slovenské národné povstanie,* the 1944 uprising against the Nazis, was barely visible through the thickening scrim of snow; the "Angry Family," as Bratislavans called it, blurred beyond distinction.

I gave you a life with meaning, I heard Stringer say as I stood on the edge of the square and looked out across the vast white space toward where the crowds had gathered throughout that November so many years earlier. I could feel the heat of innumerable bodies pressing against me, the tidal surge of it, so many people wanting the same thing. The uprising this time not against the fascists but against those who had defeated them.

How could I have said no to the life Stringer offered me? How could I have said no when my mother had died so far from home, her life so full of meaning? When the world was finally shifting, turning like that mammoth ferry of my memory, its great prow sliding forward while I held my breath?

Here was my beginning, I thought, a girl in a crowd of thousands, orphaned and untethered, an American in a country that was brimming with the promise of what America had to offer. Stringer was right; I had heard what I wanted to hear. And this is where it had brought me, where it had brought all of us. This moment of collective forgetting.

A church bell sounded somewhere, a low chime ringing over the snowbound city, and the pigeons that had gathered on the SNP monument scattered, rising upward with a papery clamor of wings. Shivering, I pulled the collar of my coat up around my bare neck and started back to Ivan's.

THIRTY-ONE

Winter is softer here than the winters I've known, almost tropical in its liquidity. Sometimes it rains for days, not a downpour but a gentle, obliging mist that settles in a whispering thrum on the deepwater bays and pebbled inlets of the island. Some mornings, when I can't sleep, I get in my rental car and drive down to Mukilteo or over to Keystone and watch the early ferries come and go from the docks. There's a ritual to it that reminds me of the abbey, each crew member in his or her place, each rope secured. The way the chains clang, and the ship groans and creaks against the wooden pylons and rubber bumpers, and the deckhands call out to one another often sounds like a kind of prayer.

On weekends I sometimes stay till midmorning, but on schooldays I leave at seven-thirty and drive toward Greenbank, toward the corner where Madeline and her great-grandmother wait together for the school bus. She's

a serious child. I can tell from the way she holds her
lunchbox, from the way she peers impatiently down the
road. Sometimes when I go by, the two of them are talking, Madeline looking up at the older woman with a puzzled scowl, her sharp little eyebrows drawn together in an
inverted V. She doesn't seem to miss me, and for this I'm
grateful, but I also know this is part of the careful way she
carries herself, and that sometimes when she's looking
down that road she's imagining me coming around the
wooded corner to meet her.

It's only a matter of time before I run out of money, a
week or two at most before my thirty-nine-dollars-a-night
room at the Bay View Motel taps the last of my savings
and I'll have no choice but to stop the car. But for now, I
keep driving. I had not intended to wait like this when I
came. My first day back I drove straight from the Seattle
airport to Greenbank. But when I pulled up to the house
and saw Madeline's bicycle on the porch and the old
metal swing set in the front yard, something caught in my
chest, and I knew I wasn't ready yet.

I'm gone to them, I tell myself each morning when I
drive by. What does another day matter? Another week?

In the afternoons I go to the beach at Deception Pass
and watch the seagulls riding the air currents beneath the
high trestle bridge. Sometimes I think about Brian, about
his mouth against mine when he kissed me that first time
in Marrakech. It seems right to me that we should each
have found an island, that he is somewhere on a beach as
well, with the soft green hills of Tortola in the distance.
That night at Ivan's when I told him about the meeting
with Stringer, he listened without saying what I knew we
both were thinking, that nothing was over, that Robert
Stringer was only a tiny part of something larger.

Dr. Delpay told me once that memory resides mainly
in our sense of smell. I didn't understand him at the time,

but I'm beginning to. There is something about the air here, the all-pervasive smell of the sea, the sweetness of wet cedar, the rich must of rain-soaked underbrush, that is so perfectly familiar. I know now that I will never remember everything, but I'm beginning to glimpse my past.

The last few days, I've grown bold enough to sit in the park across from Madeline's school and watch her with the other children at recess. Last night I walked into the woods behind my grandparents' house and spied while the two of them made dinner and Madeline sat on a stool at the counter, her feet dangling off the ground. It was just like watching myself.

ACKNOWLEDGMENTS

As ever, my heartfelt gratitude to the innumerable people at Henry Holt, SobelWeber, and Orion responsible for turning my ugly duckling manuscript into a beautiful book. Thanks to Nat Sobel, Judith Weber, Jack Macrae, and Jane Wood for their tireless readings and rereadings. A special thank-you to the incredible Vicki Haire for her superhuman copyediting skills. Thanks also to my family and friends, especially my husband, Keith, and my adoring cat, Frank.